A.J. Truman

D1527898

OUT OF MY MIND

OUT OF MY MIND
By A.J. Truman

Cover by James at GoOnWrite.com
Copy-editing by Sarah Henning
Formatting by Caitlin Greer

Thank you to Andria, Paula, Todd, and Cassie for reading, Buddy for your proofreading prowess, and Piper and Cody for your blurb mojo. A big thanks to my own Jewish mother, who always supports me in my writing endeavors, even if it's "writing porn," as she calls it. Love you! And thank you to all the readers who keep reading my books and connecting with my characters. I write these books for you, and I am so grateful for each and every one of you. I couldn't have done this without your enthusiasm and encouragement, Outsiders!

What's an Outsider, you say? Oh, just a cool club where you can be the first to know about my new books and receive exclusive content. Join the Outsiders today at www.ajtruman.com/outsiders.

CHAPTER ONE

Mac

Things were happening. Well, possibly happening. Mac put the probability at 25 percent happening for the moment.

Mac had never flirted with a guy before. Even when his gaydar went off, he ignored it. He preferred to observe, as if everyone around him were subjects in a grand experiment. Things were safer that way. After escaping his small town, quite literally, and then moving to Pittsburgh in eleventh grade, which wasn't all that different, his best survival tactic was to assume the world around him was straight and let the world assume the same about him. It had led to avoiding eye contact, unintentional celibacy, and ample masturbation. But he managed to graduate unscathed. One of his reasons for choosing to attend

Browerton was because it was a liberal campus, i.e. he could be openly gay, and flirt with other openly gay guys.

Like Gideon.

Just saying Gideon's name in his head made Mac's insides do flips that would make an Olympic gymnast jealous.

They stood next to each other at the refreshments table of a Welcome to Browerton party. It was his first night of college, and he was already loving undergraduate life.

Gideon smiled at him. Smiling was a good sign, right? Mac hitched his percentage up to 30 percent. To calm himself down, Mac imagined this as a social experiment, one of many he hoped to devise as an undergrad. *Hypothesis: Flirting is part of human instinct. Even if somebody has never flirted before in his life, he can rely on intuition to guide him to victory.*

"You can't underestimate the quality of Sprite. It has the lemon-lime taste that puts it in a class all by itself." Gideon shook out the last drops of sugary goodness into his cup. His lanky body stretched up like a beanstalk. Mac was six feet even, and he still had to crane his head back for their conversation. Gideon had dirty blond hair that dashed around the top of his head, yet still managed to make sense, and his thick-framed hipster glasses displayed large green eyes that were always exploring.

Gideon was unlike anyone he'd known back home. Not just because he was a New Yorker, which made him a little exotic in Mac's eyes. It was in his attitude and directness and volume, the way he carried himself through the world like a knife effortlessly slicing through cake.

"You've put way too much thought into pop," Mac said.

"You mean soda." Gideon arched an eyebrow that sent a spark straight to Mac's home entertainment center.

"No. It's called pop."

"Nobody calls it pop. It's soda." He said it in such a matter-of-fact way that should've offended Mac, but it just made him smile harder.

"Nobody calls it soda. In Pittsburgh, it's pop."

"I've never met anyone from Pittsburgh."

"Well," Mac put a hand on Gideon's forearm. Light touching. Eye contact. Smiling. Instinct was taking over. "I assure you that we follow the laws of the Constitution in my neck of the woods."

"Except that you say pop." Gideon didn't retract his arm right away. They remained touching for a good three seconds. Mac could hear bleachers full of people in his head cheering him on.

40 percent. Vegas would be very optimistic about these odds.

"Is it true that New Yorkers think that New York is the center of the universe?"

"It's not a thought. It's an empirical fact." Gideon flashed Mac a teasing smile. Mac liked the teasing. From all the times he had to watch straight friends flirt, he knew that teasing was good.

43 percent.

Gideon took back his arm. "Do you want a refill on your...soda?"

42 percent.

"Sure."

Mac could feel the past slipping away with each second he enjoyed at Browerton. It was a new start, much like Pittsburgh had been, only with more possibility. His

Aunt Rita had said he would love college. He lived with her in Pittsburgh, and she was more of a parent to him than his mom or dad had been.

Gideon poured him another cup of Coke. "It's interesting, though, because I could swear you have a little bit of a Southern accent."

Mac walked to an empty spot against the wall. "I do? I don't know."

"Yeah. It's there. Hiding in the background. Twangy." Gideon followed behind him and leaned only a few meager inches away on the very same wall. That had to bring him up to a 45 percent. Mac listened extra hard over the noise of the party and his heart pounding the hell out of his ears.

He looked down at his shoes. "I'm from West Virginia, originally."

"That's it!"

"But that was years ago." He would not let this conversation get awkward. Now was not the time to bring up his past. Sob stories had no place in flirting. Even a newbie knew that.

"Still makes you a Southerner at heart," Gideon said.

"It's not the South!"

"Same difference." Another teasing smile. It was a visual Mac never wanted to leave his head.

"It only comes out when I'm having fun," Mac said. Gideon's New York accent seemed to be with him nonstop. Mac wasn't complaining. It was a hot accent, all hard edges and brute force. "Say, what color is your cup?"

"*Ah*range."

"You mean *aw*renge."

"*Aw*renge?" Gideon overemphasized, and it was adorable as hell. "Who says *aw*renge? 'Look at me. I'm eating an *aw*renge.'"

Mac shoved him away, which allowed a brief touch of his chest. Gideon might've flexed for him on contact, but that was inconclusive.

"It's pronounced *ah*range." Gideon pressed a pointy finger against Mac's chest, and Mac flexed briefly, just to let him know that he visited a weightroom regularly.

48 percent.

They continued talking about classes and dorms and the soul-sucking retail jobs they worked over the summer. The words didn't matter. It was all a front for the looks and smiles and surreptitious touching. Flirting became kinda effortless. Instinctual. Mac wasn't really trying anymore. He just enjoyed Gideon's company, and the feeling seemed mutual. But the problem with talking was that it wasn't moving the percentage needle.

Gideon illuminated Mac about what matzo balls were. "It's like dough, almost like a wanton, but it's made of matzo meal, which is like bread without yeast, so it's unleavened and…it's a ball of goodness. That's all you need to know."

"And you eat it all the time?"

"You're just supposed to eat it at a Passover Seder, but my mom makes it for most holidays."

Mac pretended to know what Gideon was talking about, which Gideon was not buying.

"Passover's like the less fun cousin of Easter. You can't eat bread, and we celebrate getting to wander the desert for forty years. Jesus's last supper was a Seder."

"Really?"

"I'm ninety-seven percent sure." Gideon fixed his glasses on his ears, a nervous tic that only added to his cuteness. "How'd we get to talking about religion? What's next on the list of taboo topics? Politics?"

A silence passed between them, this one Mac felt deep within him and made him grip his cup tighter. He didn't know what to say next, but he was thinking of something fast.

"Should we try to be social?" Mac nudged his chin at the packed room. He had talked to some kids tonight, but once he saw Gideon across the room chatting away, his attention focused on getting to know the cute, tall guy. When Gideon wound up at the drinks table alone, Mac zoomed over to casually bump into him.

Gideon shrugged his apathy. He pulled out his phone. "I'm going to show you what a matzo ball looks like."

48.4 percent.

Mac proceeded to yank out his phone. "And I'll show you a map so you can see that West Virginia is firmly not in the South."

"We've only been at Browerton for twenty-four hours, and already we're expanding our horizons."

Or at least they tried to. Mac's phone was taking forever to load the image search. He refreshed, which set him back to zero. He gestured to his phone to pick up the pace, but no dice. He glanced up at Gideon, who was having similar problems.

"Everyone at the party is probably draining the Wi-Fi," Gideon said.

And that's when an idea caught fire in Mac's mind. He realized that flirting only took him so far. He was circling his opponent in the boxing ring. At some point, he had to connect with a right hook. He put his hand in his pocket and clutched his four-leaf clover keychain for some good luck.

"My dorm is across the street." Mac gulped back every last nerve. "We can just go on my computer."

Gideon looked behind Mac at the party. Mac waited like a defendant watching the jury foreman stand, ready to read his verdict.

"Great idea!"

100 percent.

Φ

Mac had to wipe his sweaty palm on his shirt in order to open the door to his floor. The layout reminded him of a submarine: long and narrow. The halls were empty. Everyone was at the mixer, or elsewhere. Mac's heart beat faster at the silence around them. His keys shook in his trembling hand. He jiggled it in the lock a few times before it opened.

Mac sat at his desk and turned on his computer. He took calming breaths in through his nose, and out his mouth. "You can sit on the bed. No need for you to hunch over me like that."

"Cool." Gideon did as instructed.

Mac willed his fingers to stop shaking on the computer keys. He was an astronaut touching down on a new planet. Planet Gay. *I can't believe I am here, in my room, with a guy, who's ON MY BED, and things are 100 percent about to happen.*

Gideon's back slumped against the wall. "So what do you want to study here?"

"Patterns." Mac spun around his chair to face Gideon. The computer was in his lap.

"Patterns?"

"Sociology is the study of patterns and trends. Our lives and our society are a system of patterns that we've honed over time, and I want to study them. What does what we do everyday say about us? They're all patterns that humans have been refining for centuries."

"You don't think people can break patterns?"

"That's what I want to find out."

"You really thought this over. My mom said that economics would be a good major for me, and I have some friends who work on Wall Street."

Mac handed over his laptop, and their fingers touched in the process. He now wished the laptop had remained on his lap.

Gideon scoured the web for just the right picture of a matzo ball. He was on a serious mission. He found his winning picture within the depths of Pinterest. A thick, large ball being raised out of a piping hot bowl of soup.

"Feast your eyes on this beauty."

Mac sat next to him on the bed. He felt every spring move underneath him. Gideon might've said something else about the matzo ball, but Mac couldn't hear anything over the pounding of his pulse in his ears. They were still circling each other. No punches thrown yet.

"Okay, so it might not look like much. You really need to taste one."

Mac took the computer from Gideon and moved it to the desk chair. Before Gideon could say anything else, Mac kissed him.

Mac could hear Gideon's breathing and his own heart rate dueling in his ears. *I am feeling Gideon's nose against my nose! I am feeling his lips with my lips!* But just as fast as the kiss happened, it was over.

Gideon scooted back. "I'm straight."

His words were the real right hook here. He stood up faster than the speed of light.

"Oh." Mac didn't know what else to say in this situation. He looked to Gideon, who didn't seem to have malice in his green eyes—just shock, and a dose of fear—which seemed to be a good start.

"I'm sorry." Mac felt his cheeks heating up faster than a stove. "I thought...I guess we got our signals mixed."

People used that expression too lightly. Mac thought about trains, and how if they got their signals mixed, they would crash and kill hundreds of people.

Gideon opened the door. He couldn't even look Mac in the eye. "I'll see you around."

The smiling, the flirting, the light touches. He thought he was on a street of green lights. *How did I get it so wrong?*

Mac ran into the hall and found Gideon hauling open the stairwell door. "Gideon."

He stopped midway down the flight. He adjusted his glasses, and it still made Mac swoon.

"Let's forget that happened." Mac waved behind him, to his room, to that fuckload of awkwardness. "Can we be friends?"

Gideon's eyes bulged open as if Mac suggested they go on a killing spree or something. "Friends? Are you out of your mind?"

Ouch. Mac wasn't expecting that. Even Gideon seemed surprised by what came out of his mouth. It looked like he was going to say something else, but he turned and continued down the stairs and out of sight.

Things had happened on Mac's first night at college, and unfortunately, he would never forget them.

TWO YEARS LATER

CHAPTER TWO

Gideon

Gideon brushed his hand against the freshly painted living room wall. He appreciated that the landlord hadn't painted his new apartment a bone white that seemed to be standard in all buildings. Beth had looked at him funny when Gideon made the guy put it into the lease agreement. He told his girlfriend to trust him. The off-white color gave his new place a warmth and coziness even before the furniture had all been moved in. He breathed in the new paint smell and smiled to himself. It was only mid-September, right before classes started up again, but Gideon already knew junior year was going to be awesome.

Boxes lined the floor of his and Beth's one-bedroom apartment. They had scored one of the best places to live in the city, thanks to Gideon charming the landlord and giving him some stock tips he'd picked up from past classes. The apartment sat above a barbershop in the heart of downtown Duncannon. It had hardwood floors, built-in shelving surrounding a brick fireplace, dishwasher, and in-unit washer and dryer—the last one being the holy grail of a college student apartment. It was slightly out of their price range, but Gideon would make it work.

Well, actually Beth's parents would make it work. Step one was buying the couple brand new furniture and paying for movers.

Gideon opened a box and thought about trying to do some unpacking until the movers arrived. He was the type who wanted the apartment set up, down to the magazines on the coffee table, before they went to sleep the first night there.

He opened a box that had picture frames wrapped in towels and sweaters. Gideon held a frame with decorative menorahs at the corners. They had made it at the Hillel, Browerton's Jewish student center, for Hanukkah sophomore year. He and Beth smiled and held up said picture frame in the shot. It was very meta.

Gideon didn't expect to have a serious girlfriend in college. But then most of his friends began pairing off with serious girlfriends, and his mom kept asking about his dating life.

Beth seemed to come along at the right time. She was from a nice family, a few towns away from where Gideon grew up. They were both active in Hillel and had many mutual friends. Dating her was an easy transition. Not much in his life had to change. And his mother loved her. She loved telling her friends about Gideon and Beth.

He sat on the toilet, the only seat in the apartment, and texted his girlfriend. *Where are the movers? Their 1-4 p.m. window is closing in twenty minutes.*

Fifteen minutes passed, and still no movers. Gideon unpacked the box of kitchen supplies his mom had shipped. He filled up the wall unit with pictures and knickknacks they had accumulated over the ten months of their relationship. Gideon had unpacked as much as humanly possible without furniture.

Have you heard from the movers? Gideon texted his girlfriend.

He stared at his phone, waiting for a response. He realized Beth hadn't responded to his earlier message.

"Gideon." Beth stood at the doorway of their apartment.

A nervous pit dropped into his stomach, not too dissimilar from the one that dropped when his parents asked him to come into the living room so they could inform him his dad had cancer, years ago.

"I managed to do what I could," he said, pointing to the wall unit and a pair of framed pictures hung on the wall. "Have you heard from the movers?"

"They're not coming." Beth could only look at him for a second before glancing away.

"What happened?" Even while asking this, Gideon had a feeling what the answer was.

"I can't move in with you." Her voice cracked. "It's over, Gideon."

Gideon needed to sit down. Too bad his only option was the toilet, which felt about right.

"I'm sorry I'm doing this now, like this. I've been thinking about it all summer."

"Way to wait until the last minute."

"There was never a good time."

Gideon sat on the polished hardwood floor. The world around him went mute, all except for Beth, who remained standing.

"I've been wondering if this really was the best next step for us, moving in together. I felt nervous. At first, I thought it was because I was moving in with my boyfriend into my first apartment, and the natural butterflies that come with that."

"Maybe it is. I'm nervous, too. We'll adjust."

"But I realized that I didn't want to adjust. Something seemed off, Gideon. Between you and me."

This was news to him.

"You never felt it?" She asked.

"What?"

"The distance."

"You mean because your internship was in Midtown and mine was on Wall Street?"

Beth shook her head no, her hair flinging out to the side. "There's always been this distance between us. No matter how close I thought we were, there was this wall. And it wasn't just me. I saw it with your other girlfriends."

That was the problem with dating a girl you had been friends with. She knew Gideon when he was dating around, so she thought she really knew him. He wasn't in the mood to be psychoanalyzed.

"You would start dating a girl, then they'd want to get serious, and you would break up with them. You have a typical playboy pattern, one I thought I could break.

"But once I started dating you, I saw how much you refused any type of intimacy. We would have these long talks, but it would feel like chatting with a stranger. Or after sex, you wanted to jump into the shower right away. You never wanted to cuddle. I thought it was because of your OCD."

"I don't have OCD."

"You had the cleanest dorm room of any guy I know."

"Since we're listing faults, can I start on you yet?"

"Don't be petty, Gideon. I'm trying to be honest with you."

"Great timing." He thought about the plush armchair they had picked out, that he would never get to sit in now. "You waited ten months to lay this all on me."

"I thought you would come around. I liked the challenge."

"I'm not a project, Beth."

"And I'm not a prop," she said back, her voice thick. "I think that we wanted to look like the perfect couple rather than actually be a good couple."

Gideon stood up. Therapy session over. "I already signed a lease."

Beth hadn't put her name on the lease, only him. Her end of the deal was getting the furniture. Gideon wondered how long this really had been on her mind.

"You can break it."

"Not without forfeiting first month's and security."

"My parents can pay you back for first month's rent. You can talk to the landlord in the meantime. I'm sure he'll find somebody to fill this place in no time. He'll let you break the lease."

Gideon studied all the details of the apartment. The enclosed porch, the molding on the borders of the off-white walls. That dishwasher. Beth seemed to read his mind.

"If you don't want to give up the apartment, you can try and find a roommate. I can ask around."

The last thing he wanted was help from her. "It's okay. I'll be fine."

"I know you're hurt, and again, I wish my timing was better."

He didn't feel hurt or heartbroken. He was angry. At her, and at himself. Because at this moment, a voice in his gut was saying he should've been the one to do this first.

Beth gave him a hug, which because he was a nice guy, he accepted. He breathed in her perfume one last time. She clicked the door shut, leaving Gideon alone with his fireplace, dishwasher, and in-unit washer and dryer.

Φ

A few hours later, Gideon's best friend Seth came over with an air mattress and a pack of gluten-free beer. Seth didn't follow the whole gluten-free craze to be cool. He had a gluten, tree nut, and peanut allergy. When they met as freshmen, he told Gideon that if he had a peanut butter and jelly sandwich, he would die, which Gideon thought made him sound bad-ass.

Seth kneeled on the bedroom floor and inflated the air mattress.

"Women," Gideon said. "They appear so soft and innocent, but they can destroy you."

"Just like almonds," Seth said. He was from Rye, a few towns over from Gideon, but managed to have a Brooklyn accent.

"It's never enough. You want to have fun and see where things go; they want a committed relationship. You give them a committed relationship, but it's not the right type of committed. It's never enough." Gideon gagged on the beer. Gluten was apparently the magic ingredient.

"Plenty of fish, Gid. Plenty of fish." Seth disappeared behind the growing air mattress. "And plenty of dating apps, too."

Gideon had done his fair share of swiping left and right before Beth, and he would go back to that well soon. But now, he just needed to vent.

"What kills me is that as she was breaking up with me, I kept thinking how I wanted to do it first. I wasn't crazy about her, and I know things weren't perfect."

"Then why'd you keep dating her?" Silence took over the bedroom. It was a valid point, but Gideon waved it away.

"I was being the good boyfriend. I was giving her what she wanted." Gideon flopped onto the air mattress. It was far more comfortable than he was expecting. "Are you sure you want to live in the dorms for another year?"

"I finally got a single! No more awkward conversations with roommates about not keeping crackers and trail mix in the room. I already installed my dehumidifer."

"Fair enough." Gideon smirked. Seth had no shame in being excited to install a dehumidifer.

"I'll ask around my dorm and my other friends to see if anyone is looking for a last minute apartment."

"Whoever moves in here would get half the living room as their bedroom. Not exactly the best deal." Gideon didn't want to give this apartment up. He doubted he could find a quality apartment at an affordable price this late in the game. His only other option was to go back to the dorms. No offense to Seth and his single, but to Gideon, that was like taking a giant step back.

"You never know. There are a lot of students on campus. Undergrads, grad students, transfer students, even new professors. Browerton is a big place."

As he promised, Seth put the word out. And it just so happened that a kid in his dorm had a friend who was friends with someone who knew a Browerton student from his Intro to Classics course last year who was in desperate need of an apartment. The news passed back through the chain to Seth, who told Gideon the student would stop over Monday night, after the first day of classes of the new school year.

In that time, Gideon scrambled to find decent furniture from Goodwill and Craigslist. His apartment had the bare essentials of a living space when his buzzer rang. Seconds later, the prospective roommate knocked on his door. Gideon recognized the short brown hair, twinkling eyes, and wide smile in a heartbeat.

Only that smile quickly turned into a scowl.

CHAPTER THREE

Mac

Mac should've known that out of all the Gideons at Browerton (which, to be fair, were probably less than ten), this one would need a roommate. He held out hope as he walked up the stairs that it would be someone else.

Nope.

"Hey." Gideon put on his best polite smile. It was a crime against humanity that he was still attractive. He hadn't been cursed with a beer gut like so many straight upperclassmen guys on campus.

"Yeah. A blast from the past." Mac had spent his time at Browerton avoiding Gideon and pretending like that night never happened. But seeing him again brought back the memory in crystal clear Technicolor.

"You're looking for a place to live?"

"Yeah." Mac peeked behind Gideon. He loved the color of the walls. And was that a fireplace he saw in the reflection of the window?

"Here, come in." He stepped aside.

The apartment was already leaps and bounds better than what Mac had seen in other places he looked. Most of the apartments he'd seen were either too expensive or barely acceptable for human living. Mac took full scope of the place. Like his friend had told him, it was a one-bedroom with a large living room where he'd reside. He pictured winter nights curling up with a book next to the fireplace. But then he remembered Gideon would probably be there, too.

"Are you still studying sociology? Like patterns and stuff?" Gideon asked.

Mac raised his eyebrows at the polished wood shelves on the fireplace. He couldn't believe Gideon remembered that. "Yeah. And you still want to be Patrick Bateman, right?"

"Right. Minus the homicidal tendencies."

"What's the rent on this place again?"

"Your share would be $600, which includes all utilities."

Mac hung his head. He wished he hadn't heard that number. That was lower than anything he could get on his own.

"I'm meeting with a few more people this week. I'll email you either way," Gideon said, a little too eagerly.

And that's a no. Mac rolled his eyes to himself. There was no way he was getting this apartment, no way Gideon wanted him as a roommate. And the feeling was extremely mutual. He took a quick stroll around the apartment before circling back to the door. He just wanted to be fully aware of what he was missing out on. Mac realized he made a terrible mistake when he walked by the kitchen. His breath caught in his chest.

This place has a dishwasher, too?

He was being messed with. Terrible guy, fabulous apartment. Somewhere, someone was laughing.

"You know, you were a real asshole," Mac said. He'd been thinking about that night for years. Knowing that Gideon was going to have a dishwasher and he'd be forced to live in a dilapidated shack at this point sent him over the edge.

"Are you talking about when you…"

"When I kissed you."

"I'm straight, Mac. I told you that."

Mac's eyes narrowed into slits. He wasn't getting off that easy. "Only after I made a move. You didn't say anything the whole time we were talking."

"I didn't know I had to."

"You were flirting with me!" Mac's voice echoed on the walls.

"No, I wasn't. We were just talking."

But Mac remembered every detail from that night. He could give minute-by-minute analysis. "You were smiling at me."

"People smile at each other when they're making friends." Gideon's calmness drove him crazy.

"You tapped my chest, like this." Mac demonstrated on himself, which Gideon found humorous. "It's not funny."

"I did? I was being friendly, I guess."

Mac crossed his arms. He had the trump card. "You went up to my room with me. That's the international symbol for hooking up."

Gideon took a step closer and crossed his arms right back at him. "If I recall, we weren't able to get on the Wi-Fi, and you said your dorm was just across the street. I pulled up a picture of a matzo ball, and then you were on me."

He was so fast with excuses and rationale. He spat them off like an automatic pitching machine.

"You really didn't know what was going on?"

"No. It was my first time away from my family. I was a naïve freshman, I guess."

It was just one night, but one Mac wasn't able to forget. Like all embarrassing, soul-crushing moments, it loved popping back into his mind at the most random occasions, usually when Mac was already feeling down on himself. It was the cherry on top of a crappy mood.

And then there were those times when Mac thought about that night, but with an alternate version that didn't have them stopping. In fact, this version had them doing more than kissing…

But that was fantasy, starring a Gideon who wasn't an asshole, who didn't make him feel like shit. Fantasy and reality never intertwined.

"I won't forget what you said to me. In the stairwell." Mac shook his head. *Are you out of your mind?* The words, and Gideon's look, still gave him a chill.

"I didn't think we could be friends, not after that. It would've been supremely awkward."

"We could've worked past it."

He seesawed his head. "You say that, but I'm not convinced."

"I guess we'll never know. You ran down those stairs like you were Forrest Gump."

"I'm sorry." Gideon knocked a knobby fist against the wall, being all smoldering without even realizing it. "It wasn't my finest hour. I freaked out."

He gave this hangdog shrug and his eyebrows sloped and his eyes went wide and that made it really hard to hate him.

"It's a nice place," Mac said, giving the apartment one more look. Because he was an idiot who enjoyed torture, he opened the door off the living room to ogle the spacious closets this place probably had.

Mac's jaw hit the floor. "You have an in-unit washer and dryer?"

"Yeah, it's pretty sweet."

"I didn't know college apartments had them. I thought it was an urban legend."

Mac dragged a yearning hand over the washer's surface. He was officially in a desperate time, and it called for a requisite desperate measure.

"Look, I know this sounds crazy, us trying to room together. I'm not a fan of it either, especially because I still kind of don't like you after what happened. But I need a place to live, okay? The only apartments that are available are ones I can't afford, ones with legitimately weird roommates, and ones that should be condemned by the board of health. I've been looking for two weeks, and this is the only decent place I've found. I'm reasonably clean, I'm courteous, I pay on time."

Gideon hung in the hallway. He was the boy in the bubble. Mac would tell him that he wouldn't catch his gay germs, but that'd probably freak him out.

"Why are you looking for an apartment now?"

"I just broke up with my boyfriend," Mac said.

"How come?"

"Ask him. He's the one who did the breaking." Mac shut the closet door. Gideon had on an earnest expression, actually wanting to hear more. "We were all set to move in together, and he pulled the plug at the last minute."

"No warning," Gideon said, as if he understood. "You know this isn't a decision they came to lightly. You'd think they could've planned ahead, before you signed a lease."

"Seriously! I paid for a credit check."

"Beth said her family was getting us furniture. I didn't budget for it. I had to buy this living room furniture from a guy whose grandmother just passed away. And rent a U-Haul to move it."

"Davis was the person I was closest to in this whole world, not counting my Aunt Rita. It was so unexpected, and so…"

"Inconsiderate!"

"Yes! Inconsiderate is the perfect word." Mac tucked his hands into his jeans pockets. "Look, I need a place to stay, and you need a roommate. It won't be awkward."

Although saying that made things awkward. Nice one, Mac.

"We'll give this a two-week trial," Gideon said. "If it's weird, you'll have time to find a new place."

"Fair enough." It would give Mac just enough time to see how awkward things might get. "I love social experiments."

They shook on it.

Φ

Two days later, Mac moved into his new apartment. He didn't have any furniture, so Gideon let him borrow his friend's air mattress. Mac enlisted his best friend Delia to help him lug up boxes on what turned out to be the last gasp of a brutal summer.

"I am sweating everywhere. In every crevice and fold and—"

"I get the picture." Mac also saw the picture, with the sweaty tips of her thick brown hair.

He pushed open the door with his butt. He instructed her to put all of his stuff in his bedroom. Gideon had picked up some freestanding room dividers from Ikea and cordoned off Mac's bedroom. It looked wonky, but it worked.

Delia stopped in the middle of the living room to marvel at the fireplace and the fine touches.

"Unpack first. Ogle later."

They went three more rounds with lugging boxes and bags up the stairs and into Mac's room. Soon, his room was packed tighter than a basement closet.

"You have a lot of crap," Delia said. Mac couldn't take two steps in his new bedroom thanks to it. He didn't know where it all came from, but he didn't want to throw any of it out.

"Is there anything in here that belongs to Davis? I'll happily throw that out, or set it on fire."

Mac wasn't going to show her the crate with the last remnants of his relationship. They'd been together for almost two years. He couldn't completely block out that period of time.

"Let's move some stuff into the sun porch."

"I moved it into the apartment. That's where my friendly duties end." Delia lay on the couch and scrolled through her phone.

Mac carried crates and bags to the sun porch and stacked them against one wall. Sweat made his shirt cling to his chest. The pile wobbled, but Mac wouldn't have to touch it until he got some furniture.

He went into the kitchen and poured them glasses of water. He joined Delia on the couch and rested his head on her lap. They met at a Rainbow Club introductory meeting freshman year. Right off the bat, Delia told him she was straight but a strong ally for LGBT students. In her hometown of Needham, Massachusetts, they had LGBT equality and protections for all minority groups. So there was nothing for her to do. "Can you imagine what it's like living in a town where the establishment is already on your side?" Mac kept his opinion to himself, that she should be so lucky. He was grateful to have anyone fighting for his rights. After the meeting, he chuckled to himself that the one friend he made was a straight girl.

"If Gideon gives you any crap about hitting on him, I'll come over and just hit him."

"You're too sweet, D. I think it will be fine."

Gideon came home a little bit later, after they had passed out on the couch, shoes and all.

"Hi. You must be Gideon." Delia sat up and shook his head.

Gideon dropped his backpack and beelined to the sun porch. "What's this?"

"What?" Mac craned his neck.

"The sun porch is not a storage closet."

"I'm working on getting more furniture, like a dresser and stuff. It'll be gone before you even know it's there," Mac said.

Gideon kept staring at the pile. "I already know it's there."

"It'll be gone soon."

"It better be. I'm not living with something like this in my apartment."

"*Our* apartment."

"No. *My* apartment." Gideon stood above him. For a second, Mac thought Gideon eyes shifted to check out his chest. But that had to be wishful thinking.

"I don't like messes. I prefer to live in a clean living space. So please, keep this in mind." Gideon removed the empty water glasses from the coffee table and brought them into the kitchen.

Delia laughed nervously, as if they were just reprimanded by a teacher. "Yeah, if you ever need someone to hit him, just let me know."

CHAPTER FOUR

Gideon

After a week of living together, Mac still slept on Seth's air mattress. He still didn't have a dresser or nightstand or any other discernible furniture. And he still lived out of his bags. Not suitcases, but garbage bags.

"You know, I saw some good dressers on Craigslist," Gideon pointed out to him a few days ago. He tried to nail his mom's tone of casual-yet-forceful suggestion, but it didn't work on Mac.

"Cool," Mac said. And it was never brought up again.

Gideon stared at the piles of packed garbage bags that lined the wall of Mac's bedroom. He hoped there was no rotting food in any of them.

But that wasn't even the worst of it. Gideon wanted to relax and do some studying in the enclosed porch while the weather was still nice. He pictured himself opening the windows and reading while a cool breeze swept through his hair. But he couldn't go in there. Half the room belonged to a pile of Mac's stuff.

Boxes and crates and yet even more garbage bags were stacked on top of one another, a Jenga tower of junk. Mac had promised that he would unpack and clean up in a timely manner. Gideon wasn't so sure. To him, it sounded like an alcoholic saying he was just going to have one drink.

Gideon didn't like to call himself a neat freak. He merely believed that a clean living space was the key to a good life. How could a person achieve success in the world when where he lived was in disarray?

Mac was the one who called him a neat freak.

"You are," Mac said as he was pouring himself a bowl of Raisin Bran for dinner. Mac ate cereal for dinner, and lunch, and breakfast. Could he not rotate in some canned soup or Chef Boyardee?

"There's nothing freaky about wanting to have a clean apartment. You need to respect your shared living space."

"You sound like an RA." Mac poured milk in his cereal. Drops splattered against the flakes and onto the counter. "I'll try harder."

"You said that two days ago. You're still on trial here."

"Where's my lawyer?" Mac smiled at his joke. "I will take care of the sun room. I just got distracted with classes starting. This weekend, though."

Gideon didn't believe him for a second. "How did you survive with your past roommates in the dorm?"

"I kept my mess to my half of the room, which I'm doing here."

"But I can still see it. The sun porch looks like an episode of *Hoarders*. Your pile of shit is on the verge of collapsing. It's not just there. You can't leave the kitchen a mess. We don't want to get ants." Gideon pointed his head at the milk droplets.

"For real?" Mac asked.

Gideon nodded yes.

"Man, you run a tight ship." Mac whipped off his T-shirt, exposing a smooth chest rippling with muscles. Gideon cut his eyes to the floor and focused full-throttle on the specks of dust on the tiles.

He pulled the dishrag off the oven handle. "Use this!"

"This is easier." Mac's arm muscles jumped around as he wiped up his mess. He left his T-shirt in a ball on the counter.

"Are you going to get a new shirt?"

"Nah. It's a white T-shirt. The milk blends right in." Mac gave him a knowing smirk and shoveled a mountain of cereal into his mouth.

Gideon didn't know why that threw him off so much, why it made it so hard to breathe for a moment. It was just a shock. No warning. Then, bam! Shirtless! Perhaps he wasn't expecting Mac to be so jacked. *Pittsburgh did a body good.* Gideon was regretting this two-week trial already.

"I thought gay guys were supposed to be super clean."

"And I thought straight guys were supposed to be slobs."

Gideon cocked an eyebrow. Touché. He checked the time on the microwave.

"I have to get ready."

"Hot date?" Mac asked.

"Yeah."

"Cool," Mac said. He seemed surprised, and maybe a touch sad, to be right.

"I'm kidding. We're throwing a party for new students at Hillel tonight."

"Sounds familiar. Don't give any naïve freshmen the wrong idea."

"I'm laughing on the inside." Gideon entered the solace of his clean bedroom with a new bed, washed sheets, and clothes that were folded or hung up. He changed into a navy blue button-down shirt with the sleeves rolled up, khaki shorts, and boat shoes. He went into the bathroom to get his puff of hair just right and spritz on cologne.

"Stop being awkward," he whispered to himself.

He returned to the kitchen, where Mac was finishing up the last bits of his dinner. Still shirtless.

"I'll be back later." Gideon froze in place. Heat strangled his neck.

Did Mac just check me out?

He felt Mac's eyes travel up and down his body for a split-second. It was so quick, and Mac was back to munching on his cereal, but Gideon caught it. He had given girls the onceover plenty of times. He knew what he saw. He wondered how much times that had happened over the past week. Gideon found himself puffing out his chest.

And did I like it?

"Make sure you put your spoon and bowl in the dishwasher when you're done."

Gideon hit on no freshmen at the event. They all looked so young. Was that really him two years ago? On his way home, he called his mom. He made sure to call her at least twice a week. He hated thinking about her all alone in their house. Talking to Gideon was the highlight of his mom's week, and she never minded telling him that.

"How was Hillel?" She asked.

"It was a good time."

"I still remember the spread they put out for parents weekend." Gideon and his mom had joked about the bagels they served, how bland and chewy they were. Any bagel not produced in New York or New Jersey was instantly inferior. It wasn't Hillel's fault.

Gideon slapped his hand against lampposts he passed.

"How's Beth?" She asked.

"She's good. Happy to be back on campus." Gideon didn't miss a beat. He didn't have any internal panic. He kept slapping lampposts.

"How's it going living together?"

"So far, so good. She has so much stuff, especially in the bathroom. I have half a shelf in the medicine cabinet."

"You never had sisters, so you don't know. We don't just wake up looking like this."

"I'm sure *you* do." He could feel his mom smile back.

"You need to send me a picture of the new furniture. I'm curious what her parents picked out."

A question like that would've tripped up an amateur. The key was to always be two steps ahead. "You know what, we decided not to do that. We realized that it was pointless to get all new furniture when at most, we'd be living in this apartment for two years."

"What about after graduation?"

"We don't know what kind of place we'd get in New York. The apartments there are smaller, and the set we were looking at might not have fit."

"Good point."

In times like these, Gideon felt like Billy Flynn in *Chicago* (the movie) doing his tap dance. It was only when he hung up that the usual cocktail of anger and guilt washed over him.

"Beth and I swung by thrift shops and got some pretty decent furniture."

"Wonderful. I'm excited to have her over for the Jewish holidays."

"I don't know if she can make it. She may be going to family in Boston. She's still figuring out her plans."

"Are you going with her?"

"And miss out on some of your matzo ball soup? Are you kidding?" His fake laugh satisfied his mom but made his throat ache.

"So Noah's still with that new girl he met at the casino. Christina," she said. Mother and son didn't need proper segues. "She's eighteen years older than him!"

"Eighteen is a lucky number in Judaism." Gideon's joke fell flat.

"It's only been two months, and he's already telling me he's in love."

"It's okay, Mom."

"Noah's always gone down his own path. But now this? Why can't he find a nice, Jewish girl, like you did with Beth? Your brother has given me enough *tsuris* to last a lifetime. I'm lucky I have you, Gideon. You've always been so good and responsible. You always do the right thing. You keep me sane."

Her words made Gideon feel pressure in his chest. Keeping someone sane was more work than just loving them. Sometimes it felt like too much responsibility.

They said their good-byes and hung up. Gideon's skill for little white lies developed over years of avoiding the Judy Saperstein freak-out. One lie after another. So harmless. It made him angry how hard he worked to present a positive front for his mom while his brother had one epic screw up after another. Then he remembered that no matter how small and insignificant it was, he was still lying to his mom. That was when the guilt sunk in.

He found his way to Seth's dorm. He needed some classic Seth neuroses to distract him.

You around? Wanna shoot some hoops? He texted.

I'm asleep, Seth texted back.

It's 10! Wake up!

Early class tomorrow.

Gideon called him up. "You are in college. People do not go to sleep at ten. You will go to your class tired like everyone else."

"Not tonight. I ate something at dinner that didn't sit right with me. Sorry, Gid." Seth sounded groggy, like he'd already been asleep for a while.

"I'm downstairs." Gideon kept up his enthusiasm.

"Not tonight."

"This is unbelievable." Though Gideon could never be truly mad at Seth. This was par for the course. He just worried that Seth was going to be single forever. He never dated. Dates didn't end at seven-thirty.

"Let's get lunch together tomorrow. My treat."

Gideon wasn't going to turn down free food. "Okay. But if there's filet mignon on the menu, I'm ordering two for myself. You've been warned." He looked up at the dark rows of windows of the dorm. One of them held Seth. "Sweet dreams."

"You too, Gid."

Gideon meandered around downtown Duncannon on his way home. To his apartment with the heap of junk and a gay guy who checked him out and who may still be shirtless. And that might not have been a bad thing.

Do not even go there, he warned himself. This wasn't the first time he'd had thoughts like these over the years. But he never acted on them, and that's what mattered. The good son would never do something so irresponsible.

He climbed the steps to his apartment and rested his head on the door. Being the good son was exhausting.

Inside, Mac watched TV on the couch. His feet rested on the coffee table, but Gideon didn't have the energy to get into that. He nodded in acknowledgement at his roommate. It was barely after ten, but he decided to go to sleep. He wouldn't tell Seth.

Gideon shuffled into the bathroom and brushed his teeth. Shave clippings dotted the sink. Again, something to deal with tomorrow. An empty roll of toilet paper hooked on the dispenser.

"Mac, what's this?" He charged into the living room and held up the empty roll.

"The toilet paper thing."

"Where's the toilet paper?"

"There's a new roll on top of the toilet." Mac remained glued to the TV.

"This isn't an outhouse or a barn. Here, when the toilet paper dispenser is empty, we put on a new roll. Like civilized human beings!" Gideon crumpled the cardboard roll in his fist and slammed his bedroom door. One more week, and then he could show Mac and his broad chest the door.

Gideon lay in bed, trying to fall asleep. His eyes were closed, but his brain continued to chug along without stopping. Thoughts of Noah and his mom and the freaking toilet paper roll fluttered through his head. There was always something with Noah. Now Gideon had to worry about him running off with this Christina girl? He felt like his family was always two seconds from completely unraveling, were it not for him.

Sometimes, when things got really stressful, he would shut his eyes and imagine the kiss with Mac freshman year, before he pushed him off. It was an out-of-body experience, the most non-Gideon thing that'd ever happened to Gideon. It gave him a few seconds where his body hummed rather than screeched like rusty gears. But now the freaking guy was living with him and walking around shirtless and that was a whole new layer of stress he didn't need.

He glanced at his phone. It was eleven-thirty, and he was no closer to falling asleep. Gideon left his bedroom to get a drink of water. Mac remained on the couch, watching TV. Gideon's TV.

"Can't sleep?" Mac asked him.

"I just needed to get a glass of water." Gideon walked into the kitchen.

"I couldn't sleep either." He heard Mac say from the living room. "If you're wondering, I'm not a couch potato like this. I just couldn't sleep. I thought this would help."

Gideon drank his water and stayed by the door. "I have aspirin if you need it."

Mac studied him. He wasn't being checked out. Something much more invasive. "You sure you're okay? You seem stressed."

"There's a mountain of junk in my apartment. Of course, I'm stressed."

"I don't think that's it." Mac was still studying.

"Good night. And turn the volume down." Gideon glanced back at the kitchen. There were no dishes in the sink.

He opened the dishwasher. It was loaded. Not well, but loaded. Loaded! It was a sight for sore eyes.

"You did this," Gideon said. He nearly had damn tears in his eyes.

"I told you I'd try harder." Mac looked so comfortable on the couch. Bits of his short brown hair stuck up in the back. It was the littlest things that made his day.

"Do you want some mac 'n cheese?"

CHAPTER FIVE

Mac

Mac and Gideon sat on the couch actually eating mac n' cheese. Not store bought. Gideon made it from scratch with spaghetti and shredded cheese. It tasted far superior to the Kraft stuff. He couldn't get over that a guy named Mac never ate mac n' cheese.

Gideon curled up into the corner, up against a mound of pillows, while Mac had taken the edge of the chaise. Despite sitting on the same piece of furniture, they couldn't have been further apart. Gideon probably liked it that way.

"Eighteen years is a big age difference." Mac drank from his beer bottle. "She could've given birth to Noah and voted for president on the same day."

"It's not just that. Noah always does this. It's like he gets some secret thrill from making my mom's life hell.

He was nearly expelled from Hebrew school. He crashed his car through a Dairy Queen, when he was on who-knows-what. And I won't get into how he dropped out of law school to become a professional gambler."

"He sounds cool."

Gideon shot him a glare that warned him to get that thought out of his head. "Our mom is a widow. Can't he go easy on her?"

"Maybe he's not doing this *to* her. Maybe he's doing this because he genuinely wants to. It's his life. If he loves this woman, then he loves her."

"That's not how it works."

"How what works?"

Gideon didn't give him an answer and shook it off.

"Thanks for listening to me talk about this." The warm smile on Gideon's face sent goosebumps zipping through his body. "I needed to get it off my chest, and I think I also wanted an outside opinion."

Mac could make out the blond stubble prickling his chin. He wanted to keep looking at it. "Yeah, thanks for the mac 'n cheese."

"My dad and I used to make it on late nights." Gideon stared at his bowl, the memory clouding his face. "It would be our late night snack. Sometimes, if I was sleeping, the smell of the melting cheese and hot noodles would wake me up, and I'd join him."

"I'm sorry. How long has he…"

"Eight years." Gideon dipped his fork into the bottom of his bowl, getting the last bits. "How about for you?"

Mac looked up in confusion.

"Your parents," Gideon said.

He looked on with even more confusion.

"You said you live with your aunt, and you talk about them in the past. I didn't want to bring it up before, but since we were sharing, I just thought…"

"I'm sorry." Mac felt himself turn red, dying of embarrassment. He didn't talk about his parents much, even though they were the cause of his constant insomnia. But barriers had fallen tonight. He and Gideon were in the middle of one of those epic conversations where walls tumbled down and people dared to bare their true selves. "I moved out of my parents' house four years ago, after my sophomore year of high school. I went to live with my Aunt Rita in Pittsburgh. They're still in West Virginia. They own a hardware store."

"A literal mom-and-pop shop. Cool."

Mac nodded. "I don't really speak to them, and they don't really speak to me." Saying it out loud made it sound ludicrous. These were his parents. And that was why Mac would rather people think what they want. It was better than the truth. "So I live with my Aunt Rita, and she's the best."

Mac could tell Gideon was waiting for more, but he wasn't going to push. When somebody dropped a bombshell, you couldn't ask follow-up questions. And like a tightly controlled press conference, that was all Mac was going to say about that.

He stood up and took their bowls and empty beer bottles from the coffee table. He looked at the time on his phone and dreaded his decision to take a 9 a.m. class. "I'll wash these," Mac said.

"No, I'll get them." Gideon reached for them, and their fingers touched for a split second, but one of those moments that defied categorization of time. Mac felt a warm rush cascade down his spine and the backs of his legs.

He wanted to gauge Gideon's response, but Gideon was already walking into the kitchen and placing them in the sink. Gideon stared intently at the dishes. A little too intently, Mac thought. More like avoiding eye contact.

"You're washing them before putting them in the dishwasher?" Mac asked from the doorway.

"Yeah. You don't want large food particles in the…" Gideon checked Mac's guilty face. He opened the dishwasher. It looked clean to Mac, but Gideon saw otherwise.

"Sorry," Mac said.

"It's okay. It's a first step. Maybe next you can tackle the Jenga Tower of Junk on the sun porch." Gideon said it with a laugh that obviously masked his strong desire for Mac to actually get his crap off the sun porch.

"I will. One thing at a time. Davis was the tidy one." Mac pictured his ex-boyfriend and a wave of sadness crashed inside his chest. "He would clean up my dorm room whenever he came over. My roommate never minded getting sexiled from the room because he knew he would come back to a tidier place."

These mourning moments hit Mac at the worst, most unexpected times. It was a reminder that things weren't the same anymore. The break-up hit Mac especially hard for some reason. It chipped at the deep recesses that he didn't want to disturb, somewhere in his mind where the memories of moving to Pittsburgh lived.

Gideon held out a paper towel. "I feel it, too. The sudden emptiness. Like just in case things are going well, bam! Here's a Beth memory."

"It sucks."

"Yep. Sure does."

They went to their separate rooms to get ready for bed a few minutes later. Mac stared at his reflection in the mirror as he brushed his teeth. He realized that he didn't think Gideon was an asshole. He was that sweet, soulful guy he first met, before his stupid remarks.

But for the sake of his living situation, Mac would keep those ideas to himself.

Φ

Mac loved the campus in the fall. Thickets of trees brimmed with orange, red, and yellow leaves. He was living in a canvas. It wasn't dissimilar from fall in Pittsburgh, but he'd much rather spend it here.

A few days later, he and Delia journeyed up north, past the tip of North campus, to the Barkley Miller Arena. They walked against the wind.

"They have hot food there, right?" Delia asked, squinting to brave the gusts of air slamming their faces. "I'm skipping dinner to go to this."

"Yes. Full refreshments," Mac said, though that was a wild guess. She'd have a good time once the game started. Well, he hoped.

"I'm only going because basketball is slightly less objectifying than football. At least this is a sport women are allowed to play. You're coming with me to a women's basketball game next time."

"Sure thing." Mac didn't mind agreeing because he knew Delia would never follow through.

They could hear the music pumping from the arena a block away. Mac's fingers tingled with excitement. He tried going to a few basketball games each year. Unlike baseball and football, basketball games moved fast. There was constant motion.

People handed out programs and hawked merchandise as a countdown clock to the game ticked away seconds in the center of the lobby. Anticipation rumbled through every inch of this place. He peeked in one of the section entrances and glimpsed the lit-up basketball court. It was bigger in person, an imposing stage.

"We're not there. We're up." Delia craned her neck back. "Way up."

They climbed up two ramps to the student section. Things calmed down at this level. Less hawking, more people finding their seats. They passed one concession stand after another as they circumnavigated the arena.

"Did we go in a circle yet, or are the concession stands repeating themselves?" Delia asked.

"They're repeating."

"And of course there's no healthy snack options, and it's all wicked overpriced. Seven bucks for a hot dog?"

"Can you save your latest protest for after the game?" Mac asked politely as they came upon their section.

They moseyed down the steep steps to their section, which was behind one of the baskets. Their seats were on the aisle, which bummed Mac out slightly, knowing people would be walking back and forth the whole game.

The basketball players warmed up, dribbling and shooting on the court. Mac leaned forward in his seat and watched everything, soaking it all in.

"The game hasn't started yet," Delia said.

"I know."

A few minutes later, she whacked him on the shoulder to get up so people could get by. Two guys shimmied down the aisle, one of whom looked miserable to be there, and the other one was Gideon.

"Of all the aisles in all the student sections," Gideon said to Mac, careful not to step on his or Delia's shoes.

Gideon and his friend plunked down next to Mac. Was it bad that Mac had begun to recognize Gideon's outfits?

"Small world," Gideon said.

"Well, it makes sense we'd both wind up in the student section."

"I guess." Gideon tapped his friend on the shoulder. "Seth, this is Mac."

"Yeah, I've seen you around." Seth held his hand out for a shake. He wore khakis and a tucked-in shirt.

"And hello, Delia," Gideon said. "Still want to hit me?"

"All day every day," Delia deadpanned.

The announcer called out each starting member of the basketball team. Mac cheered loudly, cupping his hands to make a megaphone. He caught Gideon eyeing him with a grin that made Mac blush.

"What?" Mac asked.

"I didn't know you were into basketball," Gideon said.

"Because I'm gay, I can't be into sports?"

"You're putting stereotypes into my mouth. I never heard you mention it."

"That's something that friends discuss, and we're only roommates," Mac said. Gideon seemed to take it in stride, smiling to himself.

Gideon tossed a piece of gum in his mouth and offered one to Mac and Delia. "Seth doesn't like chewing gum. He's afraid of swallowing it."

"I swallowed a hunk of Bazooka when I was nine, and if you cut open my stomach, you'd find it still intact," Seth yelled.

"I can't believe corporations are allowed to sell candy like that to little children," Delia said. "This is why obesity rates are skyrocketing."

"Soda is the new smoking," Seth said. "Have you seen—"

"*Fed Up*?"

"Yes!"

"What an amazing documentary! Of course it got buried on Netflix. That's what the food-industrial complex wants."

Delia and Seth were leaning over Mac and Gideon like they were chair arms.

"I have to eat healthy," Seth said. "I don't have a choice because of my allergies."

"And do you wonder why suddenly all of these people have nut and gluten allergies? I wonder if it's because we've been force-fed synthetic, GMO, high-fructose corn syrup crap for decades."

"You think?" Seth scratched his head. Mind officially blown.

"It's possible." Delia shrugged. "It's better than the other b.s. explanations we've been given. I want to start a petition that replaces all the candy in the campus vending machines with healthier, organic options."

"I would love that!"

The ref blew his whistle, and the players got into position for the tipoff.

"I heard that there's one organic concession stand in this place," Seth said.

"Really?" Delia asked. "Where?"

"I don't know. Want to go find it?"

Seth and Delia nodded at each other and stood up just as Browerton's player tipped the ball to his teammate. Seth climbed over the roommates, and rushed out with Delia.

Gideon and Mac shared a look like *What just happened?*

The ref blew his whistle. Players lined up for a foul shot. Gideon leaned over to Mac without taking his eyes off the court. "Tomorrow is October first. That means your two weeks are up," he said. "And I think you passed the trial period."

Mac's ears perked up. He turned to Gideon just in time to watch his face break out into a wide smile that lifted his cheeks and showed off his gleaming teeth. Mac's beating heart was a little bit more noticeable in his chest.

Gideon extended his hand for a shake. "Officially roommates?"

Mac shook it. "Officially roommates."

And just officially roommates, he told himself.

CHAPTER SIX

Gideon

Gideon couldn't unsee it. He knew that. He tried not thinking about it, but that made him think about it even more. Think about what it could do.

Where it would go.

After two weeks of being officially roommates, he and Mac had found a groove. Mac had stopped leaving plates in the sink and clothes on the bathroom floor. Gideon had come home after class the other day to find Mac sweeping the kitchen floor. He had missed many of the hard-to-reach corners where most of the dirt and dust liked to hide, but Gideon applauded the effort. Gideon had been apprehensive about letting Mac be his permanent roommate, but he used some of his powerful white lies on himself, convincing himself that there was no awkwardness between them. Mac was a decent guy, and admitting there was awkwardness meant admitting that Gideon had something to feel awkward about, and he didn't. So there.

And then there were those special occasions like today where the awkwardness literally smacked Gideon in the face.

It flashed into his mind. *It*. He couldn't even use its actual name.

Gideon let the warm water of his shower try and cleanse his mind. Droplets streamed down his face and criss-crossed through his stubble.

He had tried to ignore the Jenga Tower of Junk on the sun porch. But his eye was drawn to it. Immediately. Every day.

Mac was at class for the afternoon. Gideon stared down the tower. He could hear the Wild West duel music playing in his mind. *One of us is leaving this room today, and it ain't gonna be me.*

Cardboard boxes sunk into each other and leaned against crates with assorted flotsam and jetsam sticking out of their openings. Garbage bags stretched to their full capacity and wobbled at the top. The tower was playing chicken with gravity.

Like in actual Jenga, he went for the easy moves first. He took away the boxes and a garbage bag that weren't supporting the tower. He dropped them in Mac's room, by his bed. The tower thinned. Gideon could see the wall behind it. Well, glimpses of it.

He gripped a crate at the base that had the edge of a picture frame jutting out from its side. Gideon could make out Mac in a graduation robe with a woman with his same brown eyes and shiny hair. Aunt Rita. He could instantly tell from her smile that she was good people. He found a picture peeking out from under. It was pre-teen Mac sitting next to a cash register in what looked like his parents' hardware store. His cheeks had more fat, but Gideon recognized Mac's warm smile under there. He let it pull him in. Behind Mac were two older people, probably his parents. Gideon wondered if the picture held any answers to what happened there. He pulled out the crate to get a better view, forgetting that it was supporting the Jenga tower of junk.

"Shit!"

Bags and boxes rumbled above him, swaying back and forth. Gideon tried to reason with it telepathically why it shouldn't budge. He attempted to hold the tower steady, but it had no base. Mac's possessions tumbled forward. They splayed across the floor in a loud cacophony of clangs and smacks. The box at the top dumped right onto Gideon's head, and that's when he came into contact with *it*.

A banana careened out of the bag and nailed Gideon square in the forehead. It knocked his glasses off his face. He didn't realize what had hit him at first. *Why was Mac keeping a banana in his stuff?*

Gideon squatted down and picked it up. But bananas shouldn't be rubbery. And bananas weren't this large. Gideon put on his glasses and realized he was gripping a thick, yellow dildo in his nice Jewish boy hand.

He marveled at its weight and size and lifelike texture. But then he remembered he was holding another man's sex toy.

"Ahhhhhh!!" He threw it against the wall. It bounced off and landed on his feet. He screamed again. He kicked it into the heap of fallen junk like his life depended on it.

And now here Gideon was, taking his longest shower to date, scrubbing his hands, his arms, his face until the skin began to wrinkle. He wanted to stop thinking about what he saw, and what he touched. But the more he attempted to steer his mind elsewhere, the more his mind refused. He thought about Mac using it on Davis, on other guys, shoving it all the way in like a missile locked and loaded. He imagined Mac using it on himself, jerking himself off while he slid it inside his tight ass late at night, gasping in pleasure. Gideon might've thought about that last one a little bit too long.

His fingers pruned under the water. He didn't feel sufficiently clean, but as close as he was going to get.

He stepped out of the bathroom in a towel and found Mac in the hallway. He felt extra weird and extra naked.

"Hey," Gideon said.

"Midday shower?" Mac asked.

"Yeah." Gideon wondered if Mac was looking at him. Ever since he, um, accidentally checked out Mac when he stripped in the kitchen, Gideon had been careful about keeping his eyes to himself.

He raced into his bedroom and shut the door. He got dressed and took a few breaths. Gideon told himself he would forget what he saw eventually. *Lots of people have sex toys. My mom probably has one.*

He smacked his forehead. He replaced one visual with an even worse one.

Gideon kept his hand on the doorknob. He wondered if Mac would feel this uncomfortable if he found his stash of condoms. Probably not. Because people had sex. The earth was round. No big deal.

Why was it different here? Would Mac think of me using condoms?

Gideon opened the door. "Did class get out early?"

He found Mac in the sun porch, examining the new organization of his possessions. Gideon had quickly reassembled the Jenga Tower of Junk so he could run into a shower.

"Your shit was like a house of cards. It tumbled and fell. I figured I'd help by cleaning it up."

Mac rifled through a box in the middle of the tower. The box that had held *it*. Sweat beaded on Gideon's forehead.

"We still need to get you a dresser."

Mac turned around to face him. The non-banana was in his hands. Mac blushed. Gideon was right there with him.

"That fell out, too," Gideon said, straining through each word. He didn't know the right way to talk to a friend about his giant, yellow dildo.

"Oh, sorry."

Gideon noticed he handled it with care. "It's not going to break."

"It was expensive, so…"

"You want to take care of it."

Gideon had never seen him so red. Even though that toy attacked him, Gideon felt bad. Jewish guilt. Extending to every aspect of his life now.

"I thought it was an old banana," Gideon said, breaking the tension suffocating the room. "It's definitely not a banana."

"Thanks for cleaning up my stuff." Mac checked the last of his toppled items.

Gideon didn't understand why he said what he said next. Either his brain was two steps ahead of him, or off on another planet. But when it came out, he didn't completely regret asking the question because a part of him genuinely wanted to know the answer.

"Does it hurt?"

Mac held the dildo and looked at it to make sure that's what Gideon meant. "Hurt is the wrong word."

"Obviously, you like it."

"There's some discomfort at first, but it's an exciting discomfort, like getting your ears pierced, I think. But you get used to it. Then it feels amazing, like you're in the middle of a fireworks display."

"It looks like it would hurt."

"Well, I'd use lube, of course."

"Right," Gideon said, as if he knew any of that. For all the sex he'd had, he felt like a neophyte. "It's that amazing?"

"Are you talking about this or the real thing?" Mac asked.

Gideon gave some type of nod, and Mac seemed to get that meant the latter. He'd never been so tongue-tied. He didn't want to speak, only listen.

"Coming when someone's inside you is one of the most intense things I've ever experienced. You just lose complete fucking control." Mac put the dildo back into the crate and bolted into the kitchen. He poured himself a glass of water. "Wow, that was a huge overshare. I'm sorry."

Gideon wanted to be icked out, but he was intrigued. More intrigued than he should've been. By the actual sex act and the losing control part. He had some activity happening in his pants. He wanted to hear more, even though he knew he should leave it alone. "So are you, like, a bottom then?"

"I like doing both."

"Do gay guys do both usually?"

"I don't know. The ones I've been with, yes."

"How do you guys decide?"

"Coin toss."

Gideon hung his neck forward. "What? Like at a football game?"

"That was a joke." Mac was the only one who found it funny. Like, he was actually smiling. One of his nice, floppy smiles. *I should* not *be cataloguing Mac's smiles.*

Mac brushed past him into the sun porch. He took out the dildo and twirled it in his hand like a baton. "I was wondering when we'd have this conversation."

"What do you mean?"

"Straight guys act grossed out by gay sex, but deep down, they're curious. My gay friends have all been asked by their straight friends about their sex lives."

"Do you want to hear about mine?"

"No. I know how hetero sex works." Mac took another sip of water. "Straight guys think we're having all this unbelievable, unholy, orgy-tastic sex. Not true. It's just like hetero sex, minus a few parts."

"Excuse us for being curious. In seventh grade, we had a whole class about how men and women have sex. There was no gay and lesbian unit. It's all a mystery. We have no idea what's it like to have one of those things up…"

"Your ass?" Mac examined it in his hands. "You know, a lot of straight guys are into pegging."

"Pegging? You mean having one of those up...I'll pass," Gideon said.

"It's not as uncommon as you think." A smile spread across Mac's lips that Gideon had never seen before. It was confident and a tad sinister. "You may want to experiment and try it by yourself, even just doing a finger while in the shower."

"Nope." Gideon crossed his arms, shutting that down pronto.

"You wouldn't have to tell anyone. Not even me."

"I will pass. I will most certainly pass."

"Trust me, a lot of straight guys do it," Mac said. "They may not talk about it, but they do it."

Gideon was afraid to ask Mac how he knew that. "That's their business. Their body, their choice."

Mac slinked forward and put the dildo in his face like it was a microphone. "You could always borrow mine. Just wash it after you use it."

Mac broke into laughter.

"Fuck you." Gideon laughed, too, and just like that, they were back to normal. Two roommates joking around.

Well, almost normal.

"Would you mind putting it away now?" Gideon asked.

CHAPTER SEVEN

Mac

Delia and Seth waited on the couch while Mac got ready for Cherry Stem. The lone gay club in Duncannon finally realized the economic benefits of having an eighteen-and-up night. Mac flicked his fingers through his hair to get it the right amount of caring without looking like he cared, or in other words, "playful."

"Hurry up, Mac. You look gorgeous," she called from the living room.

"One more minute." Mac gargled some mouthwash.

Delia and Seth curled up on the chaise part of the couch both checking their phones, his arm casually around her. Mac still had to chuckle at how perfectly they worked as a couple.

"Seth, you're really coming with us tonight?" Mac asked. "You are so whipped."

"It will be fun." He turned to Delia. "Right?"

"Yes! I can't believe you don't like to dance."

"Well, I pulled both my hamstrings dancing at my junior prom."

"Why don't you do some stretching while Mac finishes getting pretty?" Delia pecked him on the lips. Seth stood up and did leg stretches against the wall.

"I'm actually done." Mac shook nerves from his hands. It was his first toe-dip back into the gay dating pool.

Delia glanced at her boyfriend, doing quad stretches now. "Let's give him another minute." She motioned for them to go into Mac's bedroom. "So how's it going living with Gideon? Is he still afraid of catching your gay germs or whatever?"

"It's going well." Mac blushed, thinking about their conversation a few days ago. On the surface, things seemed like normal, but Mac noticed little things, like how Gideon put on a T-shirt after he got out of the shower and how he didn't go near the sun porch or mention Mac's pile of shit again. At least they were both weirded out by the talk.

"You guys seem to be a good match."

"What does that mean?"

"As roommates."

"Right."

Mac took an extra second to think of him, but then pushed it out of his mind. *He's straight and your roommate.* He had to tell himself that several times over. But then Gideon would lick his lips while reading on the couch or brush past him in the kitchen, and Mac would basically need a cold shower. He needed a night out at a gay club more than ever. He needed the distraction. He reached into his pocket and squeezed his four-leaf clover keychain for some good luck tonight. It was a tradition that never got old.

"Ready?" Mac clapped his hands and headed to the front door. Delia and Seth followed.

Before Mac could open it, Gideon beat him to the punch. He swept inside, surprised at the crowd waiting for him when he arrived.

"Hi," Gideon said to the three of them. "Are you guys going out?"

"We are, but it's to a gay club," Delia said.

"You, too?" Gideon asked Seth.

"I'm being a supportive boyfriend."

"I'll come, too."

Mac and Delia traded confused looks.

"You heard me when I said 'gay club,' right?" Delia asked him.

Gideon nodded.

"So it's a club for gay guys. And a supportive boyfriend."

"Are you banning me from going?" Gideon asked, totally unfazed by Delia's salient points.

"No. Of course not. The more, the merrier."

"Great." Gideon went into his room to change. Mac and Delia communicated telepathically with more looks and arched eyebrows and nervous laughter.

"He probably doesn't want to be alone," Delia whispered. She mouthed *Beth*.

"I can stay and hang out with him," Seth said.

"No need." Gideon yanked his door open. He wore a black button-down shirt with rolled-up sleeves and jeans. Mac had a feeling the guys at Cherry Stem would take to his "straight-acting" appearance. He was finding himself susceptible.

"And you guys are awful whisperers. I want to go. It's a great place to meet girls."

"What?" Mac asked.

"Gay bars are filled with straight girls. Every girl I dated loved going to them. They don't have a worry in the world about being hit on by guys. Their defenses are down. And there are no lines for the bathroom."

"You're annoying them in the place where they don't want to be annoyed," Delia said. "A gay bar is a sanctuary where a girl can dance in peace."

"It's *our* sanctuary," Mac said. "You are a guest. But it's our safe space."

"Everybody's safe and sound!" Gideon grabbed his coat from the closet. He passed Mac his own. "But when the music is pumping and the drinks are flowing and they're surrounded by guys who want nothing to do with them, these girls will want somebody to swoop in and show them a good time."

Delia pretended to vomit. "And yet again, the straight white guy exploits a minority's sacred ground for his own personal gain."

"I'm not exploiting anything. I'm not stopping anyone from having fun. In fact, I'm clearing the way for you." Gideon pointed at Mac, who turned red from the attention. "I'm taking one for the team. Or two if I wind up having a really good night."

"I'm glad you think so highly of us deadwood," Delia deadpanned.

"Shall we go?" Seth said, pointing to the door.

"We shall," Delia said with an eye roll reserved for Gideon.

Mac locked up behind them. They rumbled down the stairs to the street. Gideon waited for Mac.

"How will I know if a gay guy is hitting on me?" He asked.

"If he shoves his hand down your pants, there's a pretty good chance he's hitting on you."

Φ

Mac didn't want to shut his eyes when he got inside Cherry Stem. He wanted to absorb it all. Every strobe light. Every thumping beat. Every poster on the wall. He felt so grateful to be here. It made him think about where he came from in West Virginia, where he had to keep his desires a secret. Or at least he tried to.

Now he was in a building filled with probably hundreds of them. Hundreds of available guys who he could openly be into. He wouldn't have to think about the one straight guy in the room. When they got into the club, Delia found her sorority sister Lorna, a girl whose red hair was a good primer on her vivacious personality. She was flanked by other sorority sisters and gay friends and made the introductions. Mac couldn't keep track of all the names, but he'd met Henry and Nolan plenty of times before. Mac introduced them to Gideon, who told all of them he was straight right off the bat.

Gideon suggested they all dance together, guys and girls, in a widening circle. Gideon needed to dance in a group in order to show he was straight. Two guys dancing together meant they were gay. Group meant friends. These were the byzantine laws for straight guys at dance clubs.

For a straight guy, Gideon knew how to dance. Mac spotted some other obviously straight guys at the periphery of the dance floor. None of them made an effort.

Henry and Nolan grinded against each other and gave each other pecks on the lips. To the untrained eye, they looked like they had just met tonight, not like a serious couple.

"PDA much?" Gideon snarked.

Nolan pulled away from Henry. "You're on our turf now. Get used to it." And he went back to running his hands across his boyfriend's body.

Gideon shot Mac a look, nodding his head at the lovebirds, as if to say "Isn't this a bit much?"

"Like Nolan said, it's our turf," Mac responded proudly.

The next song came on, and Gideon went back to dancing. Mac kept his eyes on the room, on the other guys, not on the one next to him wiggling his very cute butt.

Straight. Roommate. Cold shower.

He didn't dance like straight guys Mac had seen. Seth was pretty much stepping left then right, no rhythm. Gideon didn't seem to be scoping out the room for girls. Maybe that was part of his strategy. Mac soaked in all the attractive, *available* guys around him.

"You're staring," Gideon said.

"What?"

"You're not going to get anyone if you're gawking at them." Gideon danced closer to Mac so he didn't have to shout. "If you want to check someone out, glance at them for a few seconds, then look away. Do that a few times and see if they start checking you out. And close your mouth when you dance! It's the same as chewing food."

Mac clamped his lips shut and properly checked out a few guys in his vicinity, counting in his head for a few seconds before looking away.

"Are you counting the seconds in your head?" Gideon asked.

"How did you know?"

"Because you are concentrating awfully hard for dancing to a remixed Adele song. And your mouth is hanging open like a Venus fly trap."

Mac hung his head. Guilty. Single. Lost cause.

Gideon massaged his shoulder, which Mac enjoyed a bit too much. "Just enjoy yourself. Don't think so hard. People want to hang out with people who are having fun."

The next song came on, and Gideon challenged them to dance like no one was looking. If Gideon could sway his hips and wiggle his butt, then so could Mac. He stopped caring and enjoyed himself, just as Gideon wanted.

Their friends left for the bar, but Gideon stayed put. So did Mac. The space between them narrowed. The hairs on Gideon's arm brushed against Mac as their fingers came dangerously close to making contact. His musky cologne flitted up Mac's nose, sending all the blood in Mac's body to one central, inappropriate location. *Thank goodness it's dark in here!* Gideon wasn't following the byzantine rules for straight guys in dance clubs, but he didn't seem to care.

Mac danced a little closer. He didn't stop himself from looking Gideon up and down, taking in details like the pull of his chest against his shirt and the curve of his thigh in his tight jeans. He didn't hold himself back from meeting

Gideon's heavy eyes, which stared right back at him with an intent that nearly made Mac punch a hole in his pants.

Fuck.

Their upper arms rubbed back and forth. Mac's pinkie grazed Gideon's thumb, which flicked in reaction and massaged back. Gideon licked his lips and that feeling Mac had at the party freshman year roared back into his chest. Plus a huge boner.

He wanted to man up and kiss him, but he remembered last time. He tried willing Gideon to make the damn move. He didn't know what percent this was. Maybe there was an experiment in here about straight guys seeming gay when surrounded by other gay men.

A guy in a cowboy hat and flannel shirt had other plans, though. He snaked his arms around Gideon and grinded him from behind. Gideon's eyes bulged out of his skull like he'd just been dumped into a garbage can full of rats.

Mac pushed the guy off Gideon with more force than he planned.

"He's straight!" Mac shouted through his tightened jaw.

The guy surveyed who he just grinded and shot Mac a skeptical look. Gideon was a petrified piece of wood.

"He is," Mac said firmly.

"Then why the hell is he here?" The cowboy slapped Gideon on the butt and went back to his friends.

Gideon still didn't move. Mac wondered if he was having a heart attack. Mac's dad used to tell him if he threw rocks at a beehive, he was bound to get stung. And if you danced at a gay bar, you were bound to get your butt slapped.

"You okay?" Mac asked him. Gideon ran off.

Mac searched for him on the expansive dance floor. Smoke machines went off, puffing out smoke across the room. He tried to make him out among the clouds. He sidestepped couples as he weaved through the heart of the floor. It was no use calling out his name. The music was too loud to hear anyone unless they screamed in your ear.

He thought he saw a recognizable tuft of unruly blond hair. But the smoke cleared, and Mac couldn't have been more wrong.

The tuft of unruly hair belonged to a guy grinding against his ex-boyfriend. The guy leaned up and kissed Davis's prominent chin, then his lips. Mac wanted to move, but he was caught in a web of embarrassment. The awkward moment would not release him until he received complete degradation.

"Mac?" Davis gave him a half-wave, just as unsure as Mac as what to do in this situation.

Some part of Mac's brain had taken over manual controls. This was fight or flight, and Mac wished he could literally fly away. He didn't know where it came from, but he gave Davis a buoyant smile and a military salute.

A military salute?

Mac got the hell off the dance floor, bobbing and weaving around guys actually having a good time. He found Gideon on line at the bar.

"You'd wig out, too, if gay John Wayne put his boner against your ass," Gideon said. He immediately changed course when he saw Mac's face. "What happened?"

Mac had a jumble of possible answers lodged in his throat. "I've been replaced."

He shared his encounter with Davis, salute included.

"Where the hell did that come from?" Mac asked.

"Well, you know when people are in extreme situations, their brain can pick up skills and languages immediately? Maybe you acquired military-style fight training the second you saw Davis." Gideon shrugged. "Or maybe you just freaked out like a normal human being."

"I like your first answer."

Gideon got them bottles of water. They went outside to the smoker's courtyard and found a corner not shrouded in cigarette smoke.

"He wasted no time," Mac said. "How long do you think they've been dating?"

"Since 'Like a Prayer.'"

A guy in a pink tank top asked them if they had a light, and scowled when the answer was no. "The smoker's lounge is for SMOKING!" The guy screamed with an unlit cigarette in his mouth.

"You know what he said when he broke up with me? I'm too needy." Mac hated that Davis's words stuck in his head. "What does that even mean? How is it wrong to want to be around your boyfriend?"

"That was just code for 'I don't want to be around you anymore.'"

Mac took a sip of his water. His eyes narrowed into slits. He was onto the anger stage in grieving. "Our time together is now firmly in the past for him. Why do guys move on so fast?" He looked to Gideon for an answer.

"Do you want a polite friend answer, or can I be honest?" Gideon swished the water in his bottle.

"Please be honest," Mac said, although he wasn't sure if he wanted to hear it.

"Guys know they're going to break up with a girl, or guy, well before she knows it. The girls I've dated, I get this niggling voice in my head that says this relationship is not the one. You try to see yourself with this person, and your stomach twists in knots when you think about that future. No couple ever has that realization at the same time. Somebody's always first. Once I have it, the relationship is done in my mind, even though I have to go through the motions a little bit longer. It's like senioritis. So Davis had that realization before you. There's no shame in losing."

Mac looked out at the smokers, all enjoying their night. "Was that supposed to make me feel better?"

"No. You wanted me to be honest."

The smoker finally got his stupid light and waved it at them in victory. Mac gave him the finger. He'd never flipped somebody off. It was nice. He should do it more often.

"Did you really feel that way?" Mac asked him. "About girls you dated. Your stomach twisting in knots?"

"Something like that. It'd always start out hot and heavy. I liked that." He quirked an eyebrow. "But then in the quiet moments, when we would be laying on the bed together or when we ran out of things to say, this alarm would go off in my head."

Mac had a similar feeling when he tried dating girls in high school, but he wouldn't tell Gideon that.

"Even though you shouldn't be out here," the cigarette guy stumbled up to them and waved his cigarette at them. "I love watching you guys. You're the cutest couple."

"Oh, we're not..." Heat crept up Mac's neck.

Gideon threw his arm around Mac. "Thanks, man! College sweethearts!"

It was just for show, but it gave Mac some sort of back orgasm. Gideon's grip was stronger and more protective than it had to be. He knew how to embellish a lie in all the right places. *One million cold showers.*

The guy blew them a kiss, then wandered off to his smoker buddies.

"Why'd you say that?" Mac asked.

"It was the easiest way to get him off our backs." Gideon pulled back his arm.

Mac almost pictured them as a couple. Lying on a bed with Gideon not talking seemed better than most things in the world.

"Thanks for talking."

"Anytime." Gideon grinned, and Mac felt safe in that look. "And if you're still feeling down, Big Bird can probably cheer you up."

"Big Bird?" Mac asked before getting it. He smacked Gideon in the shoulder. "I am not calling it Big Bird. You've just ruined my childhood."

CHAPTER EIGHT

Gideon

A few days after Cherry Stem, Gideon took the train back home for Rosh Hashanah, the Jewish new year. There was no ball drop, no countdown, no celebration involved with this holiday. He and his mom sat in a packed temple as the rabbi said prayers that…well, he didn't exactly know what the prayers meant. He just knew that Rosh Hashanah wasn't about celebrating the year to come but reflecting on the year that passed.

Happy new year! Even though it's not "happy," right? Mac texted him.

"Put the phone away." Gideon's mom pointed at the open prayer book in his hands.

Gideon regretted not wearing a watch. He wondered how much time was passing, if any at all. It was like being in a Vegas casino, except less fun. The new year didn't have to be completely solemn. They were still getting to celebrate making it a whole year.

His mom craned her neck to the empty seat next to Gideon. Noah called them this morning and said he had to play in a tournament, but he would be at dinner tonight. Gideon knew that his mom was secretly hoping he would show up at services. He did, too. It was tradition. Not the Rosh Hashanah part, but the trying to make the other one laugh.

Friends of Gideon's mom walked by the aisle and saw the empty seat. His mom told them that Noah was sick and couldn't make it today. People nodded and wished him a speedy recovery, but it was doubtful if any of them believed her. She wasn't as good at the lies as he. Their disapproving looks stung Gideon deep down every single time.

"I can't believe your brother," his mom whispered to him. She had developed the distinct ability of talking without turning her head. "He chose playing cards over this?"

"He'll be at dinner tonight," Gideon said.

"It's because of her." She shook her head. "Christina probably didn't want him to come."

"He'll be here for Yom Kippur. He will." Gideon wanted to believe it, too.

"But you won't. I wanted our whole family here."

Yom Kippur was the holiest day of the year in Judaism and occurred ten days after Rosh Hashanah. If the latter was about reflecting on the year that passed, then the former was us asking the big man above to forgive all the terrible things we did over those twelve months. Gideon couldn't take off ten days from school, so he would be attending services at Browerton.

"He'll be at dinner tonight." Gideon patted his mom's hand.

She tipped Gideon's chin and gave him a smile that masked her hurt. "I'm glad you're here. You've always done the right thing."

They returned to listening to the rabbi, who was still saying a prayer. Gideon didn't know if it was the same one or a different one. His eyes landed a few rows in front, where a little kid stood on his chair. Gideon remembered being that bored in services. Now, he had to be an adult and tough it out, but he stood in solidarity with the kid. His parents ushered him down quickly, but not before Gideon caught a glimpse of his Big Bird yarmulke.

"What's so funny?" His mom asked.

"Nothing." He felt his cheeks bunch up by his eyes. He pictured Mac in the empty seat next to him, clamping his hand over his mouth to suppress his church giggles—or temple giggles in this case.

"It's a shame Beth wasn't able to make it," his mom whispered. "I think she would've loved my matzo ball soup."

Φ

Noah did make it to dinner. He came by himself. Gideon wondered if his mom had invited Christina. Maybe she was smart enough not to enter the lions' den.

"I'm glad you could make it," his mom said to Noah with a tablespoon of motherly guilt. "How was cards?"

"Good. Got next month's rent wrapped up."

Unlike Gideon, Noah had been smart and cut off his wily, Saperstein hair. He kept it close-cropped. He could be mistaken for a college student in his jeans and hoodie. It was not proper Rosh Hashanah attire, and his mom's look reinforced the point.

"I hope it was worth missing one of the holiest days of the year."

"Mom, this is how I make a living. I told you I'd be at Yom Kippur next week."

"Sadie Lowenstein's son is a partner at his Manhattan law firm, and he was able to take off for Rosh Hashanah and sit in temple."

Noah tightened his jaw. Gideon focused on shoveling matzo ball soup into his mouth. That was the one bright side to this awkward dinner. He got to eat his mom's delicious home cooking.

"Did she tell you not to come?" His mom pointed an accusatory serving spoon at her oldest son.

"She has a name. Christina. And she didn't say anything." Noah put chicken on his plate.

"Well, I'm sorry the second holiest day of the year has so inconvenienced you."

"Mom," Gideon said. "It's okay. He'll be there for Yom Kippur. It's not the worst thing if he missed one holiday."

"It is, Gideon. You wouldn't miss a holiday." She pointed at Gideon while looking at Noah. "Your brother wouldn't miss a holiday."

Unease churned in his stomach. Gideon hated getting involved. His dad had been the voice of reason in their family. But now that they were down to three, Gideon was perpetually stuck in the middle. His heart strained from the constant push and pull. Both his mom and brother were equally strong-willed. All he needed was the striped referee shirt and a whistle.

"Christina isn't leaving the picture."

Her face sank. Panic washed over her eyes. "What do you mean, Noah?"

Noah sat up straight and took a breath. "I asked her to marry me."

Gideon dropped his spoon. It plunked into his soup and splattered hot broth on his cheeks.

"When?" His mom asked.

"Last weekend."

"Last weekend? And we're just hearing about it now?"

"Yes."

Gideon didn't want to look at his mom, but he couldn't not. He tilted his neck slowly. She was as white as a ghost. Her jaw hung open like she had the wind knocked out of her.

"Noah…" she said. "You've barely begun dating."

"It's been three months. She makes me happier than I've ever been. Can't you see that?"

"She makes you happy now, but what about when she's fifty in a few years?"

"Then I'll love her just as much."

"Love?" She looked to Gideon, but he kept his head focused on soup.

"You should give her a chance, Mom," Noah said. "She's a good person."

"I'm sure she's very nice, but not as my daughter-in-law. Don't you see how crazy this is?"

"You're just worried about what your precious friends at temple will say."

"You already give them plenty to chew on," she said, her voice thick. "You're only twenty-four. You're going to give up so much of your life. Are you really sure this is what you want to do? Noah, you always rush into things. You're too impulsive. I don't want to watch you make a mistake because you didn't think it through."

"Mistake?" Noah cut his eyes to Gideon for back-up.

But so did Gideon's mom.

Gideon felt the strain tighten his chest. Enough pushing and pulling would tear him asunder. He swirled the matzo ball around his soup. He had no desire anymore to eat his mom's home cooking, but at least the food wasn't looking to him for support.

His mom stood up. "If you really thought you were making the right decision, you wouldn't have waited a week to tell us." She placed her napkin on her plate and went upstairs.

Once she was gone, Noah turned to Gideon, radiating all kinds of hurt. "Not even a congratulations or anything. Mom hasn't made any effort to get to know her!"

"She's just in shock. She just wishes you hadn't sprung it on us at dinner, after the fact," Gideon said.

"Of course you're siding with her. Because you're the responsible one. You never screw up," he said mockingly.

"There are no sides. We're all on the same team here."

"Be honest, Gid. There never was going to be a good time to tell you. Even though I love her, and even though it's my life, there was never going to be a good time." Noah stood up and tossed his napkin on his plate, just like his mother. He glared at Gideon. "A congratulations would've been nice from my brother."

The game was over. Court was dismissed. The matzo ball bobbed in the broth.

$$\Phi$$

Gideon cleared off the table and put the food into Tupperware. He stopped by Noah's room, but the door was shut. Gideon held up his fist to knock, but then what? He didn't know what to say. Whatever he would say to his brother, he should've said at dinner. But then that would've upset his mom. The Sapersteins had always been a peaceful, loving family. This level of drama was unprecedented. Rosh Hashanah was not supposed to go like this.

Can't wait to get back to campus! Gideon texted Mac.

Don't come back yet. Mac then texted him a picture of a sink filled with dirty dishes. Gideon missed their apartment. He didn't think of it as just his anymore.

I'm pretending I didn't see that, he texted back.

Gideon lay in bed, staring at the ceiling, his mind going a million miles an hour but heading nowhere. He never meant to be the responsible son. It just happened. It was a natural progression of the younger child. He saw the hard time his parents had with Noah growing up, so he molded himself to be everything his brother was not. His parents didn't deserve two Noahs. He wasn't going to be a person who ignored the consequences of his actions, who just did whatever the hell he wanted. He wasn't going to bring shame to his family. That was, well, irresponsible.

He needed a shower. That would help him fall asleep.

The hot water soothed his skin. He never understood how a shower could relax him, but they did. He kept thinking about his mom, sulking in her bedroom. She'd probably toss and turn all night, asking herself how she let this happen and where she went wrong.

Gideon turned the water warmer. He hoped that soothing feeling would kick in soon. He lathered himself up with soap, scrubbing away the day, but he still felt the stress. His hand washed his lower back, and then he let his slick fingers slip further, down the curve of his ass. Just a flicker. He pulled them back up to his chest, but it was too late. His body was already tingling.

He let them flicker down there again, descending slowly until they reached his crack. It sent a rush of pure joy through his body.

Gideon wanted that feeling back. He let his middle finger wander down further his crack and graze over his hole. It was ultrasensitive. He exhaled a trembling breath.

He checked that the bathroom door was closed. His finger went back and forth like a metal detector, dancing over his spot. His body shivered in the hot water. Gideon learned one arm against the wall for balance. *What am I doing?* He raised a leg onto the edge of the shower. He ran his hand down the crack of his ass, teasing himself, and slipped one finger into his hole.

Holy shit.

It was new. It was like nothing he'd ever felt before. It was a reckless and defiant feeling that charged through his nerves. The same feeling that had almost made him— forced him to—kiss Mac on the dance floor.

He let his finger slide in and out of his ass. Streams of water flowed down his face, onto his chest, then hit his hardening cock. His dick had never been this sensitive to touch. A few tugs would probably make him shoot.

Gideon soaped up his hand and inserted two fingers this time. He rammed them in deep, then drew them out ever so slowly. His teeth chattered as the rest of his body didn't move. *Damn.*

Gideon found a type of pleasure he'd never experienced before. His mind drifted to an image of Mac and his yellow dildo. He visualized Mac jamming it into his ass. No, *he* was the one sticking it inside that tight ass, *he* was the one making Mac writhe around in abject pleasure.

Stop thinking about this.

But his body didn't listen. It was protesting his rigid rules. His mind had been working in overdrive tonight, trying to figure out how to keep his family together. It was always working, always keeping himself in check and coming up with little white lies. His mind needed a damn break. He just wanted to feel good.

He grabbed his rock hard cock. That simple touch could've made him come in three seconds, but he did his best to prolong this feeling. He stroked his dick with his slicked-up hand while he fingered himself. He mashed his chest and head against the shower wall. He shoved that yellow toy in and out of his roommate's ass. Mac pulled his legs closer to his face and moaned for the entire block to hear. His pale ass was taking it all.

Mac whimpered out his name as a plea for more.

Gideon bit his lip. He couldn't moan. His vocal chords were frozen as was the rest of his body. Only his hands worked. In and out they went. Back and forth his fist slid over his cock. He was losing his balance. He pretended it was his fingers diving into Mac's wet, hot ass, and it was Mac's ass tightening around him.

He could barely stand as the orgasm tore through him, ripping through his insides like an unrelenting tornado. It had never been this strong, this intense. *Just like Mac had said.*

Mac screamed into his leg as he shot hot spurts over his chiseled chest. Gideon blew his load against the shower door.

He regained his breath. The water turned cold, or maybe his skin was too hot. Gideon cupped water in his hands and washed off the door.

After he toweled off, he brushed his teeth, got into his pajamas, and ducked into bed. He was grateful that the Sapersteins weren't talking to each other tonight. Nobody would question why he took such a long shower.

CHAPTER NINE

Mac

Seth didn't want to get drunk for his twenty-first birthday. He also wasn't a fan of surprises, which wasn't a surprise to Mac. Delia walked and talked as they left class, giving him the scoop on the birthday plans.

"I'm just going to have a few people over my apartment tomorrow night. There'll be some gluten-free beer, and then regular alcohol for everyone else. You and Gideon can come over anytime after 8:30."

"You know, we have our own schedules." People tended to do this lately. Just because they were roommates didn't mean their schedules were synched up. They came and went as they pleased, although Mac did have a decent idea of where Gideon was most days. *It didn't mean we were a couple.*

The next night, the roommates walked over to Delia's place. Mac found himself taking extra glimpses at Gideon, in his usual rolled-up sleeves and jeans. Same old Gideon, but Mac hadn't seen same old Gideon in a few days thanks to Rushmore Shaman. Or Russian Onyx. Or whatever that holiday was called. When he walked through the door a few days ago, luggage in hand, Mac's heart did a somersault. He instantly gave it an internal warning.

You missed him as a roommate. And a little bit as a friend. That's it.

They strolled into the chillest twenty-first birthday party Mac had ever attended. People drank their beer and cocktails while a jazz radio station streamed from Delia's phone. It was so Seth. He and Delia held hands while talking to Henry and Nolan on the couch.

"I still can't believe they're together," Mac said.

Gideon nodded, but he seemed to be somewhere else. He hadn't said much since he got back.

Everyone wound up congregating in the kitchen. Mac pulled Gideon back from joining the fray.

"Is everything okay?" Mac asked.

"Yeah. Everything's cool." Gideon headed into the kitchen and turned on his loud charm. He greeted the crowd around the drinks as if this were his party. Mac admired that ability of his to own a room.

One more glimpse.

That's enough. Mac hated that he had this attraction to Gideon and hated that Gideon's feelings for him seemed more ambiguous everyday. He forced himself to think of something else. Delia pulled him into their conversation, saving him from himself.

Mac and Gideon spent the party apart, talking to different people. Gideon held court in the kitchen, always a drink in his hand. Mac liked the relaxed, intimate setting. It gave him a chance to actually hear what the other person was saying. The lowest of the lowkey twenty-first birthday parties turned out to be a great time.

Delia buzzed off to get the birthday cupcakes ready. Henry sidled up to Mac and ushered him to the window.

"Can I ask you something?"

"Sure." Mac swiped the last of the baby carrots and dipped them in hummus.

"Is Gideon gay?"

Mac nearly dropped his plate. He laughed off the question. "No. He went to that gay bar to pick up girls."

"Or so he said. He beeped on my 'dar a little."

Mac chuckled and played dumb. He spent way too much time wondering what would've happened at Cherry Stem if gay John Wayne hadn't dry-humped his roommate. "What about all those girls he's dated?"

"He wouldn't be the first closeted guy to date women," Henry said.

That was the main talking point in this type of discussion. There were guys who dated 100 girls or were married for thirty years and still turned out to be gay. Mac knew that dating women was a flimsy excuse to prove one's heterosexuality.

"If he were gay, he'd be out." That was what Mac always told himself. Gideon wasn't the type to be holed up in the closet. He'd be just as well-liked gay as he is straight.

But Henry studied Gideon. He didn't seem convinced.

"I saw you guys come in. If any stranger had seen you, they'd assumed you were boyfriends."

"What?"

"The body language." Henry shrugged. "I wondered if you guys were secretly dating."

"You have got it so wrong."

"Have I? My 'dar is pretty damn good." Henry dumped his empty beer bottle in the trash. "It's a shame. You two would make a really cute couple."

Henry rejoined the party. Mac stared out the window. He ran through the memories of him and Gideon in the apartment. It had only been a few weeks, but it felt like longer, like they'd entered an alternate universe where they didn't fight freshman year and they'd stayed friends this whole time.

Delia brought out twenty-one gluten-free chocolate cupcakes, each with a lit candle sticking out of them. Henry shut the lights as she walked it to the dining table. Gideon led them in singing "Happy Birthday," waving his arms like a conductor. He grinned at Mac, his face silhouetted in the candlelight. Shivers of want descended down Mac's spine.

Minutes later, Mac was still by the window, surveying the party. Gideon stumbled over, his tall, lanky body knocking into an end table. He held two cupcakes and handed one to Mac.

"I'm glad somebody got wasted at a twenty-first birthday," Mac said.

Gideon rolled his eyes, still grinning. Usually, he was just an extra-social drunk, but it seemed that Gideon had crossed over into sloppy.

"Funny funny funny. You are so funny." Gideon tapped Mac's nose with his finger.

Mac's jeans tightened. *Please don't do that again.*

"I am just enjoying life," Gideon said. He shrugged his shoulders over and over, like saying "what's the big deal" on infinite repeat. It was freaking adorable.

"I'm glad. Don't let your family shit drag you down. Your mom and brother need to work that out themselves."

"They're family. I can't just abundant them."

"Abandon?"

Gideon did his classic double-point. Mac caught Henry looking at them. He turned red.

"My dad, my dad he passed away eight years ago this week. He did." Gideon raised his glass to him. Mac's heart went out to him. He wanted to give Gideon a hug, but a bro pat on the back seemed more appropriate. "He was a real gentleman. Real class act. Like fothermucking Cary Grant or something."

"I'm sure he was." Mac tried to take Gideon's cup away gently. "Do you want a glass of water?"

Gideon yanked his hand back. "What happened with your parents, Big Mac?"

Mac's insides went cold. "We can talk about that later."

"Did the mom-and-pop shop kick you out for being gay?" Gideon asked it so innocently, like a child not realizing what he just said aloud. Heads turned to them. Mac wanted to strangle him, if his own memories didn't strangle himself first.

"Shut the hell up, Gideon. You're way too drunk for this party."

"If your parents are still alive, you shouldn't ignore them. They're the only parents you got. And they may be gone soon."

Mac grabbed Gideon by the shoulders and shoved him against a bookcase. Picture frames smacked down. His head burned with anger and hurt. Once the memories started, they wouldn't stop.

"Mind your own fucking business."

Delia approached them, concern ringing her eyes. Mac released Gideon and left the party.

Φ

Mac lay in bed, unable to shut his eyes. He heard Gideon creak open the front door. Mac turned toward the wall, hoping to block out the noise.

And then he heard a knock on his room divider.

"Mac?"

"What do you want?"

"I'm sorry. I was an asshole."

"Yep. You sure were." Mac rolled around to face him. He made out his eyes and pouting lips in the soft light from the kitchen.

"You want some mac n' cheese?"

The most frustrating thing about Gideon was how hard it was to stay mad at him. Mac wondered if he was the only person to have this problem. He ripped his blankets off. "Sure."

A few minutes later, there they were, sitting on the couch, eating mac n' cheese. Mac wasn't even hungry, but he was going to finish his bowl.

"I'm sorry. I'm just still stressed about my family. It was like somebody threw a grenade on the dinner table, and I couldn't save anyone."

"Maybe that's not your job right now," Mac said. "You want to be the good son and the good brother, but sometimes it's best not to take a side. This isn't your battle."

"But it's my family. I didn't even say goodbye to my brother when he left."

There was something about the late night and the mac n' cheese that made the flood gates open in Mac.

"I wasn't out in West Virginia…" Mac started. Those gates were rusty. They weren't just going to fly open, not after being shut all these years. "In high school, I went on the computer in the school library to research this gay-straight alliance I'd heard about for kids in my region. This asshole Justin Weeks was looking over my shoulder and saw. He's the pastor's son, and he thinks that entitles him to be a dick to everyone because his dad's tight with Jesus. Word spread like wildfire. A few days later, I'm walking home from school, and I got jumped by Justin and his pals. They said they were doing the Lord's work." He could still hear their laughter. Mac raised his shirt to show Gideon the scar on his back. "I tried telling the school, but since it didn't happen on school property, there was nothing they could, or would, do. And my parents…"

He shoved the flood gates open with all the strength he had. "After two weeks of walking through school with bruises and getting looked at, I finally told my parents. It was the most awkward coming out. They went to have a talk with the pastor, who said Justin and I were just roughhousing. And my parents believed him! They went to church on Sunday like nothing had happened. They said I was being too sensitive." Mac's hands started shaking.

"Those fucking assholes," Gideon muttered. Mac had never seen him angry.

"I hated living with them. They didn't try to do anything to stand up for me. Justin didn't get into any trouble. My parents cared more about what others at church would think. We got in a huge argument. I ran away to my Aunt Rita's in Pittsburgh." Mac clenched his jaw. Here came the hardest part. "My parents told me to stay. They didn't want me back."

He picked up his keys from the coffee table. "On my first night there, Aunt Rita bought a pair of four-leaf clover keychains. One for me, one for her. She promised things were going to work out. We had luck on our side. 'May we always be each other's good luck charms,' she said to me."

Mac's keys jiggled against each other. His hands wouldn't stop shaking. They were in shock. He was in shock. He put down the keys and shook out his hands, but they continued trembling. Giving Gideon all this personal info was like dry heaving.

"How long has it been since you've spoken to them?"

"Four years."

"Fuck."

"Life in Pittsburgh was fine. I had some friends, but kept to myself mostly. I stayed in the closet and told myself I wasn't coming out until college, where it wouldn't be such a big deal." Even if he had to take out a crapload of loans to make it happen, he was determined to attend an accepting school like Browerton. Fortunately, he won some local scholarship money to make tuition slightly less burdensome.

Mac rubbed his hands together. *Stop shaking.* He felt raw, exposed. If he didn't talk about it, then he never had to think about it. That's how he got through life. Now, he didn't know what to do with all these damn emotions he had stirred up.

Gideon looked at him with kind eyes, with a sincerity that made Mac's hands shake even more.

And then stopped shaking.

Gideon held them steady with his own. His large hands maintained a firm grip. Mac was soothed by their warmth. Gideon bent down and kissed the tip of his fingers.

They locked eyes in the silence of the room, and Mac was shaking all over again. The same nerves he felt the first time they met, up in his dorm room, came rattling back.

This time, though, it was Gideon who kissed him.

CHAPTER TEN

Gideon

Gideon refused to listen to his brain. He didn't want to hear what it would say. A deeper part of him, one he had shoved down long enough, refused to stay silent any longer. Passion burned through him like that wall of fire in *Independence Day*.

His tongue licked up the salty taste of Mac's lips. He inhaled his hot breath. Mac kissed him back with equal fervor. Gideon cupped the sides of his head, and felt a man's stubble under his palms.

Gideon pulled away.

"Shit," he said. "Shit."

"Should we stop?" Mac asked.

Gideon leaned in for another kiss. Mac pecked his lips, then opened his mouth for Gideon's tongue. His felt a cage inside him get yanked open. He didn't know what flew out, but it was awfully similar to what he felt in his shower back home. Mac's story reminded him of the unrestrained glee of his Internet searches in middle school and part of high school. Before he made himself stop. Before he told himself that he was just acting out because his dad died. Before he made himself believe that looking at gay porn wasn't what good, responsible sons did.

He didn't want to be responsible. Not now. He wanted to live this moment with absolute abandon.

Gideon pulled away. This time, nobody spoke. His erection strained against his jeans. He stopped thinking. He just wanted to let things fucking happen.

Every nerve on every inch of skin was more alert than a syringe full of Red Bull.

Still, nobody spoke. Talking would ruin it. Talking would involve his brain and thought functions. He wanted the night and the alcohol to have full control.

He kissed Mac again, slower this time, savoring each flick of the tongue, each gasp of breath. Mac slid backward on the chaise part of the sofa, and Gideon laid on top on him. His hands traveled across Mac's muscular chest. There was nothing delicate about his body. It was hardy and full. Stew, not salad.

Gideon ran his hands up and down his chest and stomach, while he pressed his aching crotch into Mac's legs. Mac moaned at each thrust. He'd never heard that sound during sex. It was deep and husky. He wanted more of it. It was his new drug.

"I want to see you naked," Gideon whispered in his ear. Mac let out a gutteral moan, which he took as a *fuck yes*.

They stood at opposite ends of the couch.

Mac pulled off his shirt and let it drop to the floor. Gideon got a full view of his ripped roommate. His eyes took snapshots of the full curves of his chest muscles and every ab just below. No looking away this time. Gideon nodded for him to continue. Mac tucked his hands into the waistband of his shorts. Hearing the snap of the elastic sent a chill of anticipation through Gideon. Mac pushed his shorts to his ankles. His hard cock pointed straight at Gideon. It was like a fucking mallet. Ready to pounce. He clocked the way his thighs curved like a wine glass, the bulge of his knees. It was all Mac.

"Holy shit. You're naked." Gideon gulped back a breath. His cock raged against his pants in approval.

"I want to see you naked."

Gideon's lips trembled with excitement and a garnish of fear. He stripped off his clothes. The open air hit his exposed skin and made his cock even harder. It stuck up in the air, nearly pulling him closer to Mac.

"Holy shit. You're naked," Mac said, a smile quirking on his lips.

They stared at each other's naked bodies for an extended moment. *I'm looking at Mac naked.* He wanted to touch. He wanted to be touched.

"What do you want to do?" Mac asked.

"I want to watch you come." Gideon wanted to see the scene from the shower come to life. Mac's face flush with orgasm, his hard body coming undone.

They made out on the couch. Gideon stroked himself as he felt Mac's warm lips on his and Mac's rapid breaths in his throat. He watched Mac grip his cock firmly and that made Gideon pump his dick harder. Gideon palmed Mac's chest, and dragged a finger down the crease of his abs.

"Grab my dick," Mac said.

Gideon couldn't turn him down. No fucking way on the planet. His hand wrapped around Mac's thick, warm erection. *Fuck, I'm grabbing another guy's dick.* It was as a cock should feel, but different.

New.

Forbidden.

Mac spat on his hand and wrapped it around Gideon's cock.

"Fuck!" Gideon had never felt a pleasure like this. It was like Mac got to some secret level of a game Gideon didn't know existed. He wondered why he never thought to slick up his own hand when he masturbated.

Gideon's cock disappeared into Mac's saliva-coated fist. Gideon spat on his hand and continued jerking off Mac. Their arms moved wildly. Mac's biceps tensed. He tried to kiss Gideon again but their breathing was too heavy. Mac pushed himself back on the cushions and jutted his cock in the air, giving Gideon amazing leverage.

"Yes," Gideon whispered.

Mac hung his head back. His chest glistened with sweat and Gideon knew what was coming. His cock twitched in anticipation. Mac fucked his fist.

It was the face. Exactly the face Gideon pictured, but even better in person. His come overflowed out of Gideon's hand.

He couldn't wait for Mac to return to earth. His own dick was going to blow. Gideon returned his hand, soaked in Mac, to his own cock and stroked himself. He looked at

Mac's still-naked body, then at his own, and the image was overpowering. He shot all over his stomach.

He joined Mac in reclining on the couch. They stared up at the ceiling. Gideon's heart returned to a normal rhythm, but that was the only normal thing in this living room.

CHAPTER ELEVEN

Mac

Mac woke up the next morning not entirely sure if what happened last night really happened. But then he realized he was only in his underwear and his lips were sore.

Yep, happened.

His head pounded with a gnarly hangover, even though he didn't remember drinking much last night. Must've been that gluten-free beer. And all the excitement of what happened.

Because it really happened.

He lay back down. He was in no position to think.

Mac went over everything from last night. His talk with Henry. Gideon asking Mac about his family. Mac telling him the whole sordid, painful story of West Virginia. Mac n' cheese. Gideon's mouth coming at his.

Gideon kissed him. That was an incontrovertible fact.

He pictured Gideon naked in front of him. The light dusting of chest hair.

And then coming. They both came. Right next to each other.

Mac stuck a hand down his boxers. He was sticky.

Yep, happened.

Mac pushed himself out of bed, one hand rubbing his temples. He dragged his hunched body to the kitchen for a glass of water. The sun poured in and reflected off the appliances. Mac didn't realize how dehydrated he was until he drank the water, and then another glass.

He stumbled over to Gideon's bedroom. He held his fist at the door, but didn't knock. He didn't know what to say. The last guy he hooked up with before last night was Davis. That was a different kind of awkwardness, a normal and routine awkwardness that was accompanied with blushing and feelings. Mac was unsure how to broach last night's events.

He'd have to start thinking because Gideon swung the door open.

"Hey," he said. "I gotta take the piss of my life."

Mac moved out of the way so Gideon could shuffle to the bathroom. He put on his shirt, which sat on the floor beside the couch (*happened!*), and waited there for Gideon to finish. He tapped his fingers together, anxious as hell.

Gideon went from the bathroom straight to the kitchen for some water. Mac hung in the doorway.

"So…"

Gideon chugged his water.

"Yeah…."

And kept chugging. He was downing it all in one drink. He refilled his glass and kept drinking.

"Did you sleep okay? I'm mega hungover."

Gideon pointed at his now-half-empty glass of water.

"You've got to rehydrate," he said.

"Yeah. I had a glass this morning."

"I think it was also all that crap at the party, and the mac n' cheese. I should probably put less salt in and trust that the cheese and pasta are tasty enough." Gideon poured himself a third glass of water. Mac turned off the tap.

"Gideon."

It both hit them what happened last night. It was in their historical record.

Done. Never to be erased.

Fucking happened.

"Yeah," Mac said. He wanted to tell Gideon that it was strange, but a good strange. A strange he wouldn't mind repeating more than once. But he didn't want to be the first one to speak. There was some unspoken agreement that Gideon would have to break the silence.

"Look, last night…" Gideon said. He looked at the couch. The scene of the crime. "I was super drunk. Like beyond wasted."

"Drunk?" Mac asked, incredulous. Not too drunk to cook mac n' cheese, though.

"So drunk. And I haven't gotten laid in a few weeks. So I think it was just really drunk and really horny and it…" Gideon clapped his hands together to signify the combination. "It was….a night. But we were both just super drunk."

"Beyond wasted."

"Right." Gideon returned to his bedroom.

Mac couldn't believe what just transpired. It was the classic "I was so drunk" straight guy excuse, like something out of a movie. And if it were any other guy, he would've taken it. He would've been hurt and confused, but he would've kept his mouth closed.

But not with Gideon.

He kicked the bedroom door open. Gideon burst off his bed in surprise.

"Bullshit," Mac yelled. "Total, complete, abject bullshit."

"We were drunk."

"Bullshit! Bullshit on every straight guy who uses that excuse and expects the gay guy to accept it. We don't. We're not stupid!"

"Well, bullshit on you for making me speak first."

"Don't use the 'I was so drunk' excuse, Gideon."

"I was!"

"No guy in the history of existence is so drunk that he doesn't realize that he's jerking off another dude. If you were so drunk you didn't know what was happening last night, then you would've been too drunk to get it up. And we both know that is not true."

"Okay!" Gideon said. He slammed his door shut, as if he were afraid of the zero-percent chance that someone could hear them. "We fooled around. People fool around when they're drunk and it's late at night."

"Was this the first time you…with another guy?"

Gideon looked down. Mac could see the fragile guy behind the brave face.

"Yeah."

"Look, last night…happened. Let's not pretend it didn't."

"Fine. I just don't want to analyze it." Gideon sat on his bed, staring out the window.

An experience like this was meant for nothing *but* analyzing. Lines were crossed. New ground was broken. But Mac knew when to stop pushing, or else he'd push Gideon away. Even though they were just supposed to be roommates, he knew there was a friendship on the line here.

"You know we can't ignore it," Mac said. "I, I liked it."

He thought he saw Gideon's lips quirk up in a quick smile in the window's reflection.

"I liked it, too."

Mac took a tentative step toward the bed. Gideon turned to him.

"I still think girls are hot."

"Okay."

"I mean it. I enjoy having sex with girls. I'm not gay," he said to himself as much as to Mac.

Even if he wasn't convinced, it still stung to hear Gideon say that. In his head, he thought this conversation might go differently. *Gideon is your friend. Don't ruin it.*

"I'm not gay. But fuck, that was really cool. It was new and...I don't know."

"You're curious." Mac took another step. He was barely an inch from the bed. "Curious is okay."

"It is?"

"Lots of people are curious. I mean, that's how I figured out I was gay."

"I'm not—"

Mac held up a hand. "I know. Just because someone is curious doesn't mean he's gay."

"It's like taking geology classes," Gideon said.

Mac scrunched his brow, unable to grasp the metaphor.

"I think geology is interesting, and so I took a class in it. Doesn't mean I'm going to major in it."

"Nothing says you can't take another geology class."

Mac didn't realize what he'd just proposed until he heard it aloud.

"Really?"

But Mac considered it more. "If it gets weird for either of us, we'll say something. We're friends. I'm not going to bullshit you and put on a brave face."

"Same here." Gideon also considered it. "I kinda do want to explore."

Mac shrugged his shoulders. "We both liked it. Nothing wrong with trying it again."

"And this is just sex. Our friendship and roommateship stays same as it ever was."

"Yep."

Some voice deep inside Mac was trying to object, trying to shout from the rooftops that this would only end in disaster, that as much as he tried to rationalize this exploration, Mac was ultimately ill-equipped to handle being a fuckbuddy.

Sadly, it was overruled.

Mac sat on the bed. He held out his hand, and Gideon shook it.

"Geology class."

"Geology class," Mac repeated. The two words got his cock hard. "Is class back in session?"

"Now?"

Mac peeked at Gideon's tightening boxers. This would be his most extensive social experiment to date.

"Well, I don't usually do morning classes, but I'll make an exception since I'm feeling studious today." Gideon leaned over and consumed Mac in a lust-filled kiss.

I know what I'm doing.

Since Gideon wanted to explore, he was going to let him explore. That's what friends were for.

Φ

The roommates enjoyed another session of geology class the next night, after Mac finished studying for an exam. Which he could now barely concentrate on.

"How'd you do?" Delia asked him after class.

"It was hard."

"Really? It wasn't that bad. It was on what she said it would be."

Perhaps Delia was right, but Mac realized that he didn't study last night. He merely stared at some pages while counting down the time in his head until he could put his hands on Gideon.

"You there, Mac?" She waved her hand in front of his face. "I'm sorry Gideon was a dick at Seth's party. I probably should've cut him off."

"It's fine. I'm used to it." Mac felt his cheeks heat up. "It was standard levels of Gideon prickishness."

"Well, I hope things weren't awkward when you got home. Did you two make up?"

"In a way."

Mac's phone buzzed with a call from his aunt. He and Delia parted ways. He sat on the steps of the library and answered.

"How's my favorite nephew?"

"Favorite by default," Mac said. He couldn't help but smile when he spoke to her. There was something in her voice like lemonade on a hot summer day. "How are you doing, Aunt Rita?"

"I'm good. How's school going? Is your roommate situation working out?"

"In a way." Mac knew that joke had short legs.

"A good way, I hope."

"No, it is. It's a really nice place. Gideon's a good guy."

"I'm happy that you landed on your feet. Have you spoken to Davis at all?"

"Except for an awkward run-in, no." And Mac realized that this was the first time he'd thought about Davis since running into him at Cherry Stem. Thoughts of Gideon had replaced him, almost a clean swap.

"I still can't believe…" He could hear her shake her head. "I have to be honest. I was never a big fan of Davis. He didn't seem like the greatest guy."

"How so?" Aunt Rita had only met him a handful of times, but she had a way of reading people. She liked to say that she knew someone's whole movie just by the trailer.

"Well, you're a loyal guy. Very loyal. And I don't think he appreciated you."

"I like the way you think."

Their conversation went into a valley of silence, and Mac got a nervous feeling. It wasn't like their usual gaps in talking.

"Mac, do you have a minute to talk?"

Mac felt the concrete steps beneath him, to make sure he was sitting down. When people asked if you had time to talk, it was never a good sign. "We're already talking, Aunt Rita. Is something wrong?"

"Well, I don't know how to say this."

Mac held the phone as close to his ear as he could, until Browerton disappeared around him, and he was back in their living room.

"What is it?" He asked.

"I…well, it seems I have a tumor."

CHAPTER TWELVE

Gideon

Gideon stared at his blank notebook. He was never much of a note taker in class. He believed everything he needed to know could be found in the textbook or in the lecture slides. Only professors so in love with their own lecturing would fill an exam with questions taken solely from what they say in class.

And today? His notes were completely non-existent.

We're just experimenting, Gideon told himself repeatedly. He reminded himself of his brilliant geology class metaphor. *I'm not gay. Just curious.* Curious George, getting his banana.

They'd been ignoring the tension for weeks, but at least now they were dealing with it head-on. They'd fool around a little. The newness would wear off. The itch would be sufficiently scratched. Then, it would be behind them, and they could go back to being roommates, and friends.

And here was the conclusion to where his mental gymnastics brought him: There was a difference between doing gay things and being gay. Being gay was a whole lifestyle. Gay friends, parades, activism, assholes calling you names. Doing gay things was isolated incidents. A kiss here, a hand job there. Isolated. Not part of a lifestyle. That was his story, and he was sticking to it.

It was perfect timing. They were in the middle of the days of atonement, the ten days between Rosh Hashanah and Yom Kippur. This was the time to get in your last sins before getting them absolved on the latter holiday. And there was one sin he was dying to do tonight, something that had been tucked deep inside his brain. So he let himself take the rest of class to tune out his professor and imagine Mac exploding with orgasm all over his bed. In a few days, the chapter would end.

Φ

Tonight was a night made for whiskey. Gideon pulled out his bottle of Jameson. He took a swig straight from the bottle before bringing it into the living room. Mac sat on the couch, hands folded in his lap.

Gideon nudged the shot glass over to Mac, whose muscles poked through the tight sleeves of his baby blue polo. During geology class, he was allowed to look.

He picked up his shot glass. Mac's remained on the table. "Your Jameson is calling for you."

"I don't feel like drinking." Mac lacked any enthusiasm for geology class.

"You feeling okay?" Gideon tried to keep the energy up. Their experimentation was a house of cards. It could topple in disaster at any moment.

"Yeah," Mac said.

"We don't have to do this."

"No, it's okay. I want to."

"That was the least convincing answer in history."

Mac rubbed his palms on his thighs. Gideon was just as nervous in that moment.

"Aunt Rita has a tumor."

"Shit."

"She told me today. It's benign, but she's still getting surgery to have it removed."

"Fuck." Gideon wished he had better words, but sometimes life knocked the wind out of you and all you had left were *shit* and *fuck*. "When's the operation?"

"Next week. She waited to tell me because she didn't want me to worry."

"My mom did that, too." Gideon hadn't planned to spill any of this, ever. "I was the youngest, so I was the last to know about my dad's cancer. They think they're sparing your feelings, but the delay, the waiting, it was the worst part."

He put his arm around Mac. He hated watching a friend go through this. "I can't lose her," Mac whispered. "If I lose her, then I'll just have my parents."

"You won't. They call them benign for a reason. She'll get the surgery. She will recover."

"What happened with your dad?"

"Pancreatic. That shit is the worst. It's hard to detect, and it'll destroy you in months. It's the go-big-or-go-home cancer, although nobody gets to go home."

He nudged Mac's shot glass closer. This was the absolute best time for a drink.

"I can't drink alone," Gideon said, the shot glass in his hand. "That would make me an alcoholic."

Mac took the shot. Gideon dragged a finger down Mac's ear, which was all it took to distract his roommate.

Their mouths met in a violent car wreck of need and tension. Mac traveled up to Gideon's ear to nibble, and his stubble grazed Gideon's cheek.

Gideon pulled himself away and poured them another shot.

"I'll pass."

"You sure?" Gideon held up his shot glass and jiggled it. "I'm drinking alone."

"Then don't drink," Mac said, almost as a challenge.

But that wasn't an option tonight. Gideon gulped the shot. Then poured himself one more. For Aunt Rita, for his dad.

Nope. Not thinking of my dad right now.

They nodded and looked at the TV, then looked at each other and nodded again. Lots of nodding. Not much else.

He shut off the lamp. Darkness blanketed the apartment, with thin streaks of outside lights peeking in from the blinds. Gideon liked the darkness. It made him brave. He needed some courage for what he wanted to do tonight.

Mac began to massage Gideon's crotch through his shorts. His touch was firmer, more decisive than a woman's. He knew the equipment.

Gideon explored Mac's hot mouth with his tongue. Mac, in turn, massaged harder, turning his grip into a stroke. All of Gideon's thoughts and notions slipped away, like he was shedding armor. Gideon unzipped his jeans and let his erection into the open. He shivered under Mac's warm touch, and his heart raced as he pumped. He could barely make out anything in the dark, as he wanted it.

"I want to rim you," Gideon said with heavy breaths. Hearing the words scared him, but he wanted them to be scared together.

Mac relinquished his grip, and it was like he had turned on the lights.

"You do?"

"Yeah, I'm curious. And I like going down on girls."

"You do?" Mac asked with more incredulity.

"Yeah, it makes them happy." Gideon never wanted to have an unhappy customer in bed. He went the extra mile to deliver a good time for his ex-girlfriends. He wanted to do the same for Mac. And if they were going to experiment, he wanted to actually experiment. "Geology class."

"Geology class."

Those were the magic words.

They went to Mac's bedroom and took off all their clothes. Gideon just loved the simple pleasure of being naked with Mac. It felt both innocent and dirty. Mac got on his hands and knees on his bed. Gideon slapped that tight ass, as pale and round as a full moon. Gideon's cock was like a javelin spear.

I am about to stick my mouth on a guy's ass. He was standing at the edge of a cliff, ready to jump into the water, staring over the edge.

I am just curious. And horny. Mostly horny.

The first thing Gideon experienced was the scent. It smelled like sex, like sweaty, salty, carnivorous sex. He didn't expect it to turn him on so much. Lust dilated his pupils. The wrongness was exhilarating, and he wanted more of it. A lot more.

Gideon spat on Mac's hole and tongued it again, tasting his sweaty, musky taste. Mac quivered under his fingers. Gideon slapped his ass hard, leaving a handprint.

Mac reacted to every touch, every flinch. He was an earthquake under Gideon's fingers.

He slicked up his finger and entered Mac's ass. He took his time, letting himself savor the moment and making Mac moan for more. Gideon gave his cock a few healthy strokes.

Gideon alternated between fingers and tongue, a tag team on Mac's ass. He left no part ungraced by his touch. Mac lifted his ass in approval. Gideon's fingers traveled over the scar on Mac's back, ugly and red.

He kissed it, delicately, letting his lips linger for an extended moment.

Suddenly, this moment felt super quiet, and Gideon got freaked out for a second. He returned to the job at hand.

"Fuck!" Mac screamed when Gideon brushed his stubble against his opening. Gideon made sure to do it again. "Yes!"

Girls had moaned for Gideon. Some had even come for him when he went down on them. But it couldn't hold a candle to this, to Mac groaning in absolute pleasure, to his whole, thick, muscular body under Gideon's strict control. Watching Mac only made Gideon's cock ache to be touched, but he wanted to see more first.

"Turn over," Gideon said.

Mac got on his back. His dick spiked in the air. Gideon ran into the sun porch and fished out Big Bird from Mac's pile of junk, but it wasn't there.

"Where's Big Bird?"

"Don't fucking call it Big Bird." Mac reached up and kissed Gideon, tasting himself so freely. Gideon liked his eagerness.

Mac opened the top drawer of his nightstand that Gideon had helped him buy off an adjunct professor. He lifted Big Bird into the air, just as a streak of moonlight caught it.

Gideon slapped it against his hand. He felt its heft in his grip.

"Is it cool if we use it?"

"Yeah." Mac slapped Gideon's ass, and it vibrated in his chest. Mac got into position, with his legs pulled to his chest.

Gideon spat into his hand and got the toy all slicked up. It was definitely bigger than his fingers. He couldn't believe this was happening. Dreams literally were coming true.

Mac choked out a gasp when the toy made contact with his ass. Gideon was careful sliding it in. He wasn't hearing any noises coming from his friend. He glanced up and Mac was squirming.

"Is this okay?"

"No," Mac said. Gideon pulled it out. "Give me one second."

He opened the top drawer again and tossed Gideon a bottle of something.

"What's Astroglide?"

"It's lube," Mac said. "It's like WD-40 for my ass. Put it on the dildo. It'll make it slide in like you're closing a drawer."

Gideon was glad they could still joke. He poured a glob into his hand and slicked it over the sex toy.

"Yes. So much better!" Mac said.

Gideon pushed and pulled with ease. The dildo disappeared inside Mac. He watched Mac's hole expand and his legs shift above his stomach. Mac breathed heavily, grabbing his legs even tighter. Gideon couldn't take his eyes off Mac's flushed face. There was something about seeing Mac losing himself in the moment that was better than Gideon's times with women. Mac was the strong, silent type, and Gideon was ripping him out of his shell.

He began stroking Mac's aching cock, sending Mac into the stratosphere.

"I want you to suck me." Mac was almost begging for it.

Gideon stared at his erection in his fingers. And while he imagined this moment, getting Mac off with his sex toy, he couldn't picture himself giving a blow job. Having a guy's dick in his hand was different than having one in his mouth. Rimming was like eating a girl out, but there was no heterosexual counterpart to giving head. He got his mouth up close to Mac's dick, but he couldn't go further. It just seemed too…gay for him.

He continued jerking off Mac while plunging the toy inside him, and soon it was forgotten. Mac kept saying yes, over and over again.

Gideon pulled out the toy and slapped it against Mac's ass. Mac begged him to put it back in. Need strangled his voice. Mac yelled and writhed, possessed with orgasm. He and Gideon locked eyes as Mac spurted all over himself.

Gideon removed the toy. Mac was frozen for a second. He didn't say anything. Things weren't reverting, and Gideon was unsure how to proceed. He stood up. Maybe anal required more recovery time. But then, in a flash, Mac tumbled off the bed and got on his knees in front of Gideon.

Usually, post-orgasm, guys need to take a breather. Not Mac. He seemed even more raring to go than right before he came. He was driven by something that Gideon couldn't quite make out. Not like it mattered. Gideon happily let Mac take him in his mouth.

"Shit," Gideon said. Mac devoured his cock, jamming it into his throat. He knew what he was doing, and Gideon thought about all the times he'd probably done this before. Plus, it was different for Mac, he thought. Mac wasn't experimenting. He was getting a genuine enjoyment out of blowing Gideon.

Gideon caught that sinister look in Mac's eyes. It was the type of danger that turned him on, made more blood rush south.

His legs quaked. Gideon couldn't stand much longer. He detached himself from Mac and sat on the bed. Mac shuffled forward and returned Gideon's dick to its rightful place. His mouth went to the base. His hot breath circled Gideon warm cock. Gideon felt the sensation of a tongue swirling around his shaft. Guys knew what guys wanted, he thought. He realized that the great head he thought he'd received in the past was merely warm-up to this grand event. Gideon grabbed a fistful of his comforter. He was a goner in seconds, shooting deep into Mac's mouth.

Mac swallowed his load, sucking him dry. He sat on the floor, looking up at Gideon. Their eyes did all the talking, but Gideon wanted to break the actual silence between them. He had a compelling need to bring them back into the real world. They had ventured too far into another dimension, and Gideon craved familiar terrain.

"Good class," he said with a wink.

CHAPTER THIRTEEN

Mac

They had a few more classes over the next week. Gone was the heavy veil of awkwardness. Gideon weaned himself off pre-gay-stuff shots. Mac found himself racing home after class or a nighttime meeting, and he believed that Gideon did the same. He saw Davis in the student union with his new boyfriend and didn't even flinch.

After their hookups, they would lie in bed and talk. Mac would rest his head on Gideon's arm and rub his hand across Gideon's chest. Conversation would stretch to all types of topics into the wee hours. Families, friends, futures, pasts. Once they watched the sun rise. Since they had put their mouths on each other, nothing was considered off-limits.

It was one of the best weeks of Mac's life.

And now he was going through withdrawal. From tonight until tomorrow sundown was Yom Kippur, the holiest day of the Jewish year. Gideon had to fast and abstain from technology and sit in temple for most of the day. Mac admired his dedication. He couldn't go five minutes without checking his phone, like most normal people.

That night, Mac accompanied Delia to a birthday party for one of her friends. She and Mac had crossed paths many times before, and Mac wound up knowing a few people from class and elsewhere. That was the beauty of a college party. You were never really a stranger.

The girl's favorite color was magenta, not pink. The apartment was a wash of the color. The cupcakes had magenta food coloring, and the punch bowl runneth over with magenta-color sangria. Mac scooped him and Delia two cups worth. Delia held two mini cupcakes for them.

"I feel like this is the first time I've seen you all week," she said.

Mac blushed, which helped him blend in with the décor. "Just, busy with midterms."

"Oof. Tell me about it."

Her innocuous comment felt like a kick in the heart. She didn't question him. She didn't suspect anything.

They shared an extra-large beanbag chair in the corner of the living room. Mac held both of their drinks and cupcakes while Delia got comfortable. She then grabbed both pastries and shoved them in her mouth.

"Chocolate peanut butter cupcakes," she said with a satisfied smile, not unlike one you see on a cat being petted. "I miss gluten and nuts."

"You're a trooper. You want another one?"

"Yes. And a cookie and some crackers."

Mac took hold of the wall to push himself off the beanbag. He ventured to the other side of the living room, home of the treats, to indulge his friend's craving. He began filling up his magenta napkin when someone tapped him on the shoulder.

"Fifth row. Fourth seat from the aisle." The kid looked vaguely familiar. Surely someone who'd wear a shirt that had GAY BEST FRIEND written in big, block letters to a party had to stand out in his memory.

"I beg your pardon?"

He reached around Mac to pick up a magenta-frosted cookie for himself. "You're in my geology class."

Yes, Mac was actually in Introduction to Geology this quarter. A science distribution requirement. The irony was not lost on him.

"You always seem way too happy to be in geology class," the kid said.

Nope, not lost on him at all.

"I'm Mac."

"Rafe."

They moved around their treats to shake hands. Rafe's wild mop of curly hair seemed to lack a cowlick. It was not too far off from the unruly mess on Gideon's head.

"Some party." Rafe held up the cookies. "So are you actually into geology, or is it just a distribution requirement for you?"

"The latter. But it's interesting. You?"

"I don't know. I'm undecided." Rafe drank his punch. Mac laughed when he saw his magenta teeth.

"Do you know your teeth are magenta?"

"So are yours."

They both looked in the mirror mounted on the wall. There they were, two gays with Lisa Frank teeth.

"This is a good look for us," Mac said.

"I think this needs to be memorialized with a selfie." Rafe pulled out his phone and motioned for Mac to get close. Mac scooted into frame. Rafe snaked his hand around his waist in a classic flirty move. Subtle, yet noticeable.

"So what possessed you to wear the shirt?" Mac felt a tad embarrassed for him. His wardrobe stuck out like the sorest of thumbs.

"I'm peacocking," he said matter-of-factly.

"Peacocking? Are you going to burst into a plume of feathers?"

"Good use of the word plume. Peacocking is wearing an article of clothing that makes you stand out. It's a purposeful attention-grabber and conversation-starter. You see, most gay guys wear what you wear. The basic, generic dude outfit because they're trying to blend in. I prefer to stand out."

Mac found himself dimming next to Rafe's confidence. He had met openly gay students at Browerton. He was one himself. But Rafe seemed to out-do everyone.

"When did you come out?" Mac asked him.

"When I was twelve."

"Jesus," Mac gasped. "To just yourself?"

"To everyone. Parents, school, friends, pastor." Rafe shrugged. It was no big deal to him. Mac wondered if he grew up on a different planet than ours. He never had to live in fear. Or he never let himself.

"Where are you from?" Mac couldn't stop asking questions. Rafe was utterly fascinating.

"Arlington, Virginia."

"You're from Virginia?" Somebody had to be playing a practical joke on him. If only he had lived one state over, his life could've been vastly different. But then he might not have wound up at Browerton. He might never have met Gideon.

"Rafe, do you think gay guys and straight guys can be friends?"

Mac wondered if there was a way to answer his question with research. He wasn't sure if geology class could be considered research or tampering with his sample. Rafe didn't hesitate with his response.

"Of course." He bit into a chip. "I have plenty of straight friends."

"Are you attracted to any of them?"

"No. I'm not into straight guys. I don't believe it's a good use of my time to fall for somebody that I have zero shot with."

"Can you help it, though?"

He bit into another chip and sipped on more magenta punch. "There are straight guys that I think are cute, even hot. But there's a difference between thinking someone is good-looking and thinking about what it'd be like to date him. I don't let myself fall down those rabbit holes."

Mac didn't actively think about dating Gideon. Not when he found out Gideon was straight. He had Davis. And their time together now...well, they were falling down a rabbit hole together. But it wasn't like Rafe was criticizing his life.

"Well, next time I'm in class, I'll say hi. Or come sit in the fifth row with me."

"Or better yet," and here is where Rafe flashed a smile that announced in big, bold letters that he was flirting. "Why don't we hang out sometime, outside of geology class."

"You don't have to call it geology class. Just call it class." The word geology would forever be tainted.

"Can I get your number? I'll text you." Rafe reached into his pocket. He was a guy who did not mess around.

Mac assessed the guy in front of him. Cute, charming, smart, sweet, confident. Guys like these were diamonds in the rough at Browerton. Many of the gay guys Mac had met either came on too strong or were too in the closet. Davis, and now Rafe, were rare exceptions.

And yet something held Mac back.

"We can hang out, as friends," Mac said. "I'm not really looking to date right now."

Parts of that seemed true.

Rafe took it in stride, but Mac saw that blow he dealt to the guy's ego. "That's cool."

"I'm getting over a break-up."

"I get it. I'd like to be friends with you." Rafe said it with such sincerity that Mac chose to believe him, even though lots of guys use the friends excuse to wheedle their way up to boyfriend status. *Was that what I'm doing with Gideon?*

Rafe waited with his phone. It was Mac's cue.

"Right, sorry." Mac gave him his number and returned to the beanbag chair.

"I like him!" Delia said. She turned to Mac, but that caused them to roll into each other. They laughed over the closeness and didn't separate.

"He's a nice guy."

"And he got your digits."

"He did. But I told him I just wanted to be friends." Before Delia could chime in, he said, "Davis."

"Davis was almost two months ago. He's moved on. So should you!"

"I will. It's a process." Mac scoped out the party, searching for someone else to talk to, or talk about.

"This is another step in the process. And this step has a cute butt." She nudged her head at Rafe walking away, into the kitchen, butt firmly on display. "My dating life is on hiatus at the moment." Mac rolled away.

"Hiatus?" The word displeased her greatly. Mac's love life seemed to be her newest cause to champion. "Mac, if I ask you something, will you promise not to get offended?"

"Sure." Even though there was no way to promise that. She got serious for a moment, and if she was about to say she had a benign tumor, Mac was going to jump out the window.

"Are you hung up on Gideon? You guys have gotten along surprisingly well as roommates and are even friends. Which is great, but I don't want you pausing your life for some fantasy. Gideon's straight."

"That's what you think," Mac blurted out in defense of his life choices.

Delia's eyes bulged open. Mac bit his lip.

"I forgot to get you another cupcake." He tried to stand up, but Delia pulled him down. The fire of earth-shattering gossip burned in her eyes.

"Start talking."

There was no way he was getting around this one. Delia was a master in tunnel vision.

"What I tell you does not leave the beanbag chair. Does not."

She nodded.

"Not even Seth. Especially not Seth."

She nodded again and waved her hand to get him singing like a canary. Mac knew he was violating the ancient code of the gay-straight hookup, but he trusted Delia. She was a loyal friend.

And so in a whisper, Mac dished about his escapades with Gideon. Her mouth did not ungape. Her eyes did not unbulge. But to her credit, she didn't respond with a sassy comment, or even a laugh. She got how serious this was to Mac.

"But please, you can't tell anyone," Mac said.

"I won't. I promise." She leaned back. She had just taken a huge bong hit of information, and the new information was working its way through her system. "I had no idea."

"Neither did I."

"You think he's just experimenting?" She asked him.

"Yes." Though that wasn't the truth. The truth was that Mac didn't know the truth. He didn't want to know the final answer on Gideon's sexuality, because that would mean a final answer on their relationship. Either option scared him. He liked this gray area they were playing in.

"So that's why you don't want to go on a date with the T-shirt guy with the cute butt."

"That has nothing to do with it."

But she shot him a skeptical glare that cut through his mountain of words.

"It doesn't. I just don't feel like dating right now." It was the truth, but it also felt like a lie for some reason.

Delia didn't say anything back. She rolled over and wrapped him in a hug—well, as good a hug as she could deliver whilst on this beanbag chair.

"What's this for?" Mac rubbed her forearms.

"I love you. I hope I don't have to watch you get hurt."

Φ

When Mac returned to the apartment, the lights were on and the TV blared from the living room. Gideon sat on the couch with a bagel and cream cheese.

"How was your Yom Kippur?"

"Solemn. I brought you back an extra bagel and schmear from Hillel's break the fast." He pushed it over on the coffee table. Mac appreciated the gesture, almost too much, since it *was* just a bagel.

But he schmeared it, too.

Mac shook it off and took a seat beside him. Gideon didn't seem to be enjoying the sitcom he was watching. He put a tentative hand on Gideon's shoulder and massaged out some tension. Why did this feel like a breach to him, when they'd touched each other all over?

"You doing okay?" Mac asked.

Gideon put down his bagel. Deep lines creased his forehead. "I think we should have sex."

CHAPTER FOURTEEN

Gideon

"Right now?" Mac asked.

"After we finish our bagel and schmears?" Gideon's leg bounced up and down. *Don't think. Just do.* That was how everyone else in his family lived. He might as well join in the fun.

"Gideon." Mac studied his face, his thick eyebrows scrunching together in thought. He was still massaging his shoulder, and doing a heck of a job at it.

Gideon jumped up. His body was one of those bouncy balls that could fly off every hard surface from a light drop. An avalanche of stress rushed down inside him to his forehead. A brain freeze without the ice cream.

"My brother is having a baby."

"That's great! Right?"

Gideon paced in front of the fireplace. "He and Christina just got engaged. Because her family's religious, they don't want to have the baby out of wedlock. So they're getting married the first week in December. My mom just heard about the engagement at Rosh Hashanah, and you know how she reacted to that. This is going to destroy her." His heart raced as details from the day came back to him. "He texted me this today. Texted! On Yom Kippur!"

"I don't think Noah is as observant of Jewish traditions as you."

"Ya think?"

This was classic Noah. Dropping bombshells without warning, not caring who got hurt, leaving Gideon to clean up the mess. He probably waited until Yom Kippur to drop the news on him and his mom so they couldn't respond right away. Yom Kippur sneak attack. *Not cool, Noah.*

"Why weren't they using birth control if she's such a devout Catholic?" Gideon asked aloud. "Every girl I've been with has been on the pill, and I still used a condom."

It was the definition of irresponsible, the acme of Noah's pyramid of shit that Gideon had been witness to his whole life. This easily topped Noah getting in a bar fight. It was even more of a shitstorm than Noah leaving his passport in an Amsterdam whorehouse. Their mom was on the phone with the embassy for days to get him a temporary visa. Gideon used to think that Noah did it on purpose so he wouldn't have to come home.

"Fucking Noah." Gideon pulled out his bottle of Jameson and poured himself a shot. If Mac wanted one, he could pour it. Tonight, he didn't care if he was drinking alone. He needed it.

"Look on the bright side."

"There's a bright side?"

"A big one," Mac said, pouring himself a drink, too. "You're going to be an uncle! Uncle Gideon!"

Gideon thought about playing with a baby, holding his niece or nephew in his arms, big eyes staring up at him.

"You're going to be a great uncle. Kids are going to love you!"

"I wish I was better prepared."

"I'm sure your brother feels the same way. Cut him a little slack," Mac said. But he didn't understand. He wasn't being thrown around in the tornado, just watching it safely with binoculars.

"I'll try." Gideon kept thinking about how his mom was reacting. He checked his phone, waiting to hear from her.

But he didn't want to think about his family drama. He wanted to live his life. He joined Mac on the couch and kissed him with gusto. It was funny how easier that was getting. The less he thought about things, the easier they were.

"So, as I was saying...sex?" Gideon asked.

"Are you sure? I mean, it's sex."

"This isn't a Very Special Episode. Neither of us are virgins." Gideon lifted his eyebrows in an extra plea. Mac's tight T-shirt made him more enticed. He shrugged off the guilt he felt about making such an observation.

If my brother can get his girlfriend knocked up, then I can ogle my roommate's ripped chest.

Hesitation crossed Mac's brown eyes. Gideon didn't want to force him. He worried for a second that Mac didn't want this. Maybe he had shared too much.

"You feel comfortable...having sex?" Mac asked.

"Well, I'd be on top, so there wouldn't be much difference."

"Right. Do you want to have sex because—" Mac stopped himself to take another bite of his bagel. And then his hesitation was gone, replaced with something Gideon couldn't decipher. "Okay."

"Okay?" Gideon felt his face light up. "Should we do your bed?"

"Yeah."

They went into Mac's bedroom, where clothes littered the floor. At least it wasn't in the apartment common area. They lay on his bed.

Nerves hit Gideon. He was going to have sex. With a guy. This was real.

"Shit." Mac shut his nightstand drawer. "I'm out of lube."

"We used it up?" Gideon blushed. Those bottles weren't *that* big.

Mac tossed the empty bottle onto the floor, which Gideon pretended not to notice. "Can you pick some up tomorrow?"

Gideon did a double take. "Me?"

"I have class and homework. You only have one class tomorrow."

He was going to ask how Mac knew his schedule, but he knew that Thursdays were Mac's busiest day, too. Just one of those subconscious things roommates picked up.

"I can't pick up lube," Gideon said, desperately.

"I can't go tomorrow."

"We can go tonight."

"The stores are closed. They sell it in the student union."

Gideon huffed out a laugh. Did Mac expect him to waltz into the student union and run into someone as he asked for a bottle of Astroglide? Mac had a dark sense of humor.

"They sell it at drugstores," Mac said. "If you're going to stick your dick inside me, the least you can do is pick up the lube. It's the gentlemanly thing to do."

"The gentlemanly thing." Gideon snorted. "Until tomorrow then."

"Do you want to fool around tonight?" Mac asked, still sprawled out on the bed. Gideon could collapse on top of him and smell his warmth if he wanted to. But he decided to make Mac suffer. Who said geology class had to be so serious?

"We can wait until tomorrow. The gentlemanly thing and all."

$$\Phi$$

Gideon received the dreaded call from his mom at 10:45 the next morning. That was a good sign. She gave herself the night to think it over. Maybe it wouldn't be so bad.

Who was he kidding?

Gideon braced for impact. "Hi, Mom."

"Good morning. Did I wake you?"

"It's almost eleven."

"Well, I know how much you like to sleep late, Gideon. And you sounded groggy," she said defensively.

"Sorry. I'm up. So, I take it you heard the news."

"I did." She sounded calmer than he expected. Maybe instead of a bomb, this was a minefield, and he had to tread even lighter. "At this point, I'm not surprised by anything your brother does anymore. Noah has made it clear that he's going to do what he wants, and it's his life."

To the untrained ear, this would sound like his mom had grown and mellowed out, a real step of progress. But Gideon knew better. He hadn't spent the past twenty years being the son to Judy Saperstein without picking up on her quirks. He could hear the distinct passive-aggressive frustration and disappointment coating her resigned tone. Yes, Noah did what he wanted, and no, it would never be okay with her.

"Look on the bright side. You'll get to be a grandma."

She laughed. It was only a second, but it flashed Gideon back to when it was four of them, laughing around the dinner table, regaled by one of their dad's stories. Maybe the baby would be the ultimate bright side.

"I am looking forward to being a grandmother. And Christina and Noah will produce a very cute baby. Hopefully, the baby has her nose."

That was a joke! His mom making a joke about a potentially earth-shattering event! Gideon felt like he was in a trap, but he couldn't figure it out yet. There was the tick…tick…but no boom.

"I like your attitude," Gideon said.

"With Noah…I don't know. I tried. That's all I can say. I tried. I think your brother has a lot of anger about what happened with your dad."

Gideon wanted to remind that they were all hurt by his passing. Only Noah acted out.

"But at least I have you, Gideon. You would never do something so…"

"Irresponsible?"

"Exactly. I love our chats. There's never any drama."

But she didn't know how much work it took to keep the drama out.

"For the most part," she continued. That put Gideon on high alert.

"What do you mean?"

"When I was picking up the egg salad for break the fast, I ran into Beth's mother at the deli."

Gideon gulped back a lump of panic. He forgot that his mother preferred a deli in Beth's town. It was a rare curveball, but he could handle it. He was already on top of it.

"She said that you and Beth broke up before school started."

"We did. It was amicable. We both got cold feet about moving in together and realized it was about something bigger, that the relationship had run its course. We're still friends. It's fine."

"I'm glad it wasn't acrimonious. Why didn't you tell me?"

Gideon sensed some hurt in her voice. "You've had your hands full with Noah's whirlwind romance. I didn't want to add to your stress."

"You didn't need to do that, Gideon. You really didn't. I'm a mother. It's my job to worry about my sons."

"I know. I'm sorry."

"How are you doing?"

"I'm good." And Gideon was. He'd been happier this week than he had in a long time.

"Good. Are you paying for rent all by yourself?"

"No. It turns out that a friend of mine needed an apartment, and it worked out perfectly." A smile quirked on his lips. That was actually, mostly, the truth.

"That's a relief. Listen, you don't need to lie to me about things. I can handle it. And whatever it is, Noah's probably done much worse."

"Right." But so wrong. Gideon knew his mom would say this. It was easy to say she could handle things, but he knew that wasn't the truth. And even if Noah was a law school drop out who was having a shotgun wedding to his much-older girlfriend, he was still marrying a woman. Gideon's secret would always be worse.

"So tell me about Yom Kippur," he said, changing the subject. "Any gossip to report?"

She gave him the back home scoop about who was at temple. And things felt like normal again. Until the silence. The silence that fell on their phone call was a flare shot into the air.

"Gideon, I met a woman at temple. She's a new member. Very nice woman. She and her husband are very lovely. Her daughter is a freshman at Browerton."

He slapped his forehead.

"Her name is Hannah. She was at services. She's very pretty, and a sweet girl. I got her email." His mom pronounced it *e*-mail, as if it were still some new high-tech invention. "I'll send it over. I said that you could give her some advice, or talk to her about Hillel and classes. But now that you aren't dating Beth…Hannah is a very nice girl."

Gideon rubbed a hand through his hair, back and forth. And there was the boom.

"Mom," Gideon said through a hand smacked over his face. "I'm not looking to date right now."

"Think about it. Hannah was very excited about meeting you. Try one date. With Noah..." Her voice caught in her throat. "I still have a chance to do things right with you."

"Fine," Gideon said through gritted teeth.

Φ

Gideon wound up walking over a mile to the Walgreen's in Duncannon for the lube. He wanted to ensure that he would run into nobody from school. He kept his head down as he entered the store, lest any security cameras caught his face. Gideon buying Astroglide wasn't exactly material for the five o'clock news, but he didn't know who would have access to the footage.

When he realized that the store was pretty much empty, he relaxed. He meandered through the rows until he found the sliver of shelf space for personal lubricant. Well, at least if anyone caught him here, he could say that lube was for anyone. It was personal. Not gay, not straight.

He looked both ways, and of course, the lube was on the end of shelf closest to the pharmacy. There were probably pharmacists who scoped out the shelf all day, waiting to see the sinners buying Satan's product.

Gideon kept his eyes on the prize. Sex with Mac. He had never been this nervous about having sex. Not even his first time. *This isn't just any old sex.* It seemed like the culmination of their experimentation. Final exam for geology class, only he didn't want class to end. His fingers tingled with excitement when they made contact with the Astroglide.

He held it in his hand. In that moment, he didn't think about what sex would be like. He pictured Mac's intense sex face, staring back at him with emotion and his sinister grin. He thought of the safety of laying in bed with Mac after it was done, the same warm feeling he had after their past hookups. He let himself stand in the aisle imaging those future memories for a few seconds. It was a relief in a twenty-four hours chock full of Saperstein family drama.

Gideon walked up to the cashier. *I can do this. If she asks me anything, I won't answer.*

He didn't make eye contact with the cashier, a middle-aged woman who seemed too worn down to care that she was ringing up gay lube. This was probably a four on a scale of weirdest shit she'd experienced at Walgreen's.

"Do you need a bag?" She asked.

Gideon froze. *Oh, right. My cue.*

"No. Actually, yes. Yes." Not his finest hour. The corners of her lips curved into a stealth smile.

"Have fun."

Gideon yanked the bag and ran out.

CHAPTER FIFTEEN

Mac

Tonight was the night. Sex with Gideon.

I am having sex with Gideon.

They started off with kissing on Mac's bed, as per usual. Mac melted under Gideon's lips. He loved that they could joke and talk with each other, and then segue into making out and getting handsy without any awkward transition. It was so natural.

Like we're a couple?

He pushed the thought out of his head. He didn't want to think about anything tonight. That's how Gideon rolled. Mac saw him live in the moment when they were together. He didn't want to use his brain tonight except to remember to roll on the condom. Tomorrow, he was getting on a bus back to Pittsburgh to be by his aunt's side when she went into surgery. He was probably going to see his parents for the first time in years. Unless they didn't show up. With them, Mac never knew. They didn't even come to his high school graduation.

There was another thought he didn't need to think right now.

Mac massaged Gideon's leg, then his inner thigh. Gideon didn't push his hand away. He leaned back and got comfortable. Mac went for the crown jewels. Gideon let out a low moan, a green light if Mac ever saw one.

He stroked Gideon through his pants. Mac loved seeing Gideon lose it, his cool demeanor slipping away the more turned on he got.

Gideon took off his pants, and Mac took him in his mouth. His own cock got hard when Gideon grabbed the back of his head. Mac touched himself with his free hand as Gideon moaned louder. Mac went down to his base, fitting all of Gideon inside his mouth. He kept thinking about the epic rimjob Gideon had given him. Thinking about that day motivated him to suck harder, knowing how good they could be together.

"Just like that, baby," Gideon said, which sent Mac into hyperdrive.

He stroked and sucked as if his life depended on it, all so he could hear whatever came out of Gideon's mouth next. He slipped a finger inside Gideon's tight ass, which was warm and welcoming.

"Stop," Gideon said. "Don't do that."

"Are you sure? You don't sound sure."

"Stop, please," Gideon gasped out. "I don't want to do that."

"Not even to play? I'm not asking you to bottom."

Gideon gave him the headshake equivalent to *hell no*.

"Okay." Mac removed his finger. He didn't get it. Gideon seemed very intrigued by pegging during their initial conversation. Now, he was primed and had the chance. Stupid straight guy logic. Or "straight" guy in Gideon's case.

Mac got on his knees, giving him better leverage with Gideon's dick. He held Mac's hair and fucked his face. Mac found it a little uncomfortable, but hearing Gideon groan his enjoyment, he soon found the pleasure.

Gideon removed his dick from Mac's mouth. "Let's have sex, baby."

"You ready?" Mac asked. He knew that wasn't the brightest question to ask. What man would second-guess having sex?

"Yeah. Why don't you climb on top of me?"

Mac stood up, but then he paused. Gideon's *hell no* headshake stuck in his craw. "You seemed really into pegging when you found Big—my toy. We can do some foreplay. Gay sex doesn't have to be so monotonous and boring as straight sex. We can shake things up." Mac reached for the nightstand drawer, but Gideon pushed it shut.

"No. I'm not letting Big Bird or anything else in there."

"Okay." Mac rolled his eyes. Gideon's stubbornness was getting on his nerves. It seemed that experimentation was only one-sided. "Maybe I can rim you."

"No." Gideon sighed with annoyance. "Fine. How about I rim you, and you blow me."

The night had turned into a flea market transaction. Mac wasn't going to haggle for sex. He put his clothes back on, and Gideon quickly followed.

"Why are you so afraid of having anything down there?" Mac asked. "Scared that you'll like it?"

"This isn't easy for me like it is for you."

"This isn't easy for me, either. I'm nervous, but I feel better knowing this is all happening with a friend, with someone I trust and care about."

Mac averted his eyes. He did not mean for those last two words to come out. They were on their own mission. *This is what happens when I turn my brain off. The filter shuts off, too.* Mac waited for Gideon to respond, for him to say that he trusted his friend, that he cared about Mac.

"I'm still hungry." Gideon went to the kitchen and fished around for food in the cabinets. Mac stormed after him.

"This is horseshit," Mac said. "Typical straight guy horseshit."

"Did you eat all the saltines?" Gideon didn't look at him. He focused on foraging. Classic Gideon avoidance that made Mac want to scream.

"Fuck the saltines, Gideon. You can't be the only one calling the shots in this…whatever it is. You think that if you don't bottom, then you're not doing anything gay? Well, guess what: kissing a guy and jerking him off and letting him blow you are pretty standard homosexual acts. You can categorize and compartmentalize in your head all you want, but those are the cold, hard facts."

Gideon found a sleeve of Ritz crackers hiding in the back of a shelf. "Perfect."

Mac ripped them out of his hand, crunched them into a million little pieces, and shook them out all over the hardwood floor.

"What the hell has gotten into you?"

"You don't get to just walk away from me."

"I don't have a say in what we get to do anymore?"

"You don't get to have the only say," Mac said.

Gideon acted like Mac's words didn't dig under his skin, which hurt more than anything he could say back. Mac was proud of standing up for himself, and so instead of having Gideon say good night, he walked away first.

Φ

Mac left for the bus station early in the morning. He tiptoed out of the apartment, when the sky still had the midnight blue of pre-dawn. A part of him hoped that Gideon would rush out, charge down the steps, and stop him on the street. But this wasn't a movie.

The bus ride to Pittsburgh was a little over three hours. He gripped the four-leaf clover keychain the entire trip. Mac prepared for the emotional onslaught. He remembered what Gideon said. Aunt Rita would be fine. They call it benign for a reason. But a tumor was no match for the cold detachment of Mr. and Mrs. Daly. He wondered if they would even acknowledge them. Would he do the same? He stared out the window to distract him, but it was just trees and road signs. Not much help.

At the bus stop in Pittsburgh, Aunt Rita's friend Helen waited in her Corvette. The woman was far from rich—her stuffy, old-lady-smelling two-bedroom apartment down the street from his aunt was proof of that. But when her mother passed away, she used her inheritance to buy the one thing she'd always wanted. The car she never got to have in high school. It wasn't just a car to her, it was a new lease on life.

"Mackie!"

He blushed at the name. It was home to him.

He threw his stuff in the back seat. They gave each other a tight hug, expressing the worry and hope for Aunt Rita that words couldn't.

"She's doing good, Mackie. She's going into surgery in a little bit."

They headed to the hospital. Mac passed familiar buildings, and they gave him comfort.

At the hospital, Helen went up to the nurses station to find out if they were still allowing visitors. She worked her chatty magic. She seemed to make friends with everybody. Helen turned around and gave Mac a "follow me" nod.

Mac held her hand as they made their way down the hall. Aunt Rita was not a person who was supposed to be in a hospital. She was vibrant and had a laugh that took over a room. Thanksgiving was coming up, her favorite holiday.

"Look who I found," Helen said.

This was not the Aunt Rita Mac wanted to remember. Part of her head was shaved. Her pale skin didn't match the vivaciousness struggling to be known in her eyes. She smiled at Mac.

"Don't tell me. I look awful," she said. "Hospital gowns are not like evening gowns, I'm finding out."

She got Mac to laugh. Well, laugh with a tear falling down his face, but her humor was like a signal that this was going to be okay.

"You look great, Aunt Rita."

"Oh, shut up."

He went over and kissed her on the cheek. He pulled out the keychain. "Just in case you didn't have yours."

She held it in her frail fingers. "Mine's at home. I keep it in my underwear drawer. I like to think that'll help me with my dating life."

Helen let out a loud chortle, and Mac smiled in much-needed relief.

"Rita, what about the postman? I keep telling you he's got a crush."

Aunt Rita leaned close to Mac's ear. "He has B.O."

She kissed his keychain and handed it back. "You hold onto yours. Pull up some good luck for me."

"I will." He kissed it and put it back in his pocket.

"You didn't have to miss school for this. I'll be fine."

"That's what my roommate Gideon said. He said you're a trooper, and this is nothing."

"He sounds great. I already like him better than Davis."

"Oh, no. He's not my boyfriend." Mac blushed at the mix up, though for that second, it was a nice thought.

"Rita?"

Mac froze when he heard that voice. Helen's mouth dropped at who was behind him. His insides ran for cover. He wanted to do the same, but he balled his fists and summoned his courage. For Aunt Rita, for himself.

His parents didn't look much different from when he last saw them. Perhaps if he took a closer look, he would see more wrinkles from age and from the hard work of the hardware store. But the rush of feelings and anger and hurt flooded his system, as if time hadn't moved an inch.

"Hello, Cormac," his mother said. She came over and gave him a hug, which Mac accepted and not much else.

His father nodded hello at him. They went to Aunt Rita's side, the opposite side as their son. Aunt Rita hated talking about her condition. Mac wanted her to go into surgery in a good mood. He wanted to give her some news that he knew would make her smile.

"There's actually this guy," Mac told her. He glanced up at his parents, who did a silent recoil. "The new roommate. We're friends, but I think...Well, I hope it can go somewhere. You'd like him. He's a loud, opinionated New Yorker."

He felt emboldened by the defiance of talking about BOYS in front of his parents. Aunt Rita supported him, and she was the star of the show today.

"So he can sneak me a good bagel."

"And something called matzo ball soup." Mac smiled. The spirit of Gideon was here. "He's smart and has those black hipstery glasses."

His parents looked away, probably wishing they could unhear this conversation.

"I'll be wishing you luck while under anesthesia," Aunt Rita said.

They rolled her into surgery a few minutes later. The four of them watched her go in from the hall. As soon as she was gone, and Helen went to grab a snack at the vending machine, the happy family façade crumbled. Mac's defenses went back up to maximum strength.

"You've gotten so tall, Mac," his mom said.

"Well, that's puberty for you. You weren't around for most of it."

"I've seen pictures."

"Pictures," Mac said, as if that could make up for the distance, the distance they wanted. In pictures, they could tell themselves their son wasn't gay.

"Mac, we've tried to invite you back for holidays," his dad said firmly. "We even made the trip up to Pittsburgh, but you refused to see us."

"That's what you wanted. You wanted me gone, so I left." Four years had passed, but the pain was as fresh as the day Aunt Rita told him he was staying with her permanently. "How's church?" Mac asked with a snarl.

"It's fine," his dad said.

That was an arrow straight through the chest. "You still attend? Even though that asshole pastor and his dickface son are still there?"

"Watch your language," his mom said. "The pastor, he's…he's not the man you think."

He's a guy on the ultimate power trip who cares more about lying for his son than doing the right thing.

"He's a liar. We weren't 'roughhousing.' You know that, I know you do." Mac searched their eyes for an answer.

"We know," his dad said. "The pastor was trying to protect you."

"What?"

"We know the truth."

Mac crossed his arms. Nerves crackled in his chest. "What did he say?"

His dad looked him square in the eye, no blinking. "You were…coming on to his son, pretty aggressively from the sounds of it."

"He said that?"

"Justin shouldn't have gotten violent, but you scared him and made him very uncomfortable."

Mac almost doubled over. What kind of Twilight Zone did he leave behind in West Virginia? "You believe that?"

His parents traded looks with each other, as if to say "Yeah, of course."

"You really believe that?"

"That's what the pastor told us. His son was defending himself."

"His story's bullshit. I told you what happened four years ago! I told you the truth. He attacked me." Mac couldn't stop himself. Being near his parents sent his anger to scorching hot fire in record time. "You really think I would do that? I hated Justin Weeks. You just...you believe what you want to believe. Anything to stay in the good graces of Pastor Weeks."

"Son, life is about choices. If you choose to be so open with your...lifestyle, then you need to accept the consequences."

Mac didn't know how to answer that without screaming at the top of his lungs, which he would not do in public. "Well, at least you didn't have to deal with my lifestyle. You were happy I ran away. You wanted to get rid of me."

"Mac." His mom clasped her hands in front of her stomach, trying to stay calm. "You said horrible things to us."

"And you were horrible parents. Some things never change." Mac stared at the swinging OR doors. He prayed that Aunt Rita made it through okay. He thought time healed all wounds, but as he left the hospital that day, he realized that the real wounds, the real things that cut us, never healed. They just got a Band-Aid that could easily be ripped off.

CHAPTER
SIXTEEN

Gideon

Gideon woke up to the silence of an empty apartment. It had one of those unsettling calms that made him feel like a guy about to be killed in a horror film. He filed it under eerie. There was no Mac shuffling around, none of his plates clanging in the sink before being hastily shoved into the dishwasher minutes later.

He'd heard Mac leave early yesterday. He thought about wishing him a good trip. Instead, he stayed under the blanket and sent his Aunt Rita good vibes from his bed.

Things were still weird from last night. He didn't understand why Mac was so insistent on getting access down there. Letting a guy penetrate you crossed the line from doing gay things to being gay in Gideon's twisted universe. Every time he thought about being on bottom, about having some guy put his dick inside him, he pictured his mother's face, pinching in disappointment.

It was fucked up. He knew that.

His mom had had such a tough past few years. First with his dad getting sick, then Noah, then more Noah. Gideon wanted to do right by her. More and more, he was the lone bright spot in her life, and he didn't want to let her down. He didn't want any more whispers.

Whispers was what he called temple gossip. Temples and churches claimed that their main purpose was a place of worship. That was only a front. They served as gossip chambers for communities, places where people went to judge and be judged. He had confirmed it with his non-Jewish friends, too. The news floating in between the pews held more importance to congregants than what was being said on stage. It was like gossiping inside a church or temple allowed people to be instantly absolved of their sins.

In temple, no family ever wanted to be the flashpoint of gossip. Gideon's family was thrust into the spotlight when his dad passed away. He came for Shabbat services a few weeks after the funeral, and he heard it. He felt it. People whispered to each other and shot stealth and blatantly obvious glances at his family as they walked through the aisle to their seats.

That poor family.

That's her. The one whose husband died. Cancer.

A widow with two teenage sons. I feel awful.

The temple congregation did come together to help out his family in the wake of his dad's death. They sent cards, the rabbi paid them a visit, and members came over with homemade dinners for Gideon until his mom got off work.

But he never forgot the whispers. He never forgot the unwanted spotlight.

He heard the whispers every year, on every holiday, at every party. Anytime somebody got divorced, or bought a BMW, or got laid off. Gossip was the chum that religion fed the sharks to keep them coming back. And Noah was a prime feast.

Can you believe he got arrested?

Did you hear what Noah called his teacher?

He dropped out to become a gambler. A gambler!

My son said he was into drugs. Pot. But who knows what else.

It must be so rough on Judy not having Alvin around to help with Noah.

That poor family.

Gideon couldn't bear the whispers. He hated having to watch his mom put on a brave face. He didn't want to make her life any more stressful, any more deserving of whispers. Even if that included keeping his room extra clean. He was going to be the best son in the world.

Oh, but that Gideon. He's so smart. He got into Browerton early decision.

He's a big shot on Wall Street. Earns a fortune.

He has a beautiful wife and three adorable kids.

Thank goodness for Gideon.

His phone rang on his nightstand. He stared at the name before answering. "Congratulations."

"Thanks, brother." Noah's deep voice crackled on the line. "It's all pretty exciting."

"Exciting," Gideon repeated, as if that were anywhere near the adequate adjective.

"I can't believe I'm going to be a dad."

"Me, neither." Gideon meant it. He rubbed sleep out of his eyes. "I talked to Mom. She seemed happy."

"You always know how to make me laugh, brother. She'll come around. But you know what? Who cares. It's not her life."

That sounded a little harsh. She did give birth to him, so it is kind of her life, in a way.

"I have a favor to ask you, Gid."

"What?"

"Will you be my best man?"

The question broke through Gideon's sarcasm shield. Despite the circumstances, being the best man at your brother's wedding was still a major milestone in a sibling relationship.

"Yeah, of course," Gideon said, forgetting to be pissed at his brother for a moment. Noah was like a puppy. He meant well, but he couldn't stop pissing all over the carpet.

"Excellent!"

"So you're having an actual wedding?"

"Yeah. It's at her family's church. There'll be a reception, too. We made a deal with the bartender to serve her sparkling cider so it seems like she's able to drink."

"You haven't told her parents yet about the baby?" Gideon walked into the kitchen. No Mac dishes in the sink. He missed them.

"They're old school."

"But they can do math. And they know how to spell shotgun wedding."

"We'll deal with that later. Once the baby's born, they'll be so happy, they won't care what the math says. It'll be fine." That was Noah. Never worrying about anything. He could have five plates spinning in the air simultaneously and never think that they could break.

"Make sure you warn Mom so she doesn't say anything."

"Stop worrying about Mom."

"One of us has to." Gideon checked the dishwasher. Empty. Nothing for him to run. Mac really left no trace this morning.

"Let me give you some older brother advice, brother. Mom can be a powerful force, but don't let her control you."

"She doesn't control me."

"It's your life, Gideon. Do your own thing."

"Like you?"

"Exactly," Noah said, not getting the sarcasm. "It's your life."

Noah's hearing was not in tune to the whispers, apparently.

"I gotta go," Gideon said. "Congratulations again."

When he hung up, he found himself sitting on Mac's bed. What would the temple whispers say about that?

Φ

Gideon was doing homework on the couch when he heard the front door lock jiggle. The past two days had stretched with no sign of breaking.

"Hey," he called out to Mac.

"Hey yourself," Delia replied.

They came into the living room. He did not seem happy to be home, or anywhere near Gideon. At least they had a buffer in Delia.

"How's Aunt Rita doing?" Gideon asked. He had never met this woman, but he felt like he knew her.

"Her surgery went well." Mac walked into the kitchen, and Gideon checked out his ass. (It wasn't his fault. It was the jeans!)

Delia joined Gideon on the couch. She gave Gideon's knee a squeeze and continued where Mac left off.

"The doctors said they got all the tumor out, and she should recover nicely."

"That's great!"

Delia glanced at the kitchen, making sure the coast was clear, before leaning over to Gideon. Her hand on his knee sent the wrong kind of shiver up his leg. "Mac's parents were there. It did not go well," she said softly. "Really not well."

"Still assholes?"

"Very much so."

Mac rummaged in the kitchen, unaware of their conversation.

"I can't imagine that," Gideon said. "Your parents treating you like that."

"Me, neither. And while his aunt is getting an operation. He's a brave guy."

"He is," Gideon said, with more meaning than he probably should have. But when they were just talking or joking or, um, doing other things, Gideon forgot the fucked-up life Mac came from. Mac didn't carry around a "Woe is Me" sign. He did his best to move on with his life, something Gideon admired.

"We'll cheer him up," Gideon said.

"I'm sure you will." The curve of Delia's smile and the glint in her eye sent Gideon's mind into Orange Alert levels of panic.

Before Gideon could reply, Mac rejoined the couch. He tossed Delia a bag of peanut butter crackers and flipped on the television.

"Is it okay if we watch some TV?" Mac asked. "We talked a bunch on the way back to campus, and I just want to zone out and laugh."

"Yeah. Fine."

Mac turned on a *Simpsons* episode. It was a classic. Gideon wasn't laughing.

Φ

After a mini-marathon of peak *Simpsons* episodes, Delia yawned herself out of the apartment. And then there were two.

Mac closed the front door and sat next to Gideon on the couch. Gideon was rigidly stiff. He could trade places with a corpse, and none would be the wiser. Well, except for the heart rate, which throttled his chest.

"Thanks for your concern about my aunt. I appreciate it."

Gideon stared at the shut-off TV.

"I know it's late, but I think we should talk about what happened before I left."

"I think you've done enough talking." Gideon felt a wave of fire in his throat. "You told Delia."

The expression on Mac's face was a dead giveaway. "What?"

"Don't lie to me, Mac. We said we weren't going to tell a soul. You promised!"

Mac hung his head. "I'm really sorry. Seriously. It slipped out. But Delia won't tell anyone. She won't tell Seth."

"Why? Because you guys pinky swore? All it takes is one person, one time for her to get drunk."

"And then what? Your perfectly calibrated fortress of bullshit and lies crumbles to the ground?" Mac had on his game face, too. His dark brown eyes were like two shields ready for battle.

"I trusted you!" Gideon yelled. "I trusted you to keep this a secret. Maybe you don't care if people find out, but I do!"

"Well, don't worry, Gideon." Mac's voice was caked in a nasty sarcasm. "Because at least you were on top. You weren't doing actually gay things, per your logic. It'll be alright."

"This is a big deal for me. I'm scared shitless! This isn't a piece of gossip. It's my life."

"It's a big deal for me, too."

"It's not the same."

"Why? Because I'm gay?"

"Yes."

Mac got off the couch. He shoved Gideon against the wall.

"What's gotten into you, Mac? Things were going great. We were having fun. Then you started acting all weird, and you haven't stopped."

Mac's face broke in two, and hurt flooded out. "I *like* you, Gideon. I *really* like you."

"What?"

"I guess I'm out of my mind."

"Fuck!" Gideon yelled for the whole campus to hear. He squatted down and grabbed his head. "Fuck! Why are you doing this, Mac?"

Mac was ruining everything. Everything! Gideon wanted to hold onto what they had, how perfect it was. Their relationship was a Jenga Tower of Junk, and Mac pulled the wrong crate.

Gideon knew the look in Mac's eyes well. He'd seen it on row after row of templegoers that first Shabbat after the funeral.

Pity.

"I'm going to sleep at Delia's tonight. I'll work on finding a new apartment as soon as possible."

Gideon gazed through the window into the night as Mac packed a bag and the front door clicked shut.

Oh, but that Gideon. He's so smart. He got into Browerton early decision.

He's a big shot on Wall Street. Earns a fortune.

He has a beautiful wife and three adorable kids.

He's not gay. Only gay guys take a dick up the ass or in their mouth, and Gideon hasn't done either.

Thank goodness for Gideon.

SIX WEEKS LATER

CHAPTER SEVENTEEN

Mac

Mac rested on his bed on a cold night the first week of December. His bed and his nightstand were in the center of the room—the only pieces of furniture to his name. The rest of his junk splattered around the edges of the apartment.

He lived in a studio, and even with such small square footage, it felt large and empty, like a motel room. He could hear sounds echo off the walls. The kitchen was a fridge, stove, and oven against the wall. Paint cracked around the windows. One bad rainstorm could send the roof tumbling down.

He frowned at his humble abode. It wasn't homey like Gideon's. No fireplace. No chaise sofa. And no Gideon. Mac was proud of himself for telling him off last month and standing up for himself, but that still left him alone in a barren studio with a roof one rainstorm away from becoming a colander. He fired up his computer to watch some TV. He scammed Internet from the coffee shop next door.

Mac jumped up at the knock on the door sometime later. Delia held out a carton of eggnog in one hand and a box of saltines in the other. He took them and tossed them on the bed. She wrapped him in a tight hug.

"How are you holding up?" Delia ripped open the saltines and jammed a handful into her mouth. "Seth can't eat these, and I'm staring down the barrel of finals. Let me have this moment without judgment."

Mac held up hands up in surrender. "Eat away."

"This place has a lot of potential. It really does."

He pointed to the chipped paint and poorly patched cracks in the ceiling.

"Focus on the positive," she said. "Hardwood floors. We can do a Target run."

"I can't swing it right now." Aunt Rita was recuperating fine, but the medical bills had made money tight. Mac took on an extra shift at his work study job to help cover some of it. The money didn't matter to him. He was just happy that Aunt Rita was improving after surgery. Color returned to her face and new hair grew on her head.

"I think it's good you're living on your own." Delia brushed crumbs onto the floor. Mac didn't have the heart to tell her he didn't own a broom. "And that you're on your own, in general."

"What does that mean?" Mac didn't mean for it to come off so pointedly. Delia treaded lightly.

"You started dating Davis right away freshman year. Then as soon as you break up, you're kinda sorta with Gideon."

"I was never *with* Gideon." That come out even harsher.

But Delia held her ground. Like a good friend, she seemed to know when her wisdom was needed the most. "Maybe not technically, and not publicly. But in some way, you were." She rubbed his leg. "I thought you'd be a wreck. You and Davis were together almost two years, then he dumps you and goes with somebody else. But you were happy. Genuinely happy this fall. I saw it on your face."

Thanks to Gideon. She didn't have to say that last part. It hung in the air like a cloud of smoke at a bingo hall.

"Even if it was just some hooking up."

She was wrong, but Mac didn't want to correct her. He liked that she only knew half the story. The other half, the one with feelings and the way they cuddled and talked for hours after "just hooking up," was a secret, Mac and Gideon's own B-side. Even though there was no more Mac and Gideon.

"Fucking Gideon." Mac fell back on his bed. "You haven't told Seth—"

"Nothing." She mimed zipping her lips. "He may be a straight guy, but he's not totally clueless. I'm sure he's figured out something is up with how Gideon's been acting."

Something in Mac's head beeped wildly. "What do you mean?"

"I don't know. Different." Delia brushed off some crumbs that wound up in her hair. "Even I've seen it. He's just been in a funk."

"I wonder why he's acting like that. I mean, I thought he was happy with his new girlfriend," Mac said, thanks to some apt Facebook stalking. He wondered if his fishing was as obvious to Delia as it was to him.

"Fuck him. He's my boyfriend's friend, and therefore my friend, but between you and me, fuck him. Whatever happened between you guys, it shouldn't have ended this way. My sorority sister Lorna had a friend-with-benefit, this cute Indian guy in Kappa Kappa Sig, and after it ended they stayed friends. Speaking of Kappa Kappa Sig, they're having a holiday party, and you're coming."

"I don't know. I'm not really in the party mood."

"I will not let you become a hermit! You have a life and a six pack."

"I'll think about it." Mac opened the fridge and pulled out a can of Sprite. It was a pure impulse purchase—not to remind him of Gideon. His insides got all warm from the fizz, and only from the fizz.

"I don't hate Gideon," Mac said. "I want to hate him, for many reasons. But I can't. It pisses me off."

Delia shrugged and munched on more saltines. "Someone annoying said that love is stronger than hate, I guess."

"Even when you stop being friends with someone, you're still connected to them." Mac knew that if he let himself hate Gideon, then it would ruin every memory they had together. He wasn't ready to taint the past with that filter. "I just...I can't hate him."

Anger and hurt simmered in his chest, but so did longing. He drank his damn Sprite.

"You're a better person than me." Delia offered him crackers. He let her eat the rest of them.

Φ

Sometime after Delia left, Mac watched TV on his laptop. It was while staring at the screen as a studio audience howled with laughter that Mac realized Delia had left behind the bottle of eggnog.

He gulped down most of the drink, letting its sweet and spicy flavors distract him from the alcohol content. Mac pulled out his phone. Gideon was still in it. He was happy that Gideon was in a funk, but he felt bad if he was the cause. *Damn, why can't I just hate you?*

Mac found a different number to call, thanks to his liquid courage.

"Hey, Dad!" He said. He was more ebullient than a float at Disneyworld. Eggnog must've been spiked with holiday cheer, among other things.

"Hi, Mac," his dad said cautiously.

His dad's nervousness only pushed Mac to make up the conversation deficit. "I'm drinking eggnog in my apartment."

"By yourself?"

"Tis the season." Mac sprawled out on the bed. Life went sideways. It was quite a trip. "So Dad, I've moved apartments. Not like you need it, but I can give you my new address. I really liked my old living sitch, but my roommate and I got in a fight because I'm gay. Just like old times, huh? No bruises this time, though, at least none that anyone can see."

There was a pause on the other end. Mac's dad liked to think about what he said.

"I'm sorry to hear that, Mac."

"Are you, though? Or is this like one of those 'thoughts and prayers' comments on Facebook that people say to be nice even though they don't really give a shit."

"There's no need to use that language."

"This is kinda like what happened in high school. You said I brought it on myself. I guess I did here, too. Me and my stupid gayness. You were right again!" The TV spun and spun, sucking Mac into its orbit. "But here's the thing, Dad. I can't help being gay, even though it's mega hard. I don't want to get beat up and keep moving around like a vagabond, but I don't want to live my life as a lie. You think I'm being so audacious by living this 'gay lifestyle,' but I'm just trying to get by. It's a vicious circle. Or cycle. I don't remember the correct phrase. But anyway, how is the store?"

"I think you should get some rest, son."

Mac remembered being tucked in by his dad, followed by a kiss on the forehead. All those memories were tainted with the bad filter.

"Will do, Dad. Sorry for the cursing. I'll be sure to watch my fucking cunt cock shit damn Barack Obama mouth." Mac threw his phone on the floor. Luckily, a pile of dirty clothes cushioned the fall.

Mac did take his dad's advice and get some rest. He passed out, the side of his face mashed into a pillow.

CHAPTER EIGHTEEN

Gideon

"Relax, it's going to be great." Hannah massaged Gideon's arm and slid her hand down to interlock fingers. "It'll all work out."

Gideon rested his head against the window. The train whizzed past snow-capped mountains framed by a gray sky. He didn't realize Pennsylvania could be this beautiful.

Hannah squeezed his hand in support. Gideon continued staring out the window. "This weekend is going to be great. For everyone."

"We'll see."

Hannah laid her head on his shoulder and moved it around. "You are a bundle of stress."

"We are entering a stressful situation. I don't think I'm stressed enough."

Gideon had spent Thanksgiving weekend getting his

mom to come to terms with the wedding. When he first spoke to her about it, she seemed resigned, but as the event neared, and more people found out, her collected façade had broken apart.

"You don't want to miss this," Gideon had told her over leftover turkey. "I know you're shocked and upset and angry, but if you don't go to this wedding, then your relationship with Noah will never be the same. And you might not have a chance to make it better."

Tears ran down his mom's face in the kitchen. Gideon consoled her with a hug. He wondered if this was the role his dad played before he died.

"It's not the end of the world, Mom. You're going to have a beautiful grandchild."

"Whose grandmother is barely a decade older than the mother."

"But who will still love you and your matzo ball soup."

"The women I play mah-jongg with haven't mentioned a word about the wedding. I know they all know about it because your brother won't stop posting about it on Facebook. I see it in their eyes."

The whispers were at it again. Gideon rocked her back and forth. He set about cleaning up the kitchen and then the rest of the house. He liked seeing things in order. It gave him hope. A clean house cheered everyone up.

He saw hope in the mountains out his train window.

"Noah's wedding is going to go off without a hitch. Your mom is going to have a great time. And then we'll be back on campus before you know it."

Hannah had this way of making the biggest deals seem like trifles. Her voice sang with the tone of *It's all going to work out.* His mom was thrilled that one of her fix-ups worked out. Hannah reminded Gideon of Beth, in that she made him comfortable and their relationship was a natural progression.

Hannah kissed him on the cheek. "So, how should I introduce myself? Should I say I'm your friend, or that girl you're dating, or…"

She was fishing. Gideon took the bait.

"My girlfriend."

"Okay, then."

He and Hannah had gone on a few dates over the past month. It had thrilled his mom, and he liked the feeling of being normal again, of having a plausible story to tell people. If Hannah wanted to make things official, then so be it. It didn't matter much to Gideon, not when he couldn't stop thinking about Mac.

"You got your mom to come to Noah's wedding and be excited about the baby." Hannah offered him a sip of her water. He declined, and she slipped it in the seat pocket in front of her. "This weekend is going to be great."

Gideon remembered the hug his mom gave Christina when she and Noah came over for a post-Thanksgiving dinner. It was stilted, but he could tell she was trying.

"Thanks for bringing me with you," Hannah said.

"Thanks for coming." Gideon had pangs of guilt whenever he looked at her, like he was cheating on her. Which he was not.

He held her hand. He couldn't get through this weekend alone. Which was funny because he'd be with his family, the very people who weren't supposed to make him feel alone.

"Is there anything else? You just seem off."

Gideon looked at her and pushed down his memories

about Mac, about his now-empty apartment. "Just stressed."

A sly smile came on her lips. She dragged her hand up his thigh. "Well, maybe tonight we find a way to relieve that stress."

Her hand had the opposite intended effect. He crossed his legs, knocking it away. "I don't know. I think I'll be wiped out. We'll see."

"I didn't peg you for the guy to take things so slow. It's cute. Very old-fashioned."

"Isn't that what girls want?"

"We want *some* things."

But it was no use. An erection seemed like a Herculean task.

Hannah put in her ear buds and rested against his shoulder as the train continued its voyage to Westchester.

Φ

"Oh, Jesus," Gideon's mom said.

She wasn't being dramatic. There was Jesus, bloody and suffering, hanging from a cross on the altar. She shook her head at him in a "Can you believe we're here?" gesture.

"At least we're not the only Jews in here," Gideon wrapped his arm around her. "You're doing great."

They and Hannah stood in front of the altar while an organ played. Gideon knew this wasn't what his mom wanted. But she was being a good sport. The lines on her face were fully creased with worry and stress, more than her typical levels.

"You love your son," Gideon whispered to his mom.

"I do." They were here for Noah. "I do."

"Are we sure Jesus was Jewish?" Hannah asked them.

"I don't know any Jewish person with hair that smooth."

And then Gideon heard a sound he thought he'd never hear today: his mom hysterically laughing. She bent forward and heaved out laughs, giggling so hard her face turned red and tears beaded at her eyes.

"Although I guess if he can walk on water, he probably doesn't need a hair straightener," Hannah said.

Gideon looked behind them at the guests finding their seats, probably wondering what the hell those Jews were laughing about in their church. But he didn't stop his mom. Her laughter was music to his ears.

"Thank you, Hannah." His mom held Hannah's hand. "I needed that."

"Whenever today gets to be too much for you," Hannah said, pointing to Jesus. "Just think of his hair."

"I like this one, Gideon. At least I'll get to plan one Jewish wedding." His mom dabbed at her eyes with a handkerchief.

A pit belly flopped in Gideon's stomach. "Not for a long, long while."

"I know." His mom raised an eyebrow, as if to say not too long. "Well, Hannah, let's go find our seats. Gideon has to go with the wedding party. I have lots of questions to ask you."

"Can't wait!" Hannah walked to the pew with his mom. She turned around and flashed panic in her eyes. Gideon gave her a thumbs up for encouragement.

Φ

After the Catholic mass that would not end, Noah was officially a married man. The reception took place at a banquet hall down the block, one whose décor probably made Gideon's mom want to claw her eyes out, but she was putting on her strongest game face.

"It's very nice," she said to Noah's new mother-in-law, the ultimate test of her strength.

At least there was an open bar. Gideon headed straight for it like an oasis. He had the bartender make him a double. Some part of him told him to take it slow, but it drowned in a sea of gin.

Gideon meandered through the gathering guests, doing his best not to stumble. He didn't know most of them. Noah invited very little family. His mom wanted to keep it a small wedding since it was last minute, but Gideon knew the real reason. He felt grateful that he was spared having to engage in awkward chitchat with distant relatives who still thought he was in middle school.

Hannah grabbed his arm. "Easy there. You don't want to fall into the wedding cake."

"That's from *28 Days*! I love that movie! One of Sandra Bullock's best!"

The deejay (another test of his mom's game face) put on the first song to get everyone on the dance floor. Hannah reluctantly pulled Gideon onto the floor. She held him close, and usually he'd be all on it. Why wasn't he now?

Stop being an idiot! He told himself. *Pull it the fuck together.*

He and Hannah swayed to the beat, and he let his body loosen up a little bit. Not too much. Not like how he was at Cherry Stem. Straight guys weren't supposed to dance that way. Straight guys weren't supposed to let their thighs rub against another guy's legs and fingers weren't supposed to touch. Hannah reached her arms around his neck, which because of their height difference she could barely get up there. For a second, he pictured it was Mac. He thought his feelings for Mac would've waned by now, but they only grew stronger, like they were planning a hostile takeover of his body.

Gideon did his best Seth impression on the dance floor. Stilted and rigid. *Christina's family doesn't need to see Noah's brother acting weird.* Being a blah dancer was taking so much out of him. It was like holding his breath over and over.

"I'm going to the bar." Gideon pushed away from Hannah. "Do you want anything?"

"Slow down, Gideon," she said, somewhat forcefully. She was a good person. Gideon hated doing this to her.

I'm not doing anything to her.

He leaned against the bar and ordered another double. Noah bear hugged him from behind.

"You're married," Gideon said. "And you're going to be a father."

"Thank you for the life recap, brother."

The bartender mixed Noah a gin and tonic. Noah tossed a fiver into his tip jar.

"Hannah's nice," Noah said, but there was a weight to his words that set Gideon on edge. "How long have you guys been dating?"

"About a month."

"And you brought her to the wedding?" That was a question that didn't require an answer. He was just making an observation.

"She's really cool," Gideon said.

Noah tasted his drink and *aaaahed* in delight. "Do you

have a second for a brother heart-to-heart?"

"Sure?"

He walked with Noah into the hall, away from the little kids—Noah's new nieces and nephews?—playing tag. Gideon wished he'd gotten his drink first.

He placed his drink on an empty chair and put his hands on Gideon's shoulders, as if he were about to give him a pep talk. *Shouldn't this be the other way around?*

"Thank you for getting Mom here. You are the glue of this family," Noah said.

"Of course."

"I know what I'm doing is unorthodox, to say the least. But that's how I'm choosing to live my life. And it's okay for you to do the same." Noah had a look on his face that Gideon couldn't read. "You don't have to do everything she says."

"I know."

"I'm trying to impart this advice before it's too late, brother."

Noah tried to fix Gideon's tie, but he smacked his older brother's hand away.

"What are you getting at Noah?"

"Hannah is a really cool girl. She's the type of girl Mom loves. Just like Beth was. But that doesn't mean you need to date her."

"I'm not dating her to make Mom happy. Hannah makes me happy."

"Do you even know the difference?"

"What's wrong with wanting to make your parents proud? Mom and Dad did a lot for us. Mom's been through so much. So yes, I do want to make her happy."

Noah made Gideon look at himself in the hallway

mirror. "Fuck. She's done a number on you."

Gideon shook out of his brother's grip. "I have no idea what the fuck you're talking about. Speak English."

"Do you remember when we used to play hide-and-seek when we were little kids? Do you know where I always found you hiding? Under my bed with my *Sports Illustrated*. Funny thing was, you never tried reading the articles. You would just stare at the players."

"How many gin and tonics have you been drinking today?" Gideon checked to make sure his mom or Hannah weren't looking for him.

"I thought you would've figured it out in college," Noah said. "Gideon, you don't always have to be the responsible one. Hannah may be what they want, but I don't think she's what *you* want. Since we're both adults now, I don't have many opportunities to give you sage advice. Hell, you've always been smarter than me. But this whole experience with Christina has made me appreciate going my own way. You need to do the same, brother. You should be with a person that makes you truly happy, despite what Mom or those dipshits at temple think."

The deejay put on another classic dance tune that Gideon would've loved to dance to—*with Hannah*. It summoned them, but Noah wasn't moving. Gideon's love for his brother flipped to anger, in a Jekyll and Hyde swap. Years of pent-up rage exploded out of him. No net, no dam, no extra-strength lock could hold it in any longer.

"I don't want to be like you, Noah! You don't care about who you hurt when you find your own fucking path. You make a mess, and I pick up the pieces."

"Nobody asked you to!"

"Nobody ever does! That's not how family works.

You live in your own world and do whatever the fuck you want. Your life does not exist in a vacuum. Your actions have consequences.

"Do you know how hard this has been on Mom, what you've put her through? For years!" Gideon gained added respect for his parents. Their oldest son wasn't just a troublemaker. He was a completely self-absorbed troublemaker. "I can only imagine the stress you caused Dad for all those years."

Noah's eyes sparked with anger. Something finally got a rise out of him. "Dad loved it. He laughed when I would goof off. He told Mom I would straighten myself out, just like he did. Mom was the one who freaked out. We all had to fall in line. Heaven forbid people gossip about us. You were young still. She could still get to you." Gideon wanted to hear more about his father, another glimpse that he was too young to remember. "I'm sorry, Gideon. I should've been there before she could get to you. But I'm trying now."

Gideon glanced at his red face in the mirror. He could've blended into the over-the-top floral arrangements.

"I'm trying to help you. You don't want that life. I care about you."

"You don't know anything."

"You're gay, Gideon!"

Gideon stormed out of the banquet hall. To his right, the bridal party was lining up to be introduced by the deejay, another thing his mom was going to hate. He ran left, down an empty hall. He burst through the double doors and cold December air hit his face.

"Gideon, wait!"

Gideon stepped into the snow. The air cooled his head.

Noah followed seconds later.

"Where are you going?"

"Fuck you, Noah."

"Tell me I'm wrong."

The brothers stared each other down. Gideon thought about all he had done for his brother, for this family. He was glue, and all Noah ever tried to do was break them apart. "You can't stand that she loves me more. You think this will help her get on your side."

"Listen to yourself, Gideon. Just listen to yourself."

Gideon ripped off his boutonnière and threw it at his brother's feet.

"What are you doing?" Noah asked.

"Enjoy your wedding." Gideon stomped through the snow, away from the church.

"Are you serious about this?"

Gideon didn't answer him. He didn't think about his mom or Hannah or Noah. He charged through the snow with the determination of an Everest climber. *To hell with the consequences.*

CHAPTER NINETEEN

Mac

It took until mid-December for the first real snow to hit campus. A few inches of white powder blanketed the buildings and piled up on sidewalk corners. Mac took his nightly walk to the grocery store to pick out dinner. Frozen meals were the best. There was no cleanup involved. Just toss away the carton. He focused on that rather than the pathetic, "party of one" vibe they gave off.

He pulled a chicken pot pie from the freezer. It seemed festive. He caught a glimpse of himself in the glass reflection. His baggy parka hung over a sweatshirt and his rattiest jeans. He felt like he had lost his life a little. It was wrapped up in Davis and Gideon. And now with the pot pie, he was on his way to losing his six pack, too.

Mac put the pie under his arm and walked to the cash register. One register over, Gideon was buying a rotisserie chicken and bottle of Sprite.

Shit. Of all nights when I let myself go full homeless person. Gideon wore his jeans that made his ass extra round. Mac assumed there was a button down shirt with the sleeves rolled up underneath his jacket.

He took baby steps behind the magazine rack to stay hidden, but the cashier looked his way.

"Four sixty-nine." She had a booming voice that was louder than any microphone. She motioned for him to come forward and pay.

Mac slid over a five from his hiding spot. Gideon picked up his grocery bags and headed for the door. Mac breathed a sigh of relief. But a second later, Gideon pivoted on his foot. He forgot his damn wallet at the checkout.

And that was when he got to feast his eyes on his pathetic, frozen dinner-eating, parka-wearing ex-roommate.

The cashier made change and gestured for Mac to get moving. She had a line and no patience for college drama.

"Hey," Gideon said.

"Hey." It was pretty much a vocalized grunt. Mac eyed the door, then Gideon. He made the mistake of looking up into those green eyes. They were a fucking trap. But at least he seemed to be just as awkward and uncomfortable here as Mac.

"Were you able to find a new place?"

"Yeah." Mac couldn't tell if his heart was racing because he wanted to get the hell out of there or he wanted to stay. *Why can't I just hate you?*

"That's good." Gideon pointed at the chicken pot pie. His bags swayed in his hand. "Dinner?"

"Yeah."

"Me, too. Chicken and soda."

"You mean pop." *Fuck.* Mac said it without thinking. That was a joke, and jokes were only for friends.

Gideon's lips curved up into remnants of a familiar smile Mac still liked to picture. Nothing beat the real thing, though. "I mean soda."

For a second, it seemed like things were like back to normal, back in the geology class (tossed) salad days. Before Gideon ran full force back into the closet. But those days were long gone.

"Have fun with Hannah." Mac swerved around him. Right when he thought he was free, Gideon grabbed his forearm. Mac's parka was so thick he couldn't feel any of his warmth.

"Mac…" Gideon's eyes dove into his. They radiated hurt and tiredness and a million other things that were on his mind.

So say something, dammit. I can't be your mind reader.

Gideon let go, and as Mac walked out into the chilly air, he knew he had to do the same.

He texted Delia: *still going to that party tonight?*

Φ

The Kappa Kappa Sig holiday party could've been one of the Rainbow Alliance parties for all Mac knew. He counted at least seven gay guys. At a frat party. Delia told him that after one frat brother came out last year, two more did, then two of their pledges.

"I guess you *can* catch it," Mac said with a smile. They hustled through a packed dance floor to Delia's friend Lorna. She was there with the same guys from Cherry Stem. All that was missing was uptight Gideon, in his button down shirt wiggling his butt. That brought a brief smile to Mac's face.

Henry and Nolan danced like nobody was watching, PDA central. Or maybe they wanted to be watched. They waved to him.

"Where's your friend?" Henry asked.

"He's at a basketball game," Delia chimed in, saving Mac.

Henry gave an exaggerated nod, as if basketball were code for something. Mac wondered how long it took Henry's 'dar to go off about Gideon.

Henry realized his cup was empty. "I need a refill. You want one?"

He didn't tell Mac what it was, but it had to be either jungle juice or beer. Mac nodded okay.

"Let's go!" He slapped Nolan's butt like a sled dog, but without saying "mush."

"You know, you don't have to slap my butt all the time," Nolan said.

"You have a slappable butt. Own it." Henry slapped it again, and they were off.

Delia introduced Mac to the two guys remaining, Greg and Ethan. They talked to each other in the corner of the dance floor, by a row of windows strung with lights. Mac found out that Greg was the frat brother who came out last year. His ears perked up.

"Was this after you guys had started dating?"

"Yeah...kinda," Greg said. He was tall with short brown hair and a killer smile, which was on full display. "We were friends-ish first."

"Friends-ish? Like friends with benefits?"

"Yeah...kinda. Except we didn't really like each other all that much." Greg turned to Ethan who reluctantly nodded in agreement.

"I mostly didn't like you, because you were an ass," Ethan said.

"Nah, you liked me from the start," Greg said with a smirk.

Ethan blushed, bolstering Greg's argument.

"But it worked out," Mac said, hopeful. "You came out, Greg."

Greg and Ethan traded a curious look. "What's going on?"

Mac spilled the whole story about Gideon to them, swearing them to secrecy. Gay guys knew the code of silence, especially with closeted guys. Mac had found people who could understand what he was going through. Ethan had conquered the gay holy grail, turning a closeted straight guy into a public, serious boyfriend. Henry and Nolan rejoined the conversation halfway through, drinks in hand.

"It's Gay Everest," Henry said. "Yeah, a few people have made it to the top, but most people give up or die trying. I don't get the whole obsession with lusting after straight guys or straight-acting guys. I'm gay. I want somebody who is gay, not a guy who is trying to be straight. It's like a weird game. It's probably daddy issues or some shit like that. No offense," he said to Greg and Ethan.

"You know what the difference is between Drunk Henry and Sober Henry?" Greg asked Mac. "Nothing."

"I'm laughing on the inside," Henry deadpanned. Then he turned back to Mac. "But seriously, I've seen too many guys spending their days pining after a straight guy or a guy in the closet. We live in one of the best times in history. There are more out gay men than ever before. Why waste your time on the ones who won't even hold your hand in public? Move on dot org."

Nolan removed Henry's cup from his hand. Mac listened to Drunk Henry, though. Gideon obviously didn't want to change, and Mac couldn't wait around for him. Why should he spend his time hoping? The world was his oyster.

"Do you guys think straight guys and gay guys can be friends?" Mac asked, as if he was conducting a survey.

"Absolutely," Greg said. "One of my best friends is straight."

"Yes," Ethan said. "Of course."

Nolan nodded yes.

Henry tipped his head side to side. "Only if the guy is ugly."

"That's kind of offensive," Ethan said. "I have lots of attractive straight guy friends, and it's never been an issue."

"Who are these attractive straight guy friends of yours?" Greg asked playfully.

The jungle juice was sweet going down Mac's throat with an alcohol kick at the end. "I feel like dancing."

He was at a party. People were dancing. He didn't want to keep thinking about Gideon. Hence, he should dance.

Mac danced in place, letting the alcohol and music take hold of him. The other guys joined in. Henry and Nolan nosedived right into PDA central. Nobody cared about the stupid straight guy dancing rules. Guys danced with guys, by themselves, with girls. It was all good. Delia and Lorna danced around Mac, as if part of a ceremony. They moved further into the depths of the dance floor.

The opening bars of Mariah Carey's "All I Want for Christmas Is You" came on, and the crowd yelled their applause. The three of them danced themselves silly. Mac spilled some jungle juice on his sweater, but he didn't care. Nothing mattered except dancing. It was the greatest release. A few times, he pictured Gideon with his heavy, determined eyes staring at him like at Cherry Stem.

"No," Mac said to himself. He couldn't stay glued to the past. The present was waiting for him.

Delia gave him a head nod to her left, to a guy dancing in an ugly Christmas sweater vest, one popular among senior citizen women doing arts and crafts. But the pants he wore were modern, and tight.

She wiggled her eyebrows, and Mac knew what that meant. "Are you going to do anything about that?" They screamed at him.

Mac remained dancing in place. No comment.

Delia got closer to him, and with a forceful movement of her hips, she shoved him into Rafe.

"Sorry," Mac said.

Rafe's bright smile and wild hair were here to party. He was as cute as Mac remembered.

"Well, this is a total surprise. I never expected to run into you at a frat party." Rafe was extra smiley. He grabbed Mac's arm to talk in his ear. All classic flirt moves.

Mac placed a hand on the small of his back. He had some classic flirt moves up his sleeve, too. "Geology class is over for the quarter, and you never sat next to me."

"I kinda got the feeling that's what you wanted."

"You did?"

Rafe shot him a look warning him not to go down that path. And he was right. Ignorance and denial were Gideon's strong suit, not his.

And Gideon is in the past where he belongs.

"You're right. I was an idiot," Mac said. "I got hung up on some straight guy."

"Don't they all."

"Gay Mistake 101. It was a bad rabbit hole." Mac brushed a curl out of Rafe's eyes. "But I'm out."

Geology class was over.

"Good."

They danced together until the end of the song. Delia sang into her fist. Mac wanted to absorb this night into his bloodstream.

"This is the part where you ask me out," Rafe said. "Before I dance away."

Mac got right up against Rafe's ear, putting a tight arm around his waist. His erection poked against Mac's thigh. "Let's do lunch tomorrow. Not breakfast. I'm not that kind of gay."

"Neither am I."

Mac tugged on a Rudolph broach on Rafe's Christmas sweater vest. "I'll see you then."

CHAPTER TWENTY

Gideon

Gideon hadn't turned on his phone since he got back to campus. As if he wasn't already dealing with the wedding fallout, right after they got back to campus, Hannah dumped him. He didn't blame her. He'd left her alone at a wedding of strangers. And then right after he dumped her, he ran into Mac at the grocery store, giving him the coldest of shoulders. He didn't want to deal with the world. His phone sat in the nightstand drawer, taunting him, waiting to see who was going to blink first.

He wondered what kind of message Noah left him, or that Noah left no message at all. He had emailed his mom that his phone was busted and was getting fixed. Another white lie. They were so convenient. At some point, Gideon stopped thinking of them as lies and more as beats in a story he was constantly weaving.

"Oh, I got really nauseous at the reception. I needed some fresh air, and then I went home and took some Advil."

"Oh, my roommate moved out because he was on the waiting list for a dorm room, and a slot became available. It's cheaper than rent. We were on a month-to-month agreement."

"Oh Hannah, I texted you that I was leaving the wedding. The reception in that area is terrible."

Spin spin spin.

Gideon reached a breaking point when he got back from class a few days later. He turned his phone back on and rejoined the world. His phone buzzed with texts from Seth and his mom.

He scrolled through his Instagram. All the smiling faces on his feed made him more depressed. Delia posted a picture from some frat party. Mac had his arm around this guy with a stupid sweater vest. *Well, Mac's moved on.*

If only Gideon could do the same.

He shuffled to the kitchen. No stray cups on the counter. The dishwasher was full of clean dishes. Exactly how he wanted it.

He made himself a cup of coffee and sat on his sofa. Behind him was Mac's bedroom. The dividers remained in place. Gideon didn't bother looking inside. It was going to be empty. No bed. No clothes on the floor.

His phone rang in his pocket.

"Hey, Mom."

"How are you feeling?" She asked with concern. Gideon had to remind himself about his stomach bug.

"Better. Yeah, feeling better."

"Are you sure? You don't sound great."

"I just woke up from a nap." He shielded himself from the glare of the sun.

"Have you gone to the infirmary yet?"

"No. I'm feeling better."

"Well, you can never be too sure. That bug might be part of something bigger. I mean, for it to cause you to leave your brother's wedding..."

"Mom," he said before restraining himself. He took a breath. "I'll go to the doctor this afternoon, to be safe."

Another story beat.

"How was the rest of the reception?"

"It was…it was nice. Your brother seemed very happy. And Christina's family is very nice, too."

Gideon shuffled his mug around the coffee table, watching it leave a ring of steam and condensation in its path.

"Did Noah say anything about me leaving?" He couldn't believe he was using his mom like this, but hell if he was going to extend an olive branch to Noah. Just because he was older didn't mean he was wiser. It didn't mean he knew anything.

"No. I told him you texted me saying you weren't feeling well, and he understood. He was too busy drinking and carousing with Christina's family." Gideon's chest constricted with the same old stress. "It was his wedding. He was having a good time."

"I know." He could hear her eye roll over the phone. "Gideon, I have to be honest. It seems strange that you felt so sick that you had to leave in such a hurry. Some of my friends asked me how it went, and I had to tell them that my son left his brother's wedding early. It wasn't like you, Gideon." Suddenly the conversation turned away from familiar topics. It was no longer about the disaster that was Noah. It was about Gideon.

"Is everything okay?" His mom asked, that familiar concern in her voice. Was she ever not concerned? "You've been acting strange, and remember, you can talk to me about things."

"What do you mean?" Gideon went over his behavior of late. Save for the wedding incident, it was in line with previous Gideon experiences. He did not break story continuity.

"Well, the wedding, for one."

"I told you I was sick!"

"Don't raise your voice." Even though he was twenty, her reprimanding tone still shut him up. "And we haven't talked as frequently. I'm lucky if I can get a hold of you once a week now. And just now. You never raise your voice like that."

"I just have a lot going on." *No no no.* This was the wrong kind of lie. It was vague. It threw up red flags.

"Are you on drugs?" She asked, completely serious.

"No!"

"I worry. You hear these stories about good kids who go away to college and become drug addicts or die of alcohol poisoning or get hazed in their fraternity."

"I'm not in a fraternity, and I'm not on drugs. You don't need to worry about me."

"I know I don't, but I still do."

Gideon went to the window and drew the blinds. The glare off the snow made the sun unbearable. His apartment was now dark like a vampire's lair.

He composed himself and remained in character. "Mom, it's been a tough quarter. With Beth and all the drama with Noah, and having a heavy load of classes— I mean, these professors are tough—it was a lot."

The beats may have changed, but the story kept on rolling.

"Don't worry, sweetie. We all go through rough patches. You'll make it through. I have full faith in you."

"Thanks, Mom." He appreciated her supportive words, even if he still heard worry in her voice.

"And how is your roommate situation? Did you find a new one yet? Hopefully, this one is more dependable."

"I hope so, too," he said. Because the story kept on rolling.

Φ

That night, Gideon and Seth shot some hoops at the gym. Seth had picked up his game in the past few weeks. Usually Gideon played with his friend to feel better about his skills, but he was getting schooled by a guy who didn't eat half the foods in existence.

"Damn, have you been practicing with Delia or something?" He asked after Seth blocked his shot.

Gideon dribbled around him. Or he tried. Seth stole the ball.

"You are like Jewish LeBron."

"What's going on with *you*? You used to have game." Seth weaved the ball through his legs.

"Used to? I still do." Though Gideon didn't feel too sure about it. His charming, fun, social self seemed miles away. This fall had brought too much shit. "So what's Delia up to tonight? Hanging out with Mac?"

"Is that your attempt to find out what's been going on with Mac?"

Gideon stole the ball from Seth before his friend could question his blushing cheeks. "I just want to make sure the guy is doing okay in his new place. Where's he living?"

"Those crappy apartments on Pine Street. It's small."

"Empty? I had to pull teeth to get Mac to invest in a used nightstand."

"He just got a dining table and chairs so people could come over."

"He did?"

"Yeah. Rafe helped him pick it up."

Gideon completely airballed his shot. "What's a Rafe?"

"This guy Mac has been hanging out with."

"Like a boyfriend?" *The guy in the stupid sweater vest.* Gideon picked up the ball and almost flattened it in his hands.

Seth shrugged. This was gossip overload for him. "I think they just started hanging out like a week ago, nothing official."

"This is a pretty big step, though, picking out furniture. I mean, Beth and I didn't do that until ten months of dating."

Seth looked at Gideon as if he had crazy all over his face. "I think Rafe just went with him to the seller's house?"

He tried to picture what a Rafe would look like. That was not a name you heard in Westchester. Maybe that was what Mac liked. Gideon pivoted, on the court and on this conversation. "Good for him for getting some furniture. Maybe next he'll get a Swiffer."

"I guess." Seth picked up the rebound and positioned himself for a three-pointer, which bounced off the rim. It was closer than he'd come in their past games. "Why do you care so much?"

Gideon couldn't tell if there was a tone to his voice that belied something else, like maybe he and Delia had been having some conversations lately.

"I don't." Gideon swished his shot, and that was that.

Φ

Except it wasn't. Because after their game, instead of going back to his apartment, Gideon's feet brought him to the crappy apartments on Pine Street. The main door was unlocked, allowing Gideon to look for Mac's name on the mailbox and access the stairway. It was Gideon's hands that had a mind of their own and knocked on Mac's door. And it was Gideon's eyes that absorbed every inch of the Mac who stood in the doorway, the same, strong Mac that had screamed with orgasm and cuddled in bed.

"What are you doing here?" Mac asked.

It wasn't the way Gideon wanted to start this conversation. Mac's instant offense made Gideon feel super awkward. He poked his head in.

"I wanted to check out your new place." Mac did what he could with what looked like an apartment that hadn't been kept up in years. It was one of those shady college apartments where the landlord didn't fix anything because he knew there'd always be a college kid dumb enough to rent it as is.

Exhibit A: Mac.

A few items of basic furniture gave the place the shape of an apartment.

"It's nice," Gideon said.

Sitting in one of Mac's new dining chairs was the Rafe. The guy's rainbow socks peeked from under his jeans.

"This must be Rafe." Gideon plastered on his best smile.

"And you must be Gideon." He didn't know why, something about the smile this guy gave him instantly made Gideon dislike him.

"I'm Mac's old roommate."

Rafe nodded. Still with that smile. It made Gideon itch.

"There's not much to look at." Mac remained at the open door. "It's a studio."

"I'm glad you found a place."

Mac didn't respond, which prompted Gideon to act like more of a jackass. He pointed at the two guys.

"So are you like a thing?"

"Gideon, can you leave?" Mac pointed to the door. Gideon got the hint. Didn't mean he was going to take it.

That was a yes or no question, and you didn't give me a yes or no answer.

He swung on his heel and checked out the pathetic lineup of appliances that was passed off as a kitchen. "Oh, no dishwasher. Probably no in-unit washer and dryer, either."

But there was a full dish rack next to the sink. For some reason, Gideon took pride in it, like it was his influence.

"This studio isn't so bad. It's a healthy step up from a dorm room. Actually, though, a bachelor unit is a step up from a dorm room. With those, you just get a hot plate."

"Thank you for the insight." Mac nodded his head out the door. He didn't find a lick of this entertaining.

Not like Rafe, whose smile was holding back laughter.

"What's so funny?" Gideon asked him.

Rafe looked him square in the eye, shrinking him to petri dish size. "You."

"What does that mean?"

Rafe got up and in his face. "It means Mac wants you to leave. So leave."

This guy wasn't worth making a scene over. Gideon strolled to the door. As he stared into Mac's unblinking eyes for a sign of their old relationship, he realized how much he missed their talks most of all. He would've loved to stay up unloading the wedding drama with Mac over some mac 'n cheese. He didn't want his fuckbuddy back. He wanted his friend. He wanted his lover. But neither was a sufficient enough word for what they had.

Mac's eyes were a pair of big, brown vaults, and Gideon didn't have the combination anymore.

"I'm really glad everything worked out," Gideon said right before his throat choked up with emotion. He barreled down the steps before his stupid emotions got the best of him.

CHAPTER TWENTY-ONE

Mac

People never knew when their lives could change on the dime. It could be any day. And so when Mac woke up the next morning after that incredibly awkward meeting with Gideon to his phone ringing, he expected it was Delia or Rafe. Or hell, even Gideon with an apology.

It was Helen.

"Mackie…" The dreary, adult tone of her voice already told Mac bad news was next. Helen sobbed. "Well, your aunt…she passed away yesterday."

He was all logic, the only thing keeping him together. He had to know the cold, hard facts.

"The doctors said she was supposed to make a full recovery. She was fine when I spoke to her."

"And she was. She was feeling better and getting back to her old self at home. But I came over, and she was on the floor. They said a blood clot had developed after surgery and it got into her bloodstream and caused an embolism in her brain. I don't even know what all that means!" Helen let out a few sobs. "But she's gone, Mackie. She's gone."

"But she survived a brain tumor!" Mac yelled. "They said it went okay."

Mac's jaw tightened and rusted shut. He didn't let one tear fall. This wasn't fair. This wasn't how it was supposed to go.

"I know, sweetie. It hurts."

"Do my parents know?" He asked with businesslike efficiency.

"The coroner's office called them since your dad is next of kin."

His parents got to hear the news before him. Equally unfair. Mac pinched himself, hoping this was some nightmare. He missed his stupid, petty college bullshit drama so much right now. He didn't miss Aunt Rita yet. He still couldn't believe she was gone. Aunt Rita in the past tense did not compute.

Mac's stomach clenched with a new level of worry. "Helen, where are they burying her?"

"Pittsburgh," she answered.

He breathed a sigh of relief. He only had to deal with his parents, and maybe a few other relatives. He didn't have to go back to West Virginia. Helen gave him the information for the funeral service. Mac was already online booking his bus ticket before she hung up. He gripped his four-leaf clover keychain until his fingers turned white.

"Where was my damn good luck?" He asked it. Then he threw his keys across the room.

$$\Phi$$

Helen waved to him when he got off the bus, but it wasn't her usual enthusiastic greeting. Just a wave to let him know where she and her Corvette were. Mac didn't sleep on the bus. His body was exhausted but his mind was wide awake. He got in the car and shut the door.

Helen pulled him into a hug. His side dug into her center console.

"Oh, Mackie," she said to him, to herself, to the world. He rubbed her arm. He didn't know what to say back. *This fucking sucks* didn't seem appropriate. "Let's go home."

She meant to her house, where Mac was staying. Not his real home. It was understood that Mac didn't want to sleep alone in the house where Aunt Rita died.

"Are my parents in town yet?"

"I assume so," Helen said. "I got a call from your mother about the time and location of the funeral. They're working with the funeral home."

Mac whipped his head to face her, his jaw rusting in place again. "My mom called you?"

Helen nodded. She glanced at Mac, surprised. "She and your dad are putting together the service and arranging the burial. They've been notifying friends and family."

Not all family, apparently. Mac checked his phone. No missed calls. No texts. No emails.

"Do they have your phone number?"

"Yeah," though Mac wasn't completely sure.

"I'm sure they assumed that I would call you," Helen said, desperately trying to sound positive.

"But what if you hadn't? What if you didn't have my number?"

Mac's vision went blurry with anger. He sure as hell wouldn't shed a tear over what his *parents* did.

"I know this is a tough time, but maybe it's these experiences that help people reconnect. Grieving is a communal activity."

And I'm not part of their community. Mac's distance from his parents had been tough over these years, despite all the good times with Aunt Rita and his friends in Pittsburgh and Browerton. He had people, but just not the two people he wanted most. Yet he thought, in the back of his mind, that whatever happened between them could be repaired. That no matter how bad things had gotten, no matter how much time had passed, that they were his parents and he was their son, and that fact would triumph.

Looks like I was fucking wrong.

"It's going to be okay, Mackie."

Mac looked out the window, never feeling more alone.

Φ

Mac watched TV in Helen's living room, which smelled of lavender and cigarette smoke. The TV was merely background noise to him, so the house didn't feel so quiet. Helen had to run some errands to prepare for the funeral, like getting her dress dry-cleaned and picking up some food for Mac to eat while he stayed with her.

He stared at his phone on the glass coffee table. His parents would do the right thing. He knew that he could call them, but he was scared of being right. At least now, he lived with a sliver of hope that they were trying to get a hold of him.

He didn't know how much time had passed, but the sun was still out, and the house was still empty. It was that time of December when the sun looked to be perpetually setting, tinting everything with a constant magic hour glow. Mac checked online, and friends had sent and posted their condolences. *At least the Internet cares.* He searched the comments on his profile for one in particular, for an avatar with wild blond hair and dazzling green eyes.

Nada.

Mac sat upright on the couch. He couldn't recline, couldn't relax. He had to get out. He had to get fresh air.

In the garage, he found an old bike belonging to one of Helen's sons. It creaked when Mac got on and creaked even louder when he pedaled, but there was air in the tires and he was moving. He biked through Helen's neighborhood, past the cookie cutter homes with their identical snowed-over lawns.

Aunt Rita didn't live far from Helen. On warm days, they would walk over to her house for a barbeque. These familiar streets were more of a home to Mac than any part of Kingwood, West Virginia.

He turned right onto Ryder Avenue. A fresh lump appeared in his throat. Their house was just around the curve in the road, past their neighbor with the duck-shaped mailbox.

On this familiar street, there was a familiar car in Aunt Rita's driveway. A red pick-up truck. Mac had a new lump in his throat, this one far more powerful and indestructible.

He opened the front door and heard voices inside. He followed the noise into the living room, where his parents were surrounded by open boxes.

"What's going on here?" Mac's body was already in fight mode.

"Mac," his mom said. He looked at his father.

"Hello, son."

"How'd you get in?" His mom asked.

"I have a key." Mac dangled it for proof. "Since this is my home."

Crumpled newspaper lay on the floor. The box in front of his mom was labeled DONATIONS.

"What are you doing? The body is still warm and you're cleaning out her house?"

"We're only here for a few days. We want to make the best use of our time," his dad said.

"Why don't you spend that precious time mourning your sister?"

"I am," he said firmly. "We are doing what we can, but we also have to get back to the store."

"Priorities," Mac huffed.

"We closed the store for a non-holiday for the first time in twenty years to come up here. You remember what it's like," his dad said heavily. "There's only so much we can do up here."

"We're not throwing anything out yet," his mom said. "Just making preliminary piles of what would most likely be donated."

"You couldn't even wait a few hours. Were you even going to ask me if I wanted anything? Since I live here and all." Mac raced upstairs, realizing he was in the house where the only person who ever loved him died.

He burst into his bedroom. It was still intact. But he had an icky feeling as he tiptoed to Aunt Rita's room. He pushed the door open slowly. Her bed was stripped and the closet looked ransacked. He yanked open her underwear drawer. Completely empty.

Mac launched down the stairs like a rocket of pure fury. His parents continued packing up. "Where is it?"

They looked up, blank stares.

"Where's the keychain? The four-leaf clover keychain? It was in her underwear drawer."

His dad scratched his face. His apathy was a punch in the gut. "I don't know what you're talking about."

"She kept it there."

His mom shrugged, as if Mac was just talking about a stupid keychain. "That tacky souvenir? I think I threw it out."

"What? You shouldn't be throwing anything out. This isn't your house!"

Mac tore through the Hefty bag against the wall. His heart crumpled in his chest. He wouldn't let them see him cry, and it took everything to hold the tears back. They wouldn't have that satisfaction.

May we always be each other's good luck charms.

The keychain was a damn needle in a haystack. His fingers slid against the sides of the trash bag. He pressed his eyes shut, hoping he could feel Aunt Rita's spirit in this house. His thumb touched metal. He peeled off a ketchup-soaked Burger King wrapper covering the keychain. He wiped grease and more ketchup off the four-leaf clover. The anger was hot and liquid in his veins, lava ready to spew.

He ripped a glass shell out of his mom's hands. She jolted back, afraid of her son. *Good.*

"Mac!" His father yelled.

"What is your problem?" He yelled back. "You don't get to throw out somebody's stuff!"

His mom didn't try to take back the shell from him. "Look, I know this is sudden. Going through her stuff is another way for your father and I to remember her." She sounded somber, and Mac was glad in a way that Aunt Rita's death actually meant something to his parents. They weren't devoid of emotion and compassion. Only when it came to him.

"You should've called me. This is my house, too! What were you going to do with my stuff?"

"We don't know. We were going to talk to you about it at the funeral," his dad said.

Mac took in his final glances of Aunt Rita's house. He didn't want his last memories of this place to be of his parents ripping it apart. "You never told me about the funeral. You didn't even call to tell me she died." Tears fell down his face. "You knew how much she meant to me. You didn't even call. What the fuck is wrong with you?"

"Watch that mouth of yours, Cormac." His father pointed a stern finger at him. "You made it clear in the hospital how often you wanted to hear from us. Communication is a two-way street."

"Fuck you and your two-way streets. I hate you. I used to be mad at you and hurt, but now I really hate you." Mac clutched the keychain as he headed to the front door. "Don't touch my room."

Φ

More family than Mac assumed would come showed up to the funeral, people he hadn't seen in years. He was glad that they cared about Aunt Rita.

This was the first time Mac had stepped foot inside a church since West Virginia. Aunt Rita was not religious. He imagined how much she would hate this service. The pastor preached from the front of the church, and people looked to be in their own worlds.

Mac didn't sit with his parents. He had a pew to himself. A few family members he recognized said hello and kissed him on the cheek, but they didn't sit with him. They didn't ask him to join him.

"Let us remember and cherish the times Rita brought joy into our lives. Let us not dwell on the sadness we feel now, for sadness is only temporary." The pastor made eye contact with Mac. At least one person here did.

He zoned in and out of the sermon. He thought about the good times with him and Aunt Rita instead. Grand pronouncements about the meaning of life and death were a snooze compared to remembering their Christmases and the smell of the kitchen when Aunt Rita made pancakes.

He wondered what was going through his parents' heads, if they were in mourning at all. They didn't talk to Aunt Rita much. When Mac first moved in with her, they would call for updates, just to make sure he hadn't dropped out of school and spiraled out of control. Mac didn't want to speak to them, and soon, they stopped asking to speak to him. He believed that that parent-child bond was unbreakable, but it was just as tenuous as any other relationship. As sturdy as a damn tissue.

The ceremony moved out to the graveyard. The sun would not stop shining, which really pissed Mac off. It was the type of winter day everyone dreamed of. Crisp breezes and blue skies. Aunt Rita would've loved it, but she couldn't get to enjoy it.

His family congregated on one side of the casket, while assorted friends spread out around them. Mac stood off to the side. He was alone, unflanked by family. Even Helen had her two grown sons at her side. The crisp breeze morphed into a strong wind that slammed into his side.

Aunt Rita's casket was lowered into the ground. That was, so to speak, the final nail in the coffin. She was dead. She was gone. And she was never coming back. She would never get to meet Mac's future boyfriends or attend his wedding or see what would become of his life.

Mac sobbed into his sleeve, deep sobs that made his body shiver. He outsobbed Helen in the car and anyone else at the funeral. His face was soaked and hot. He was the only one making noise with his crying, as the rest of the funeral stood in solemn silence. He squeezed his four-leaf clover keychain between his fingers as hard as he could. Emotions ripped through his chest. His head vibrated with his crying, for Aunt Rita, for being alone in the world.

He felt a calm as the wind stopped.

Only it didn't stop. Someone shielded him.

An arm maneuvered around his waist and pulled him into a warm body. Mac wiped the tears off his face. He looked up, and Gideon's green eyes shined back at him.

CHAPTER
TWENTY-TWO

Gideon

He missed those brown eyes so freaking much. Mac radiated a need that emboldened Gideon, made him stand up straight and puff out his chest. It wasn't until he looked away from Mac and saw people staring at them that he realized how gay he was being in public. A man and woman across the plot shook their heads and grimaced. It was Mac's parents. He just had that feeling. He could sense the disappointment coming off them in waves.

As soon as the funeral ended, Mac pulled Gideon away from the cemetery. They said no goodbyes, and nobody came up to say goodbye to them. Gideon hailed a cab and took them back to his hotel in downtown Pittsburgh.

Mac sat in the desk chair in his hotel room, glassy-eyed. He looked like he just came from battle. Gideon rubbed his shoulders.

"How did you…"

"Delia told me. Then I called around to funeral homes in the area, found a last-minute hotel, and booked a bus here."

"You did all that?"

"I want to be here for you." He spun Mac around to face him. Gideon's stomach did a somersault when those brown eyes were on him. "I missed you so much. I'm sorry for pushing you away. I feel like I've been pushing my whole life. Pushing to be somebody I'm not. Pushing anyone away that could expose who I really am."

When Gideon had left Mac's apartment, things started to become clear. He let himself see who he really was and think what he really wanted to think.

"Do you know what would go through my mind when I dated and hooked up with girls?" He squatted down to get eye level.

Mac cocked an eyebrow, afraid to hear the answer.

"I would say 'Good job' to myself. I would tell myself I was doing the right thing." Gideon shook his head. *Always the good son.* It was so fucked up. "I spent so much time trying to convince myself that I didn't want the things I wanted."

Mac placed a comforting hand on his shoulder. "You're not the first gay guy to feel this. You are gay, right? This is you coming out?"

Gideon nodded, silently grateful that Mac took those words out of his mouth for him. He still felt a ripple of shame when he heard them. He wasn't ready for the world's reaction.

"What was going through your mind on the night we

first met?" Mac asked him.

"I thought I was lucky that I got to meet a cool guy on my first day at school."

"And when I kissed you?"

The memory was still vivid in his mind. "I freaked the hell out. It all happened so fast. It was like going from having secret, fleeting thoughts about skydiving to being thrown out of an airplane." Mac chuckled at the analogy. It was better than geology class. "I panicked."

"I've never been that forward," Mac said.

But now it was Gideon's turn to be forward. He brushed his lips against Mac's, breathing in his warm taste, realizing just how much he missed it now that he had it back. He planted tender kisses along Mac's freshly shaved cheeks.

"What if I told you that I really liked you?"

"Then strap me into a parachute because I am ready to skydive." Mac pulled Gideon against him, the kisses turning passionate and hungry.

Their lips were magnets to each other. Mac dug his fingers into Gideon's unruly hair and pulled him closer. It was different from the times in their apartment. For the first time, they could kiss each other without any pretenses, their true selves laid bare.

Gideon hugged Mac into his chest. They couldn't kiss each other fast or hard enough. Mac shoved his hands up Gideon's shirt. His fingers prickled against the hairs on his chest and stomach.

Gideon pulled away mid-kiss. He felt an intensity shaking his core. He needed this. He led Mac to the bed. They took off their suit jackets.

"Are you sure?" Mac asked.

"You tell me." Gideon opened the nightstand drawer and pulled out the bottle of Astroglide. "I figured if all went well today, we'd get to use it. And if you had rejected me earlier, I would've come back here and used it on myself."

Mac laughed. Gideon wanted to make him laugh and smile, especially today. This kid had been through so much. Gideon wanted to make him feel good.

For weeks, Gideon was a house where the lights were shut off. He tried turning the circuit breakers, but they didn't do a thing. Kissing Mac, feeling that hard body against his made Gideon the brightest house on the block.

Those ferocious lips brought him back to life, and Gideon wanted all of him. Mac lay across the bed, his muscular frame sprawled out on the comforter. Gideon's lips moved from his mouth and slid down his neck. Mac shivered at his touch. He groped Mac's cock through his pants. His hands hovered over a Hanukkah gift all wrapped, waiting for him to tear it open.

He looked up at Mac as his mouth moved further south. Mac's eyes asked if he was okay. *Hell yes.*

He unbuttoned and unzipped Mac's pants. *There's a dick in my face*, Gideon thought. *A big one.* He wondered what others would think. He closed his eyes and forced all of those thoughts out of his mind. They were other people's words, other people's beliefs. He focused on what he truly wanted.

"What's wrong?" Mac asked.

"Nothing." Gideon's lips curled into a smile. *There's a dick in my face.*

He let Mac enter his mouth, as much as he could. He relaxed his jaw, and Gideon took in the sweaty taste of him. He focused on the now. No analysis. No neurosis. He had one of those rare experiences of living in the moment. He slapped the hard dick against his tongue. Mac groaned in delight. Gideon would never get tired of that sound, especially knowing that he was the cause.

Gideon moaned as the hot, throbbing cock filled up his mouth. Mac grabbed the headboard to steady himself. He lifted his hips, sending his cock further inside Gideon's mouth. Gideon rubbed himself over his pants. A rogue finger of his found its way to Mac's ass. He pushed it in. Mac gasped like no one was listening.

He pulled out his finger and tried to stand up, but Mac yanked him into a kiss that dared to suck his lips off. His tongue tasted the insides of Gideon's mouth. Their warm bodies locked each other in a tight embrace. Mac's erection branded Gideon's leg.

"Get on your back," Mac commanded. His heavy-lidded eyes conveyed such force and lust that Gideon would've walked to China if Mac told him to.

Mac whipped his shirt off. His pecs and biceps bulged as he undid Gideon's pants and threw them on the floor. The cold hotel room air hit his bare legs and ass, but the heat coming off Mac made for a potent shield. Mac slapped his ass. Gideon spread his legs further.

The anticipation sent him spiraling. He felt a finger circling his ass. Now he was the one getting impaled by the dildo in his fantasy. Except this wasn't a dream, and it was going to be much better than a yellow sex toy.

"Yes, baby. Yes." Gideon slammed his head against the mattress. Mac pressed in further. It was ten times better than what Gideon did to himself in the shower. He hated that he'd passed this up, any of it.

Mac licked his aching hole. As much as Gideon enjoyed rimming Mac, he had to say that receiving was overtaking giving at a fast clip. Gideon dug his fingers into the sheets. He was on horniness overload. He had to stroke his dick. It couldn't be ignored. He needed to get out the urge boiling over inside him.

Gideon jerked himself off while Mac ate him out. The bottom half of his body was a roller coaster zooming around loops at full speed. Mac shoved two fingers inside him. Gideon cried out and stifled his voice against his forearm.

"Don't do that," Mac said. "Don't cover it up. I want to hear you. Every sound."

He followed Mac's order. He'd never let anyone call the shots like this. He didn't have to think. He just had to react. With his free hand, Mac massaged Gideon's balls.

"Yes!" Gideon yelled out, damned if any other hotel guests heard him. His words had to wait for breath that wasn't coming fast enough. Mac removed his fingers, and instantly Gideon was dying of want. His cock had never gotten this hard in his hand.

"Want to...kiss you," Gideon said, his body feeling a million amazing things at once. Mac's imposing frame leaned over him. He tasted all of himself on those lips.

"How far do you want to go?" Mac asked.

"All the way, baby." They gazed deep into each other's eyes. Gideon saw past the sexy haze that clouded Mac's vision, into his heart. Gideon had a place there. He kissed Mac softly, a brief respite in the passion.

Mac slapped his ass hard. He pictured the mark of Mac's hand, branding him like property. Gideon was nervous, but he rode it. When he had to make sharp turns in his car, he put his foot on the gas and went faster.

"Do you have a condom?" Mac asked.

"No. Is it okay if we try without? I haven't been with anyone since Beth over the summer. Have you?"

"Not since Davis, in the summer."

"Not Rafe?"

Mac crossed his arms and arched his eyebrow. "Not Hannah?"

They both shook their heads no.

Mac prepared Gideon with lube, which was cold compared to everything else that had been down there.

"Is it going to hurt?" It was finally happening, the final frontier. No turning back.

"Yes, but hopefully the good feelings will outweigh the bad." Mac rolled on the condom.

Gideon didn't know if he was talking about sex or life in general. But he trusted Mac.

"If it hurts too much, let me know, and I'll stop."

He sucked in a breath when he felt the tip of Mac brush against his opening.

"You okay?"

"Do it, baby," Gideon said.

"You've been calling me baby a lot." Mac kissed Gideon's neck.

"I know."

Mac eased himself inside his ass. Gideon mashed his lips shut and grunted. Mac kissed his shoulder in support. He kept going.

Gideon felt whole, but uneasy. It was a new sensation his body was trying to process. He didn't stop Mac. He pulled out slowly, then slid back in.

Don't think. Just feel.

Oh that Gideon. He has a dick in his ass. The whispers! Gideon focused all his mental power on blocking them out. He stared up at Mac, sweat dripping down his cheeks. Their feelings were stronger than stupid gossip.

Stay in the moment.

"Stay with me." Mac cupped Gideon's chin and directed him to look into Mac's eyes.

That shut up every whisper.

Gideon's grunting turned to moaning. His mind was dizzy with the thickness filling him up. *There was dick inside me.* Just thinking about it drove him wild. The more wrong it sounded, the more right it felt, like all of life's best things.

The added pressure made his own cock harder. Mac ran his fingers through Gideon's hair. His breath danced on his neck. Gideon was taken over by Mac. His dick rubbed against Mac's tight stomach.

Golden rays of setting sun spliced through the blinds, giving them a magic glow. Mac pumped into Gideon's ass with passion and strength. His hands traveled up Gideon's sweaty chest and flicked his nipples.

And then that intense feeling Mac had told him about in their apartment, the feeling of knowing you're about to come while getting fucked, overtook Gideon. His whole body shook with anticipation as it built and built. His body tried to clench, but couldn't because of Mac's cock. He was powerless against his orgasm ravaging through him. Fucking powerless. It was wonderful. Mac fucked him harder, grunting into his ear. Gideon's body was defenseless. He surrendered to the moment. His legs were about to give out. Every muscle in him spasmed. Mac held him tighter, sensing he was close.

"You're gonna come for me?"

"Baby, I am."

Mac slammed into him in deep thrusts. Gideon's body shook like it was getting electrocuted. He was going to yell so loud that everyone in the hotel would hear them. But Gideon still had some modesty. He bit into his arm as he shot hot white streaks against his stomach. He thought he might have lost consciousness for a few seconds.

"Holy shit," he whispered.

"Intense, right?"

"Holy shit." It would take him a few moments to regain speech and motor functions.

Mac fucked him in speedy hits as he raced to orgasm. He doubled over as he came inside Gideon. When he was finished, he collapsed onto the bed.

"So how was it?" Mac asked with a curious smile. He kissed Gideon's shoulder and rubbed his chest.

Words and Gideon were not on the same wavelength. He was still catching his breath.

"Gideon?"

His mind was mush with afterglow, but he managed to say something.

"I'm gay. I'm really, really gay."

CHAPTER
TWENTY-THREE

Mac

Mac dreamt about Aunt Rita. He imagined her resting happily in heaven. She peeked through the clouds at her funeral. As Mac looked up, she winked at him. It was going to be okay, he thought the wink meant. But then Gideon wrapped his arms around him, and Aunt Rita winked again.

Mac woke up in Gideon's arms. Gideon nuzzled his chin into the crook of Mac's neck. His chest hair bristled against Mac's back.

It was going to be a good morning, a good day, good week, good everything. For the first time since being back in Pittsburgh, Mac felt hopeful. He filled up his lungs with stuffy hotel room air. The smell of sex lingered in the room.

Mac replayed last night, particularly the part when he had sex with Gideon. It was better than he imagined, because it meant something to the both of them. He wasn't alone anymore. It was like Aunt Rita had this all arranged, and she really was winking from heaven above.

"Morning," Gideon groaned. He pulled Mac backward into a kiss. The first signs of his stubble burned Mac's cheeks. Gideon's stubble came back barely a day after shaving. Mac found it undeniably hot.

"You called yourself really, really gay last night," Mac said, giving him a quick peck on the lips.

"Well, considering what I had done just moments before, was it really a surprise?" He had that growly voice of just waking up. Mac felt himself pitching a tent in their lovely hotel bed.

"I'm proud of you, Gideon." Mac stroked his hand. "I know that wasn't easy."

"Well, you're the first person I've said that to, so I still have a ways to go." Gideon leaned on his side to face Mac. "What I went through is nothing compared to what you had to endure in West Virginia."

The tent collapsed. Mac gulped back a lump in his throat. He didn't want West Virginia anywhere near this bed. He kissed Gideon, putting their conversation on hold for the foreseeable future.

Gideon's phone buzzed on the nightstand. Mac tried to pull him back, but nobody could ever resist that siren call. iPhones were more addictive than heroin.

"I'll just let it roll to voicemail." Gideon turned around to get his phone, and in two seconds, he was out of bed. He gasped at his stark naked body and scrambled to find his boxers. Mac watched this scene with some amusement.

Gideon clicked on the phone. "Hey Mom, can you give me a second? Yeah, yeah, just one second." He held the phone to his chest. "I'm talking to my mom while I'm naked!"

His eyes had the familiar panic of their first meeting as freshmen. Gideon darted around the hotel room, searching frantically for his boxers while his phone was pressed into the crook of his neck.

"Yeah, Mom. Sorry, one second. I just need one more second. I was coming out of the bathroom from brushing my teeth and I have the coffee maker going. I just need to shut it off so I don't burn the place down."

Mac pointed to Gideon's boxers, hanging off the desk lamp. Gideon pressed his hands together as if he were praying and mouthed "Thank You."

"No, Mom. I don't have class this morning...yeah, well I do have that class but it was cancelled because my professor has a stomach bug...yeah, I think it's food poisoning." He sat in the desk chair and tried to put his boxers on, but his arm couldn't stretch because there was a phone connected to it.

"Hey, Mom. I'm going to put you on speakerphone for one second. I just need to do something with both hands for one second. Okay, you still there?"

Gideon gave Mac the quiet hand signal popular with all librarians. He placed the phone on the desk carefully, took a quick breath, and put Mama Saperstein on speakerphone.

"Mom, you still there?"

"Hello? Gideon, can you still hear me?" His mom's heavy New York accent was like listening to a cartoon character for Mac.

"Yeah, Mom." Gideon yanked on his boxers, and then his jeans with such intensity that Mac thought they were going to rip.

"I'm getting an echo. Do you hear that?"

"Mom, that's speakerphone."

"So what kind of stomach bug does your professor have? The temperature is dropping, and I don't want you getting sick again so soon after your brother's wedding. Are you bringing hand sanitizer to class with you? I saw this special on *Dateline*, and you know what has the most germs?"

Gideon took her off speakerphone and put the phone to his ear. "What, Mom?...Oh, really?" He put the phone to his chest and mouthed "doorknobs" to Mac.

That made sense.

"I think he just got food poisoning...no, he doesn't eat at our dining halls. I don't know what he ate. I don't actually know if it's food poisoning. That's just a guess."

Mac reminded himself to stock up on hand sanitizer before he took the bus home. He was curious what restaurant Gideon's professor ate at, but then he remembered that this was all complete fiction. Gideon should've majored in creative writing because he knew how to tell a story.

Gideon sat on the edge of the bed. "Yeah, Mom. I'm fine...no, I haven't spoken to Noah. I will." Mac wrapped his arms around Gideon, and his body tensed underneath. "He said that? Okay. I'll call him this week. Yeah, yeah. I'm fine."

Gideon got off the bed and stood by the closet, across the room. "If I was in a funk, I would tell you. If something was really wrong, I wouldn't hide it from you.

Actually, Mom, I need to run. I'm scrambling some eggs, and they're starting to burn. We'll talk later, okay? I love you."

He hung up and held the phone to his chest.

Mac had to catch his breath. Just watching Gideon was beyond exhausting. He couldn't imagine having to live like this. Even though Mac's family kicked him out, at least he never had to lie about anything. He wondered how many lies Gideon had told his family, how many lies those lies created. And Mac could tell that he kept track of everything. He never got tripped up.

"You want some breakfast?" Mac asked.

Gideon remained by the closet. He was probably on some adrenaline high talking to his mom, and he was still coming back down. Mac got out of bed and slowly snaked his arms around him. Gideon rested his forehead on Mac's shoulder. The exhaustion came off Gideon in waves.

"It's going to be okay." Mac rubbed his back. "Breakfast?"

"Okay," Gideon said into his shoulder.

They got showered and dressed. Mac used a tissue to open the door of their room.

Φ

Mac tapped his finger against the window of the taxi for the entire ride. His stomach twisted into a thousand tangled knots as if it were made of wires. He and Gideon were on their way back to Aunt Rita's house to pack up his room. He paid for a month of a local storage locker. Mac would figure out what to do over Christmas break. Mac hated to think that the only remaining part of her life was stuff to be packed into boxes.

Gideon covered Mac's tapping hand. "Nervous?"

"Just a little. I really hope my parents aren't there."

"Don't worry. I got your back. You won't be facing them alone."

Mac managed a smile. This whole weekend had been a whirlwind of emotions, and he was wiped out on every level. He had done so much adulting. He wanted to go back to his college life of parties and classes.

And Gideon.

"I'm curious, did you ever try to bring charges against this Justin Weeks asshole?" He checked to make sure the cab driver had his eyes on the road.

Mac shook his head no again. Gideon's forehead creased with anger.

"You never pressed charges or tried to sue for damages?"

"Are you serious?" And Gideon was, which made Mac let out a nervous laugh. "You think when some good ole boys get in a fight in Kingwood, West Virginia, they bring in lawyers to sue for damages? You think there's a hate crime ordinance in my tiny town?"

Mac shot Gideon a get real look. They lived in the same country, but grew up in different worlds. Gideon didn't say anything for the rest of the trip.

"Fuck," Mac said upon seeing the red pickup truck in the driveway.

Gideon massaged his shoulders, like a manager getting his boxer ready for a fight. "You got this."

Mac opened the door with his key. The living room was all packed up. Every knickknack, every piece of personality that made his house a home was in a box, ready to be sent to the past. Or donated.

"Hello?" Gideon called out to the seemingly empty house. Mac gestured for him to keep his voice down.

"Hello?" His mom called back. "Who is that?"

"It's me, Mom," Mac said, not wanting to answer her question just yet.

His mom met him halfway down the stairs. She eyed Gideon and didn't say anything. Not with her mouth, anyway. But Gideon didn't show an ounce of fear.

"Hello," she said to the non-Daly in this house.

"I'm Gideon. We're here to begin packing up Mac's room."

She turned to Mac. "Your father and I are cleaning out the attic. Aunt Rita has a lot of junk."

"Maybe you should let Mac take a look at some of that junk before you toss it out. It might be his." Gideon crossed his arms.

"Okay." His mom seemed nervous. Mac felt bad that they'd spent two long days packing up the whole house, while also attending the funeral. They must've been exhausted.

They all walked upstairs. Mac's dad gave a nod of acknowledgement from up in the attic.

"You were at the funeral yesterday, right?" Mac's mom asked Gideon.

"Yeah. Is this the room?" He pointed to Mac's door.

"Wait," his mom called out, but Gideon did no such thing.

He opened the door. Mac's room was packed-up. Nothing hung on the walls. Nothing sat on his desk. It was so bare, like a hospital room.

"We didn't know when you were coming back, so we went ahead and did your room," his mom said. "But you can look through. How long are you staying before you go back to school?"

Mac was upset, but understood. He knew time was precious, and he appreciated the help. It seemed like his mom was trying extra hard to be nice, like maybe she felt bad about two days ago with the keychain.

"You had no right to do this," Gideon said before Mac could open his mouth. He was in full Pitbull mode. "Mac told you he would be back."

Mac's dad stepped in. He wasn't as tall as Gideon, which diminished his intimidation strategy. "We didn't know when that would be, and we can only be in this house until the end of the month."

"He said he would be back, and here we are. You should've *believed* him. But I know that's not really your forte."

"I don't follow," his dad said.

"You seem to have this tradition of not believing your son, taking the word of a douchebag preacher over him, and basically leaving him out to dry."

"I don't think you know what you're talking about," his dad practically growled.

It was like watching a car accident in slow motion. Mac wanted to yell at somebody to hit the brakes, but his voice was out of commission. All he could do was watch.

"You couldn't wait to clean out her house and go through her stuff the second she died. Are you planning to sell those assets? Some of them are Mac's, which he purchased with his own money."

Mac's parents traded confused glances. It was weird, but even though he was angry with them, he felt like they were being disrespected, and it stung someplace deep within him.

"You really should stay out of this. It's a family matter."

"Don't you talk to me about family matters, Mr. Daly," Gideon shot back. His ears were tinged red with fury. "Family is just people you can kick to the curb whenever you want, right? Your son gets the shit beat out of him, and you don't do a goddamned thing to stand up for him. You just cozy up to the pastor. What? To save face, and your store? To avoid the whispers at church? Then you send him away. You don't try to get any type of justice against his attackers. Is that what family is to you? Not like it matters now." Gideon held Mac's hand in a blatant sign of defiance.

Mac hated what he saw. His mother looked down, and his father could barely hold on to his stoic expression. Gideon landed direct hits, but why didn't it make Mac feel better?

"And yeah, I'm his boyfriend, or something like that. I mean, we haven't really DTR'd yet, but at least somebody in this house cares about what happens to your son." Gideon's glare could slice through stone.

Mac's parents stared at him speechless. His dad barreled down the stairs, and seconds later, Mac jumped when the front door slammed.

"Mac, is that what you think?" His mom asked him. "That we don't care?"

He couldn't answer. His body had completely shut down.

The front door clicked shut quietly for her exit, but hurt just as much. Gideon seemed a little shaken by the drama, but he held Mac's hands and kissed him.

"I'm sorry I didn't get to see your childhood bedroom all put together."

Mac nodded, his voice still paralyzed. He stayed quiet for the rest of the afternoon while they packed up odds and ends in his room and checked to see if anything in the boxes could be brought back to Browerton. He couldn't even appreciate that Gideon had just called him his boyfriend.

CHAPTER TWENTY-FOUR

Gideon

On the bus ride home the next day, Gideon's hands were all over Mac, in a loving way. Massaging his shoulder, rubbing his leg. He didn't care how they looked. He was emboldened with a need to help the man he cared about.

"I thought about you," Gideon said to Mac. The bus drove through an endless stretch of deserted highway in Pennsylvania. "Over the years, sometimes the thought of you would pop into my head. I would pass you on campus, and I would have these fleeting moments where I wondered about what would've happened if I let you keep kissing me freshman year."

Mac interlocked their fingers in a tight grip. "You don't have to wonder anymore."

They snuck a kiss while those around them were glued to their smartphones and tablets.

"I thought of you, too," Mac said. "I hated it. Whenever I made friends with a guy in my class, I heard your stupid voice in the back of my head, telling me I was out of my mind thinking we could actually be friends."

Gideon wanted to smack his freshman year self. Maybe Mac was out of his mind for giving Gideon a second chance. But he wouldn't screw this one up.

Mac rested his head against Gideon's shoulder and fell asleep for part of the journey. Gideon loved being his pillow. A man in the row across the way shot them a look that cut Gideon to the bone. He hated that this stranger made him feel that way, but he wasn't going to give him the satisfaction he wanted. He turned to the window. He knew on some level, the whispers would always be with them. The world was changing, but not fast enough.

"We'll figure out what to do with your stuff," Gideon said. "Don't worry about your parents. Don't give them another thought. They don't deserve your energy."

Mac gave him an uneasy smile. It was the same reaction Gideon noticed when he brought this up earlier. His face drained of color like it had in Aunt Rita's house. Gideon thought he would be more excited that someone was standing up for him to his parents.

Gideon kissed his ear. What Mac needed most right now was support, and Gideon was happy to be the supportive boyfriend. "It's going to be okay."

They reached the Welcome to Duncannon sign. Gideon felt his body clench up a touch. Back in the real world, where Gideon Saperstein didn't canoodle with his male ex-roommate.

Φ

Seth was a very methodical dribbler. He seemed to go into deep thought and used the rhythm of the bouncing ball to coordinate his attack.

"Sometime this century, man. Or else I'm going to steal." Gideon only pretended to play defense. He used these extra seconds to prepare himself for coming out to his friend.

"You can try to steal. Doesn't mean you're going to be—"

Gideon stole the ball and dribbled up to do an easy lay up. He bounced it back to Seth. "Eight-four."

Seth returned to his methodical dribbling. Gideon was dribbling in a way. He found himself stalling all night long. This was Seth. His best friend. He was cool with Mac, but maybe that was because Mac was Delia's friend, not his.

Gideon feared the whispers. The whispers could be non-verbal. They could be the different looks Seth would give him, or maybe Seth wouldn't want to change in the locker room with him anymore.

He blinked, and Seth dribbled around him and sunk a two-pointer."You're off your game," Seth said. "Eight-five."

"I just…I figured I had to let you score just a little to make it a fair fight."

Seth checked the ball to Gideon who immediately spun around him and headed for the basket.

"So where were you these past few days?" Seth asked. "Did you go home or something?"

The ball hit Gideon's shoe and almost rolled away, but he caught it. "I did. I had to see my mom."

"A week before we're out for winter vacation?"

"Yeah. It was nothing. I just had a funeral." That was kind of the truth. "My Great-Uncle Mort. He was ninety-two. So I went back to Westchester for the funeral and to sit shiva." Gideon couldn't stop. He had gotten used to lying so much throughout his life that it was second nature. Once he started a lie, he had to keep unraveling it. Watching his friend believe him made his heart ache.

"I'm sorry, man."

"It's fine. He was old." Gideon dribbled up to the basket. He didn't take the shot. He thought about all the shots he never took.

"I'm sure he was a great guy. I lost my grandpa almost a year ago. He was ninety-nine, but it still hurt."

"It's…" Gideon kept dribbling. "Yeah, the service was nice. People made speeches."

STOP

But Gideon couldn't. This was what he did. Lies on top of lies. Giving the people the stories they wanted.

Oh that Gideon. He traveled home on a moment's notice to be by his family's side when his great uncle Mort passed away. He's such a good son. He's not "going through anything." He's always doing swell.

"Are you going to take the shot?" Seth asked.

Gideon bounced the ball up and down. He chucked it against the wall. The slamming sound echoed in the gymnasium. The ball rolled down the court. Seth didn't touch it.

"Um, I think you airballed."

Gideon went to the wall. He leaned forward, like he going to hurl. How was lying so easy and so freaking hard at the same time? His stomach and head were sandbags being dragged across the ground.

Seth's shoes squeaked over to Gideon. "Let me get you some water."

"No," Gideon said.

"You miss him, don't you?"

He shook his head no. He took deep breaths. "There is no Great-Uncle Mort."

"I was talking about Mac."

Gideon flung himself straight up, like a rubber band snapping back into place. He and Seth exchanged a look that dug deeper than their friendship had ever gone.

"The last time we played basketball, and I told you about Mac and Rafe, well...you seemed jealous. Really jealous." Seth shrugged his shoulders, and Gideon saw the infinite wisdom of his friend. He had been watching the whole time.

"I...I really like him." Telling the truth helped him breathe better. Unlike lies, where he had to keep telling them, there was only one version of the truth. "I was in Pittsburgh. I went to Mac's aunt's funeral and told him how I felt."

Gideon bounced on his toes. More truth! "Delia told me about his aunt passing away. She's known about Mac and me for a while."

"So I was the only one who didn't know?"

"I'm sorry, man."

Seth didn't seem mad. More of a little brother feeling left out of the cool older brother stuff.

"You don't know how hard this is, not telling anyone." And Gideon braced himself for the biggest truth of them all. "I'm gay, Seth."

"I can't believe I was the only one who didn't know," Seth said with a smile. It was the perfect reaction.

"I didn't know how you'd react. Are you okay?"

Seth hugged him. It was the best bro hug Gideon had ever received.

"You're happy. I'm happy."

"Really?"

Seth looked at him as if he belonged in a mental institution. "Of course. You're my best friend."

Tears pooled in Gideon's eyes. He couldn't be crying on a basketball court. He tried to stop it, but they fell anyway. Telling the truth had possessed his body.

Seth picked up the basketball and checked it to his best friend.

"Eight-five."

Φ

Gideon was on such a high from his game with Seth. He felt indestructible. A new version of his true life was being formed. He couldn't wait until he got home. He had to call his brother the second he left the gym.

He sat on a bench in the freezing December cold.

"Hey," Noah said cautiously.

Gideon wasn't going to waste anymore time. "I'm sorry, Noah. I'm sorry I left your wedding."

Noah didn't say anything for a few moments, and Gideon's throat closed up with fear. "I wish you hadn't run."

"Me, too."

"You didn't get to watch Mom cringe when they served iceberg lettuce in the salad instead of romaine."

It felt good to laugh.

"Noah." This would never be easy, he realized. There would always be a lump in his throat before he told people one of the most personal parts of himself. "You were right."

"I always am."

"I was…I mean, I am…"

"I know, brother. I know. It's been a long road." Noah always put everything so well. "Have you told Mom yet?"

"No. Has she said anything to you?"

"No, she's just worried as usual."

"Because of what you told her," Gideon said. "When I spoke to Mom a few days ago, she said that you said I was 'going through some stuff.'"

That had caught him off-guard during his phone call in his hotel room, more off-guard than talking to his mom while a naked guy was in his bed. He figured that it was a screw you move from Noah for ditching his wedding.

"I had to tell her something. You bailed on my wedding! She likes to worry, and you gave her something to worry about."

Noah had a point. Gideon picked at peeling white paint on the bench. "I'll tell her."

He just hoped that his admission wasn't drowned out by the whispers.

"I know you will. I say just rip off that Band-Aid."

Noah lived his life by ripping off Band-Aids. Acting now and thinking later.

"Thanks for being an awesome big brother, Noah."

"I'm not that awesome. I should've been there for you more growing up. I was so into my own shit. I kind of imploded when Dad died. I hoped you would just follow my lead, but you went in the opposite direction."

Maybe there was a part of Noah in Gideon, a part that made Gideon kiss Mac for the first time, the part that made him book a bus ticket and hotel room five minutes after hearing about Mac's aunt. Noah might have been a troublemaker, a *vance* as their grandmother would call him in Yiddish, but he followed his heart.

"There's nobody else who I'd want as my brother," Gideon said.

"Just 'cause you're gay doesn't mean you need to get all mushy on me. I'm already bawling at the first ultrasound photo."

Gideon remembered he was going to be an uncle. "How does he or she look?"

"Like an it. Kind of like a potato."

"Did you tell Christina's parents yet?" Gideon got up and began his trek back to his apartment, where Mac would be waiting. His feet were nearly floating down the street.

"We just told them. We told them and showed them the ultrasound picture at the same time, to soften the blow. Her dad gave me this look that almost made me shit my pants, but now they're focused on the baby. So it all worked out."

"It all worked out," Gideon said. He hoped that saying held true when he spoke to his mom, whenever that would be.

CHAPTER TWENTY-FIVE

Mac

After spending the past few days sleeping at Gideon's apartment, they decided the logical thing would be for Mac to move back in with him. Mac spoke to his landlord, who said that if Mac could find somebody else to move in, he would let him break his lease. The landlord wasn't going to do any advertising. It was up to Mac.

Mac and Gideon put the word out to their friends. In the meantime, Gideon continued to cover his rent and Mac covered his, both barely, and they got to enjoy sleeping in the same bed together.

Among other things.

Mac came back to his studio apartment after class to pick up a change of clothes and start doing some cleaning, just in case he had to move out fast. Even though he'd only lived in this apartment for a few weeks, he had managed to leave his mark. Dishes overflowed in the sink, which was strange since he never cooked. TV dinners stuck out from under the trash lid. Clothes were spread out like lily pads on his floor. Dust bunnies tumbled along in the corners. Mac was tired of looking at this place and eager to be a full-time resident with Gideon.

One reason why Mac never was able to clean in the past is that whenever he started, he would fall down a rabbit hole of looking at old pictures and old papers and letting memories play in his head. He and Gideon brought back some of Aunt Rita's photo albums and scrapbooks, more stuff he could look through. He found a framed picture of him and Aunt Rita on Christmas with their matching Santa hats. A pang of sadness hit him square in the gut. He believed she would have loved Gideon.

There was one picture he had forgotten all about. He and his parents at Disney World outside Thunder Mountain. He was six and having the time of his life. It was one of the few pieces of evidence showing his dad capable of smiling.

Mac considered calling his parents. He hated how they left things in Pittsburgh. He appreciated Gideon defending him, but he didn't like seeing them attacked. And his mother asking him "Is that what you think?" threw him for a loop. Some dark corner of his heart refused to let him outright hate his parents, the same corner that wouldn't let him hate Gideon. Maybe it was a survival instinct to keep certain people in our lives.

He held his phone in his hand, pressing his fingertips onto the screen but not dialing. Someone knocked at his door, rescuing him from his awkward moment.

"It's open," he called out.

Rafe stood in the doorway. Mac had an epic "oh shit" moment.

"We were supposed to have a date tonight."

Mac searched his memory, then searched his phone.

"We texted when you were on the bus to Pittsburgh. I said I'd come over when you got back and bring you chicken noodle soup." Rafe held up a container of what could only be chicken noodle soup. The secret ingredient was guilt. "I guess you forgot."

"Why don't you come in?" Mac cleared off space on one of the dining chairs.

"Is this a date, or is this where you break up with me?"

"Break up? We weren't exclusive. We weren't even dating, technically." That didn't matter to Rafe, he saw. Rafe was someone who went all in right away. "Please, sit down."

Rafe came in, shut the door, and had a seat. He waited for an explanation.

"This has been a really weird time. My aunt just passed away, and things with my family are worse than ever." Mac stopped himself. He wasn't going to drag Aunt Rita into his mess. "Gideon and I reconnected. I'm sorry for not telling you sooner. I should have." Rafe was one of the good guys. He deserved better. "I'm really sorry."

Rafe slouched in his chair, like a kid in detention. "So Gideon's officially gay now?"

"He is. He's in the process of coming out."

"And you guys are like together-together?"

"We are."

Rafe gave an exaggerated nod, which Mac did not trust. Curiosity got the better of him.

"What?" Mac asked.

Rafe didn't hesitate. He leaned forward and had a dark look clouding his eyes. "You're just jumping from guy to guy. Once you broke up with Davis, you started messing around with Gideon. You and Gideon got in a fight, you started dating me. And now you're back with Gideon. I'm guessing this apartment is the first time you've been on your own."

Mac looked at him like he was crazy. The kid must've been heartbroken. "I'm twenty. Of course I've never lived on my own."

"Not lived on your own. Been on your own. Been able to stand up for yourself. When Gideon barged in here, I was the one who got him to leave." Rafe stood up and surveyed his surroundings. "You can't even keep a one-room apartment clean." He kicked a box on the floor. "You can't even unpack and get some basic furniture. It's like you just expect other people to do things for you and clean up your messes."

Mac stayed frozen at the table, heat burning between his eyes. "You didn't seem to mind any of this when we were dating."

"I thought we weren't dating. Maybe I dodged a bullet then." Rafe picked up a dirty T-shirt off the floor. "You were wearing this at the Christmas party."

Mac ripped it out of his hands. "You don't know what it's like, Rafe. You grew up in cushy Arlington where everyone was so happy you were gay. You didn't have fists slammed into your face. You weren't practically disowned by your own parents. You don't have to put on your game face whenever you see your mom and dad, just wondering what they're going to say that will make you feel like complete shit!"

Mac kicked his nightstand crate over. Memories splayed across the floor. He hoped the Disney World picture shattered. "I'm not perfect, Rafe, but I'm doing the best I can."

Rafe looked toward the door. He was the scared freshman, far too young and sheltered for the shitstorm that was Mac's life.

Mac stared him down until he got the hint to leave. He left the chicken noodle soup behind. Mac sunk to the floor. Someone reached inside of him and yanked out all his dirty secrets.

He instinctively began to text Gideon, but he stopped himself. Rafe's words reverberated in his ears. His apartment had been downgraded from mess to outright disaster. Mac put down the phone. He went to the narrow closet next to the front door and rummaged for the cleaning supplies Delia had forced him to buy. They were still in the shopping bag, in their original packaging. He pulled out the dustpan and brush set. He got on his knees and chased every single dust bunny in his apartment into submission. He shoved his overflowing garbage into a trash bag and tied it up. He lined his trash can with a fresh garbage bag and filled it up with dustpan after dustpan of trash. Next he filled up his sink with hot water and soap and soaked his dishes, then set them out on the drying rack, which Delia also forced him to buy. He made hard choices with his boxes of memories on what to throw out and what to keep. He got on his hands and knees and scrubbed his hardwood floors with a washcloth soaked in warm water.

Three hours had passed. He had laundry in the washer and the soup heating on the stove. He sat at the dining table, making a list of what he needed to buy for the apartment. Mac had this feeling swell within his chest, which he couldn't describe, but it was like a compass telling him he was going in the right direction. Maybe Gideon was onto something about being a neat freak.

He texted Gideon to come over later for dinner and a movie. He was cooking. Well, he would go to the supermarket and pick up one of those pre-made meals that just had to be heated up. But still, he was in charge of dinner.

CHAPTER TWENTY-SIX

Gideon

Gideon took the stairs to Mac's apartment three at a time, basically jumping up each flight, ready for whatever dinner Mac had concocted, and ready to see his man. He enveloped Mac in a deep kiss, complete with tongue.

They sat on Mac's bed. Gideon couldn't help but notice how clean the place was. Had Mac done this all himself?

"The place looks great, by the way."

Mac pulled lasagna out of the oven. The box peeked out from the trash, but Gideon would let him have all the glory.

"Smells great!"

They ate at his dining table. The whole time, Mac seemed distracted, like how he was on the bus. After all the drama that happened with Gideon and him hooking up and then his parents, Gideon had to remind myself that Mac lost his closest family member. He was still fragile.

Gideon rubbed his hand over the table. "I really admire you, Mac. You've handled all of this so well."

Mac gave him a half-smile, mostly for show.

"What's wrong?"

"I hate how I left things with my parents." Mac hung his head, and Gideon could feel waves of stress coming off him.

"I can't imagine what you're going through. But don't forget what they did. They believed you were hitting on that kid. They pretty much sold you out."

"Maybe they were just as scared as me," Mac wondered aloud.

Gideon hated how Mac's parents had this control over him. Despite everything, Mac was still trying to be the good son.

"If they want to make things right, they should make that first move."

After dinner, Mac and Gideon sat on his floor and went through more of Aunt Rita's photo albums. Mac showed Gideon all of his embarrassing school pictures. Gideon didn't tell him that he found every picture of Mac freaking adorable, bad haircuts and all. Even as a third grader, that ear-to-ear grin held so much kindness.

"Holy shit." Mac reached into a folder in the back cover of one photo album. He pulled out a handful of old letters.

"Oh? Did Aunt Rita have a secret lover?" Gideon scooted closer. Mac's smile faded, and he showed Gideon the envelope.

"These are from my dad." Mac's eyes widened. He studied the letter in his hand, but couldn't bring himself to open it.

Gideon was just as curious as him. "How old is that letter?"

"I don't know."

"Are you going to read it?"

"Should I? It might be personal."

Gideon nodded, but he could see the curiosity lighting up his boyfriend's face. "I mean, there's only one way to find out if it's personal…"

"I'll just read one letter."

"Great compromise!"

Mac took the letter out of the envelope and unfolded it in his hands. Gideon could only know what was in it by Mac's face. But Mac wasn't giving away much. His face turned to stone. His eyes traveled down the page at least three times. He picked his head up and had a dazed expression.

"What did it say?" Gideon asked.

Mac handed it over, stood up, and did a zombie walk to the kitchen area.

Dear Rita,

Enclosed is the monthly check for Mac's expenses. It's a little bigger than usual so Mac can buy some back to school clothes. I can't believe he's going to be a senior. I still can't get over some of the colleges he's thinking of attending. I can't believe I might have a son who attends Carnegie Mellon, The University of Pennsylvania, or

Browerton. Not bad for a guy who barely got through community college. I'm so proud of him, Rita. I know he wants nothing to do with us, but I hope he knows that. Thank you for sending pictures. He's really getting tall. Maybe we can all spend Thanksgiving together this year. I guess that'll require one of us to swallow our pride. We think about him everyday. Thank you again for taking him in. We miss him, but we know he's safe in Pittsburgh.

Love,
Sean

"Holy shit," Gideon said under his breath. He grabbed the stack of letters. They were probably all of the same variety.

Mac poured himself a glass of water. "Why didn't they tell me?"

"Maybe they didn't want you to come back." *Because it wasn't safe.* Gideon's stomach sank with a nasty feeling for all the things he said to Mac's parents. "You hadn't seen them since Aunt Rita got sick?"

"No. I remember that Thanksgiving. She suggested my parents come up, but I refused. I was so angry at them."

"You missed out on an awkward family holiday."

Mac wasn't smiling, though. He looked worse than when Gideon started talking. "I need to call them."

He took out his phone. His thumb hovered over the screen. Gideon got up and wrapped Mac in a tight hug, practically swaddled him.

"They didn't believe me," Mac said. "They took the pastor's word over mine. They thought I hit on Justin and that I caused this. Even if they let me stay in Pittsburgh to avoid the bigoted assholes back home, they still thought that I brought on what happened to me. They didn't stand up for me."

Mac collapsed against Gideon's chest. Gideon rubbed his back. "Baby, you need to relax."

"I don't know what to think. This whole time…"

"Breathe. Just breathe." Gideon rocked them back and forth for a few minutes. He kissed Mac's head.

Mac looked up at him with those eyes that plugged right into Gideon's soul. Their lips met in an instant. They kissed each other with a hungry need.

All of this emotion had given Gideon a wicked hard-on. He pushed Mac backward on the bed. Their lips refused to budge from each other. Gideon ran his hands through Mac's hair, then swooped them down to his tight stomach and muscular legs. Mac quivered under his touch.

He wanted to remember every second of this. Gideon unbuttoned Mac's jeans, then his own. He pulled out their cocks and massaged them together, rolling them around in his fist. He spat in his hand and slicked them up real good. Mac moaned into his chest. Gideon pressed his weight into him.

He panted and gulped down air as he continued to stroke them. Mac's fingers rubbed Gideon's back, softening his tensed muscles. Their dicks fucked Gideon's hand, and he was going to shoot at any moment. But not yet. He wanted more. His anger and fear had turned into lust, and he wanted to consume Mac, the way Mac had done to him in their hotel room.

"I wanna…have sex." Gideon breathed deeply. He inhaled Mac's soapy, musky scent, and it made his cock harder.

Gideon got off the bed and shoved his pants and boxers to the floor. His cock flopped in the air. He kicked his shoes to the far reaches of the studio and stepped out of his pants. He tossed off his dark green sweater and chucked that into the kitchen area.

"Don't go making a mess," Mac said with his sinister smile. Gideon didn't realize how much he missed it. "I just cleaned."

"Oh, we're making a fucking mess tonight, baby." He yanked Mac's pants and underwear completely off. They landed by the front door. He motioned with two fingers for Mac to sit up. He slowly lifted his shirt over his head. His fingers grazed the ridges of his abs and firm pecs. He breathed in the scent of Mac's shirt, then threw it onto the dining table, where it landed on the leftover lasagna.

"Should I get Big Bird?"

Gideon glanced down at his raging boner. "I don't think we need it."

Mac took lube and a condom from his nightstand drawer. He placed it on his stomach. Gideon positioned Mac on the edge of the bed and shoved his legs back to his head. He gave his ass a nice little spit shine. But not too much. This wasn't a night for foreplay. It was one for action. Some cosmic force was pulling Gideon to Mac.

He got Mac and himself prepped for entry. He leaned over his boyfriend and whispered in his ear "I'm falling in love with you."

He knew it was fast, that they'd only known each other a few months, but the words weren't going to stay inside him. Gideon worried that maybe it was too much for Mac—

"Me, too."

Or maybe it was just right.

He entered Mac's warm opening, and instantly his knees quaked. Mac arched his back. His thick cock lay against his stomach.

Gideon leaned over his boyfriend and smoothed his sweaty hair back. He kissed him along his jaw line and that sweet spot where his neck met his shoulder. Sweat trickled down Gideon's chest into the creases of Mac's stomach.

He didn't want to stop touching Mac. His hips, his ass, his legs, his feet, his elbows. It was all manna from heaven to him. He pushed Mac's legs closer to his stomach as Gideon slid deeper inside him.

Mac reached around and slapped Gideon's ass. Gideon admired his flexibility. They looked into each other's eyes, and Gideon saw enough hope and love to help them weather this storm.

It's going to be okay, Gideon told Mac telepathically.

"You're gonna make me come," Mac said. Not the response he thought, but a great one nonetheless.

"That's the point." Gideon sped up, banging his cock into Mac's ass in short bursts. Mac spread his legs, allowing Gideon to thrust deeper.

Mac grabbed onto a patch of Gideon's wild hair. He grunted with orgasm and covered his chest and stomach with streaks of himself. Gideon lost all balance and the room went white as he shot hot spurts into his boyfriend.

He cleaned the both of them up with Mac's T-shirt, then tossed it back on the ground. Gideon promised Mac he would do laundry in the morning. They lay on the bed together, basking in the afterglow. They fell asleep soon after. Gideon was an extra strong big spoon, holding Mac tight. He didn't want to let him go.

$$\Phi$$

Gideon woke up a few hours later. Mac wasn't in bed. He was standing at the window, gazing out into the darkness.

"Can't sleep?"

Mac turned around. His face told Gideon sleep was the furthest thing from his mind. "I'm going back to West Virginia."

"When?"

"Tomorrow."

Gideon sat up, fully awake. Streaks of light spliced through the blinds.

"I'm going to West Virginia to talk with my parents. I need to fix this."

"How long are you going to be gone?"

"I don't know. Winter break is starting, so everyone's going home this week."

"So I won't see you until January?"

"I don't know." The moonlight silhouetted Mac's strong frame.

"I can go with you, for moral support, and just in case you need to find solace in another hotel room." Gideon smirked, but Mac didn't react. He was already in West Virginia.

He rejoined Gideon on the bed. "I am so grateful for what you've done, but I need to fight this battle myself."

"I want to help you."

"I know you do." Mac brushed down a clump of Gideon's bedhead. It didn't make any difference, but it made Mac smile. "I have to stop letting people fight for me. I am so lucky that I've had people in my life who care about me this much to stand up for me. It's my turn to stand up for myself."

Gideon noticed how scared Mac was, but he was pushing through. That was the very definition of courage.

"I don't know if it's going to work, but I need to try and make things right myself," Mac said.

Gideon wrapped his arms tight around Mac and kissed him.

"You do what you gotta do, but don't get too comfortable back on the farm," Gideon said.

"We don't have a farm."

"You know what I mean." Gideon tapped at Mac's chin. "I don't want to lose you."

"You won't."

Sometime around four, Gideon managed to fall back asleep. When he woke up the next morning, Mac was gone.

CHAPTER TWENTY-SEVEN

Mac

Mac stepped off the bus, groggy from his nap. Rain splashed against the pavement of the bus station parking lot. It looked like it wasn't going to be a White Christmas in Kingwood, West Virginia. A fog enveloped the trees and mountains, as it usually did. "It's God's whipped cream," Mac's dad once said to him when he was little. It felt like eons ago.

He had little memories like that pop into his head on the ride down. Instead of preparing for battle, Mac chose to remember the good times with his parents. He thought back on holidays and early mornings cleaning the store with his dad or reading a bedtime story with his mom. It was easy for Gideon to hate his parents. He only saw one side of them. He only saw the after, not the before.

The town of Kingwood wasn't large, and even though it was spotty with sidewalks, it was still manageable to get around on foot. His family's store was about a mile and a half from the bus station. One hundred years ago, this town was just an intersection with a gas station and general store. Now there were strip malls and big box stores, but that small town spirit remained.

Mac remembered it well.

He strolled down the main strip. Lights were strung around the lampposts. Rain be damned, it was Christmastime!

He let the memories wash over him. He had lots of great times in this town, until he got gay bashed. Then the small town charm gave him the cold shoulder. If the pastor hadn't wielded so much power in town, then maybe he would've had a shot at fairness. A slim chance, but a chance. Mac spent years trying to move forward. Instead, he had just repressed.

The store looked the same, for the most part. His dad had installed one of those spirally energy-efficient light bulbs above the front door. And they replaced the old Santa-themed holiday welcome mat with a more generic Christmas tree design.

"You can do this," he said to himself. He grabbed the door, but before turning, something caught his eye. His dad had tried to paint over it, but the traces of graffiti streaked the outside of the store, just above the grass. Mac could only make out hints of an F, then an A. He didn't need to know the rest.

The door to the store swung open, giving Mac a shock.

"Mac?" His mother held her hand to her heart.

"I took an early morning bus."

Neither knew what to say next.

"Can I come in?"

His mom nodded and stepped aside. She looked Mac up and down, as if she hadn't had a chance to really see her son in a while.

The interior of the store hadn't changed. He always thought this store felt especially homey. It was like a second home to him, from the signs behind the register, to the long scratch on one of the tiles in the paint supplies aisle.

"Where's Dad?"

"He's just finishing up in the stockroom."

"Is he still lugging around heavy boxes?"

She straightened out an end cap display. "He still lifts with his legs."

His dad came back into the store, rolling a dolly of boxes filled with inventory. Even though his dad was still tall and strong, Mac saw age start to get the better of him. The crows feet, the hair that's more salt than pepper, the slower gait. He knew his dad would try and tough it out until they carried him out of the store.

He spotted Mac and left the boxes in the middle of the aisle.

"I took an early morning bus," Mac said, answering the obvious question.

Nobody knew what to say next. Mac pulled his dad's letter out of his pocket. "I found this."

He registered a modicum of surprise on his dad's stoic face. His dad didn't give up much more.

"I didn't know," Mac said.

"And we didn't want you to know," his dad said. "You would've made Aunt Rita rip up all those checks, and you would've taken on two afterschool jobs or even dropped out of school to make up the difference. Anything than accepting charity. You're stubborn."

"Takes one to know one."

His dad cracked a sliver of a smile.

"Why didn't you want me to come back here? I ran away to Pittsburgh because I was hurt, because you didn't believe me. I would've come back, but you didn't want me."

"We were protecting you, Mac. Some people in this town would not have welcomed you back," his mom said.

Mac thought of the graffiti on the side of the building.

"Things didn't go back to normal once you left," his dad said. "We didn't want to risk you returning and getting in trouble again."

"You also didn't want to ruin your relationship with the pastor."

His parents traded a look that admitted some truth in that statement.

"You know that I didn't hit on Justin Weeks."

"It was a very…." His dad searched for the right words. He probably wasn't used to having a talk like this. "It was a very turbulent time, okay? One day, everything was fine, the next you're…"

"Gay?"

"Yes. And getting in a scuffle with the pastor's son. You kept insisting that we do something, but I didn't know what to do. I just thought it was a fight. I got in my share of fights growing up."

"You let yourself believe that."

"I didn't know what was going on. I'd never met a gay person, and then you tell us this story. The pastor told us what happened, that you hit on Justin, and we believed him…because we were scared." His dad hung his head, ashamed by the admission. "Our lives are in that church. Our friends, our neighbors."

"And they were more important than me."

"The comments and looks and names didn't stop once you left. It felt like there was a police spotlight on us whenever we went anywhere. Word got out about what happened. I didn't want to expose you to that anymore than you'd already been."

Another battle for Mac. Another person who had to fight it.

His dad sat on a step ladder. He was tired on every level. "Your parents aren't perfect. It was a turbulent time and we tried to make the best decisions we could. Should I make you come back home and face Justin Weeks and this town for another two years, or do I make you stay in Pittsburgh where you can live your life, even if you hated us for it? Here." His dad opened a box of wrenches, and without thinking, Mac stocked them on hooks. He didn't have to remember where they went. That information was programmed into his head.

"You blamed me, Dad. Justin looked at my computer. He and his friends followed me when I left school, and they cornered me and beat me up. I didn't do anything wrong. I didn't go down the street like a one-man gay pride parade." Mac had tried denying what was on his computer when Justin and his crew asked him, but they saw through his stammering lies. "Why didn't you stick up for me at all?"

"It was complicated, Mac," his mom said, trying to soften the blow. Her face was all pain. "We were scared."

"I was scared, too. School was hell for that month before I ran away." Mac stared at them with wide eyes, with such intensity that he felt his voice echo in his throat. "I was born gay. It's in my blood. Nothing anyone could do could ever change that. I can't stop this. I can't change it. It's who I am." Tears streamed down his cheeks. He let them fall. He wanted his parents to see this. "Those guys, they found out, and they attacked me for being something I can't control. And everyone turned their backs to me. But I thought that I still had you. That's what hurt the most, knowing that you didn't have my back."

They didn't say anything for a few seconds. Mac hung the wrenches. He didn't know how long the silence would stretch

"I'm sorry," his dad said, a quiet and humble admission. "There are so many things I'd redo if I could, but time only moves in one direction."

"We love you, Mac," his mom said.

His dad wrapped him in a tight hug, and Mac didn't realize how much he'd missed this.

"I love you, too." *Damn, it felt good to say that and mean that.*

"Here for the holidays?" His mom asked, a hopeful note in her voice. Mac hadn't spent Christmas with his parents in four years, which was a depressing thought. "I'll make a pecan pie."

"I'd like that."

"Is your, uh, friend with you?" His dad asked.

"No. And he was just trying to defend me. He didn't know the whole story. I didn't either."

"I like him! He's got spunk!" His mom said and helped Mac unload the box of merchandise. They all laughed at her outburst, and wounds in Mac began to truly heal.

CHAPTER
TWENTY-EIGHT

Gideon

Gideon picked up his clothes off Mac's floor, got dressed, and shuffled back to his apartment. He was in dire need of coffee, but instead, he got an even bigger jolt.

His mom. On his front steps.

One of the barbers from downstairs was waiting with her, peering through the front window. He was totally old school, with the white smock and everything.

Gideon darted across the street and joined the fray. "Mom, what are you doing here?"

"Gideon!"

"Is this your son?" The barber asked her in his thick Italian accent.

"Yes. Thank you," she said.

"We do not own the apartments upstairs," the barber said. He still had a comb in his hands and was pointing it at his mom. "This is our shop. We do not own the apartments."

"I'll take it from here." Gideon clapped the barber on the shoulder. He sneered, ready to be done with this screaming lady and her son. Good thing Gideon never got his hair cut there.

Gideon opened his door. They trekked up the steep staircase. "What are you doing here, Mom?"

"I feel like I've barely heard from you these past few weeks. We don't talk as frequently, and when you do, you just…you just haven't seemed like yourself, Gideon." Pain crossed her face. This was already an Orange Alert situation for her. "And I know that today is the last day of finals, so I wanted to surprise you and pick you up. We could get breakfast at that kitschy pancake house I like and catch up on the drive home."

Gideon unlocked his apartment door. He tried to mentally calculate if any of Mac's stuff was laying around. *Did I leave out the Astroglide?*

He spun around, his back pressed against the door. "Mom, can you give me a second just to clean up?"

"You want me to wait out here? Gideon, I used to clean your room and wash your dirty underwear. And it was really dirty."

"Just one second. Please?"

She gave him one of her trademark passive-aggressive sighs. "Okay."

He pecked her on the cheek. As soon as he stepped inside, he was a tornado of catastrophe avoidance. He zipped around the apartment, swiping up any of Mac's clothes and any sign of sex. That meant shoving condom wrappers deep into his trashcan and covering them with old papers. The whole thing lasted thirty seconds, but it probably was an eternity to his mom.

Gideon opened the door. "Welcome!"

She gave him a suspicious look. "I'm surprised your apartment would be messy. You've always been so good about cleaning."

"I know. I had a friend stay with me a few days. They were fixing the roof in his apartment. There were leaks, so it was easier for him to move out for a few days and crash on my couch." *Spin spin spin.* Gideon hated every word that came out of his mouth. Lying wasn't second nature. It was an addiction.

His mom took a seat on the chaise section of the couch, Mac's preferred spot. Gideon thought about Mac, who was sitting on a bus to West Virginia at this moment. When he woke up and realized Mac was gone, Gideon had texted him *Good luck.*

"Do you want anything to drink?"

"I'll have some coffee."

"Me, too!" Gideon scrambled into the kitchen and turned on the coffeemaker. He was out of the line of fire, but it was short-lived. His mom joined him.

"Is your friend still staying with you? I don't see any of his stuff."

"He went home last night. I was just cleaning up some stuff he left behind. I'll give it to him when I see him again." He shut down during these moments, and some lying instinct took control of his body. Each lie made him feel dirtier. His mom drove all this way to get caught in more of Gideon's lies.

"You seem nervous, Gideon."

"I'm not nervous."

"Are you all done with finals?"

"I have my last one this afternoon, then we can take off." He got to tell the truth! What a glorious feeling!

Coffee dripped into the pot. "Any word on Noah and Christina? Noah and I talked, and I apologized for getting sick and leaving his wedding."

"That's good. They aren't taking a honeymoon, for obvious reasons. Gideon."

His mom stared at him. He pulled his attention away from the pot.

"Why weren't you in your apartment when I arrived? Did you not sleep here?"

He could handle this. He was always two lies ahead. "I pulled a really late night at the library, and so I crashed at Seth's dorm, since he lives right by there."

It worked. "I didn't realize you still had a final left today. I can occupy myself until you're done. There are some cute stores along this street." She poured herself and Gideon a cup of coffee. "How is Seth? You told me he has a girlfriend, right?"

She walked back into the living room and reclaimed her spot on the couch. She laid back and enjoyed the chaise. "I may need to take a nap here. But I won't bother you. I'll let you study in peace."

Gideon stood at the doorway of the kitchen and watched her sink into the cushions. She was relaxed and happy. She would get to spend quality time with her son and by the time they reached Westchester, her worrying about Gideon would be long gone. *Because I am the Good Son.*

He had gotten so good at telling the right story that it was practically automatic. Second nature.

He could do this forever.

Forever.

"Mom." His voice trembled, and she sat straight up. Her mother radar was back on high alert.

"What is it, Gideon?"

He held onto the doorway for support. The words were there. In his mind. On his tongue. He just had to push them out.

"Gideon?"

"I'm gay." And with those two words, the catalogue of lies and stories he had built and carefully curated went up in flames. Goodbye, Good Son.

"Are you sure?" She wasn't moving from that couch. It was her fortress. "You've had all those girlfriends."

"I'm sure, Mom."

She had never been this reticent. For now, he was assuming it was a good sign. If she wasn't talking, then she was processing.

"This is all so sudden."

"Is it, though?" She'd raised him. There had to have been signs like Noah saw.

"I mean, when you were younger maybe, but you seemed to grow out of it. And you were dating girls. Maybe you can still date women and just do your business on the side." She tried to smile, and it was the equivalent to an out of tune violin.

"Doing my business? Like urinating?" He sat on the far side of the couch. "I'm not going to do that, Mom. And not just for me—I don't want to subject a girl to that life." He thought of Hannah and Beth and all the other women who were unknowingly, or knowingly, marrying gay men because it was the responsible thing to do.

"I know," she said quietly.

"I know this is hard for you, and it's unexpected, but I'm happy."

"It wasn't completely unexpected." She dabbed at tears in her eyes. Gideon swiped her a napkin. "The way you'd been acting this fall. It was an idea that crossed my mind, but then you were dating Hannah."

"I was doing that because I wanted to make you happy. No." Gideon wasn't going to do that. He had himself to blame for his actions, for his lies. They came from *his* mouth. "Because I wanted to do what I thought was right. I was too scared to be me."

He hated seeing her cry, and knowing he was the cause. He imagined Mac beside him, holding his hand. *We will get through this.*

"You know, all I wanted was for my two sons to marry two nice Jewish women and carry on the name and traditions of our family."

"That can still happen," Gideon said. "I want to have a family someday."

Her eyes clouded over. She picked up her coffee, but put it back down. "When I said this wasn't completely unexpected…"

"What?"

"When you were little, your father and I had a conversation. He'd found you under your bed reading the Fruit of the Loom catalogue, specifically the men's underwear section."

Gideon's cheeks burned with embarrassment. *Why does everyone remember these memories except for me?*

"He had a feeling you were gay," she said. "I thought…I don't know. I thought you were just bored with your own books, but he seemed pretty sure."

Gideon had always wondered what his dad thought of him. Of course, his dad loved him, but he'd never get to see the person Gideon became, personality and all. But if he could, he probably would've hated all this lying and deception. *I wasn't making you proud.*

"What did he say?" Gideon asked her.

"He said 'Well, if my son is gay, then my son is gay. It won't make me love him any less.'"

Gideon wiped his tears on his sleeve. His mom used her napkin.

"I'm so sorry, Gideon, for making you feel like you had to lie all this time. That couldn't have been easy. Although I must say, you're a very good liar. It's a little scary."

No more. Those days were over. "It's going to be okay. I know this isn't how you wanted things to go, but that's life. And it could be worse."

She grabbed his hands. Her fingers were boney, but forceful. "I love you. You will always make me proud."

She kissed him on the cheek. They hugged, and it was the first hug where there were no walls between them.

"You know, Frieda Feldberg's son is gay, and he's in medical school."

Gideon closed his eyes, ready to crush her spirits again. "Actually, I have a boyfriend, and he's not Jewish. But we're still a million miles away from kids or marriage or even dating, and he doesn't seem like a practicing Christian, so I think we would probably raise the children Jewish, assuming we adopted."

"I look forward to meeting him," she said, with some levity in her voice like she finally found the sense of humor in all of this.

"I love you, Mom. I just want to be a good son to you."

Her eyes bore deep within him with all their motherly power. "You are a *great* son."

Gideon was still dealing with aftershocks from the conversation, but he never felt so hopeful. Gone were the walls. He was free.

He sat back and sipped his coffee. Being the Great Son had its perks.

CHAPTER TWENTY-NINE

Mac

Mac spent the next week reconnecting with his parents. His mom cooked him eggs for breakfast, and his dad happily added shifts at the store to Mac's schedule, even though he never said he would work there. He didn't have to. It was an unspoken agreement. If your last name was Daly, you worked at the store. They couldn't make up for lost time, but they were moving forward. Days were spent at the store, and evenings were reserved for long family dinners. They sat around the table well after they were done eating, catching up. His parents asked him question after question about college life. They wanted to know about every class and activity. Well, not all activities. Geology class would not come up in conversation. Mac made sure of it. They even asked a question or two about Gideon.

"He's from New York, right?" His dad asked after a meal of chicken pot pie. Real chicken pot pie. No frozen dinners allowed in the Daly household.

"Yeah. Westchester."

"I had a feeling. He was kind of abrasive."

"That's just his natural charm."

Even though they were only a few days from Christmas, business wasn't picking up. While a hardware store wasn't exactly a destination for holiday gifts, Mac clearly remembered the holiday rush when he was younger.

"There's a new Home Depot along the highway," his mom explained while they were closing down the register one night. "It opened last year. We've definitely been affected."

"Is it bad?"

She wobbled her head back and forth, but put on a brave face. "Your dad is working harder than ever. We've had to cut staff. I feel like we're fighting a losing battle. Usually, your father wouldn't give up until there were no other options, but he's starting to come around. Maybe it's time for a change."

Mac appreciated his mom opening up. "Pittsburgh is a great town."

"I want to go somewhere warm. I loved that trip when we went to Disney World." She had a wistful twinkle in her eye, and Mac wondered if there was any part of her life that wasn't built on sacrifice. "You just wanted to ride every single ride over and over. You wore us out. I'd put you to sleep and then lay out by the pool and read magazines with the stars shining above."

"It was a fun trip. From what I remember." Mac thought back to the Thunder Mountain picture.

Mac ended his shift early since it was pretty dead. When he got home, he did the dishes and swept the kitchen floor. He grinned at his handiwork. His parents' jaws would drop. If only Gideon could see him.

Mac's phone rang with a familiar name that made his heart swell. "Hey, you."

"How's the Mountain State?" Gideon asked. "I looked that up."

"Good job."

They spoke every day. Gideon loved hearing about Mac's progress with his family and may have asked more questions than Mac's parents. Mac was like a witness who could not leave the stand.

"Well, I have some good news for you. My mom says hi, and she can't wait to meet you."

Mac sat up straight and pressed the phone to his ear. "Did I hear that correctly?"

Gideon laughed, and it was music to Mac's ears. "I can't wait to see you, Big Mac. I miss you, and I'm still falling in love with you."

Mac could feel his smile through the phone. "Same here."

Despite working a tiring shift at the hardware store, Mac had energy to burn. His parents wouldn't be home for another two hours. He decided to go for a jog. Today was a winter reprieve. No precipitation and fall-like weather. All Mac needed was a hoodie.

Sidewalks were sporadic in his town. Kingwood wasn't a place for walking. Mac jogged along the road. The waning rays of sun illuminated the majestic mountains around him. He inhaled crisp air into his lungs.

Mac checked his phone and found a text from Rafe. *I'm sorry how things went down. I was shocked and hurt. Maybe we can meet up for coffee in January? As friends…*

Mac smiled at the screen. *I'd like that. What you said stuck with me. I'm in West Virginia now, standing up for myself. And it worked.*

Sweet. Have a Merry Christmas.

Talk soon.

Mac put away his phone.

The sun zipped behind the mountains as if it were playing hide-and-seek. Lampposts became less frequent, and darkness took over the roads. He stayed on the side of the road and shielded his eyes from the powerful car lights.

He jogged with a smile on his face. He never thought a week like this would ever happen again. He'd had that same thought about geology class, though that was where comparisons ended.

A pickup truck's lights nearly blinded Mac, but they didn't pass. They pulled over to the side of the road.

A familiar face smiled through the windshield. Justin Weeks. Mac's stomach pulled into a tight knot.

Justin was on the shorter side. He looked scrawny, but he was all muscle. Mac spun around and walked toward home, toward the lampposts.

"Mac Daly," he said.

Mac's heart leapt around like crazy in his chest. He slowly faced Justin.

"Holy shit. It's Mac Daly. I was driving, and I says to myself, I says that can't be Mac, can it?"

His laugh made Mac taste the blood in his mouth all over again.

"I haven't seen you in years." He slammed his car door. The sound echoed in Mac's chest. "What are you doing back?"

"Seeing family." Mac could barely hear himself. He wanted to run. Adrenaline surged through his veins, telling him to get the hell out of there.

"Your parents seemed like nice people. It's a shame they got a faggot for a son." Beer coated Justin's breath. Some life he led. "I thought we got rid of you."

"You and your dad are liars."

"We're doing God's work, Mac. You can't just go around living this homo lifestyle. Not here."

Mac got a good look at his face, a face he'd remember forever. He punched Justin, connecting a right hook with his nose. "God's work, Justin."

Justin stumbled back. Mac savored his victory for a second, then he bolted as fast as he could. His body was possessed by a strength more powerful than adrenaline: fear. He didn't look behind him. He didn't waste one precious second.

He couldn't focus on hewing to the side of the road, not when all that mattered was getting home. He couldn't see in front of him, only the lights in the distance. His pulse pounded in his ears. All he could hear was himself gasping for breath.

Don't look behind you. Don't look behind you.

But he did. The sound of the engine was too close to ignore.

The truck's lights overpowered him. The heat of the car kicked up against his legs. Mac's chest heaved with breaths that couldn't come fast enough. He heard Justin's laugh.

"Aaah!" Mac screamed out as something smacked into his back. *Was that a baseball bat?* He stumbled away from the car, and in the darkness didn't see the railing. He lost all sense of gravity and what was up and what was down as he fell.

He tumbled over rocks and into the forest. His body smacked against thick tree trunks and pointy bramble. He wailed in pain to the night sky and blinking stars and the quiet trees. None of them cared to listen.

The last thing he thought of before he blacked out was the comfort of Gideon's bed.

CHAPTER
THIRTY

Gideon

Winter vacation was spent catching up with Noah, updating friends on his sexual preference, and vegging on the couch watching TV. All of his friends showered him with supportive statements and bro hugs. If he'd known coming out was going to be this easy, he would have done it sooner. He was lucky, and he knew it. He knew it could be so much worse, like getting-the-crap-kicked-out-of-you worse. The only awkward moments came from his mom, though he supposed that was to be expected.

She knocked on Gideon's door whenever she wanted to talk with him, even when his door was wide open. She would tap gently, and her eyes would squint, as if she might catch her son watching gay porn.

"I'm fine, Mom," Gideon assured her. He saved that for after she went to bed, naturally.

He never brought up anything about Mac or being gay around her. They would go about their business and talk about celebrity gossip or random people from temple, and then all of a sudden, his mom would burst out with a sentence like "How did you meet Mac?" or "Does this have anything to do with your father passing away when you were young? Should I have tried to remarry?"

Out of nowhere. It was never a dull moment with Judy Saperstein.

"This has nothing to do with Dad," Gideon said. They were eating matzo ball soup at the kitchen table. His mom had prepared a vat of it in preparation for Gideon's return. "Noah married a woman."

"But he was older when your father passed away. You were so young. Nobody should have to lose their parent at that age."

"It's nobody's fault. I've met guys who are amazing athletes who are gay. I've met frat guys who are gay."

"I know. You're right." She rubbed his free hand. "I'm still getting used to this."

Gideon didn't mind the deluge of awkward, random questions. It felt nice to tell the truth for a change. He cut his mom's matzo ball in half and scooped it into his bowl. She never ate her soup. She only liked serving it.

"So Mac is from West Virginia, but grew up in Pittsburgh?"

"Yes. His parents own a hardware store."

She let out an ahh and a large head nod. A hardware store owner in Westchester was as common as a stockbroker in Kingwood, West Virginia. Mac's parents might as well have spoken a different language.

Gideon checked his phone again. No sign of Mac.

"Is he having a good time with them? Does it snow in West Virginia?" His mom asked.

"I don't know. I think so." Gideon had texted him two days ago but hadn't heard back yet. They'd been texting and talking on the phone every night. It was a routine. Mac knew all about patterns, and he was breaking this one.

"Is something wrong?"

"No." Gideon slurped his soup. "Actually, yes." No more lies. He had to remind himself that he didn't have to hold things in anymore.

He put down his spoon and told her that he hadn't heard from Mac. "That's not normal. How long does it take to shoot off a text?"

"It's only been two days, Gideon. Have some patience. You kids, today. Needing to text each other all the time."

"What if you hadn't heard from me in a week?"

"That's different. I'm your mother. It's my job to worry. Maybe he's busy getting ready for Christmas." She said Christmas funny, like she was asked to name a sex act. "Are you going to celebrate Christmas now?"

"No! I still prefer Jewish Christmas." It was a favorite pastime of Gideon's. Movies and Chinese food on Christmas day, just as baby Jesus intended.

"He's fine." She wiped a stray matzo ball crumb off his chin with her thumb. A mother's work was never done. Her soothing tone helped make Gideon feel better, but he couldn't escape the nagging feeling that something wasn't right.

For Jewish Christmas, Seth and Delia joined him and his mom. They met up at the theater, and Delia and she hit it off. They both found somebody who loved to chitchat as much as they did.

Movies on Christmas Day was no longer just for Jews, apparently. People crammed in the lobby and concession stand lines stretched over five people deep. His mom reserved the seats with their coats, while the three of them tackled refreshments. They each started in a different line to see who would get there first. When it became obvious that Seth had the golden touch, he and Delia joined him.

"Gay guys are so adorable." Delia blatantly observed a gay couple in her old line, two guys in their twenties who held hands. Gideon had a strange mix of emotions battling inside him. He wanted to raise a fist in solidarity while telling them to not be so obvious. This gay stuff was hard work.

"You shouldn't stare," Gideon told her.

"I'm not staring. I'm fantasizing."

"If they were two girls and you were a fifty-year-old man, you'd be called a pervert."

"It's a double-standard I'm willing to back."

"I just realized there is nothing here for me to eat." Seth gawked at the menu in bewilderment.

"What about popcorn?" Delia asked. "Gluten-free."

"But they might make it in peanut oil."

"Those bastards."

Gideon was only half-listening. A few high schoolers in front of them were staring at the gay couple and snickering to themselves. Not in a Delia-fantasy way. His blood pressure rose, and his appetite for concessions vanished.

"I'll just get some SweeTARTS."

"We'll ask about the popcorn." Delia squeezed her boyfriend's hand. Nobody made a stink about *that*.

The snickering in front of them grew louder, or maybe they were the only wavelength Gideon was tuned into. He also caught football-coach-looking guy in his former line eyeing their hand-holding with a disapproving scowl.

"Have you heard from Mac?" Gideon asked, desperate to be lost in conversation. "I haven't heard a peep in three days now. I emailed him last night, and haven't gotten a response."

"No," Delia said. "But it is Christmas."

"And I'm his boyfriend. Shouldn't he be wishing me a happy Jewish Christmas? He hasn't tried reaching out to you?"

"I could also get Sour Patch Kids, although all that sugar makes the roof of my mouth sore."

"Not now, Seth." Gideon was already on edge from the stares and whispers. He upgraded Mac's ghosting to a disappearance. "Can you try calling him?"

"Now?"

"Yes." There was no wiggle room on this.

Delia took out her phone and dialed away. Gideon made her put it on speakerphone so he could listen.

So he could listen to it go to voicemail.

"Hey Mac! We wanted to wish you a Merry Christmas!" Delia said. "Hope you're enjoying your ham. We'll be eating popcorn and lo mein. Love you!"

"Something's wrong," Gideon said. "Mac's never taken three days to respond to anyone, and he was returning to a town full of people who hated him."

"Okay, now I'm scared," Delia said.

Mac could be buried in a ditch or fed to the cows or something crazy like that.

"I have an idea." Gideon took out his phone and did a frantic Google search for Mac's family's store. When it came up, Gideon remembered that it was Christmas day and would probably be closed. Still, he called and got the store voicemail.

"Due to emergency circumstances, we will be closed through the end of the year. We look forward to seeing you in the New Year," Mac's dad said in a drone.

"Shit." Gideon hung up the phone. Worry flashed in Delia's eyes. "This is not good. Do you have his parents' number?"

She shook her head no. Did any kid have their friends' parents' number? Gideon searched online for a home number. There had to be some phone number on some page on some corner of the web. The Internet wouldn't let him down.

And the whispering laughs struck again. Gideon glanced up from his phone. The annoying high schoolers were taking pictures of the two men, giggling like the circus had come to town. The gay couple put their hands back in their pockets, which killed Gideon most of all.

"What the hell is your problem?" He said to the teens. "Put your fucking phone away."

"What?" One of them said. They had those shit-eating grins on their faces, total nervous laughter that only inflamed Gideon more.

"It's a gay couple. It's legal. Welcome to the twenty-first century. Don't film them," Gideon growled. He ripped the phone out of the kid's hand. "Delete it or I'm breaking your phone."

The kid gulped back all his stupid laughter. His fingers shook as he removed the video.

"And apologize."

They did. Looking down at the ground the whole time, but they did. They stepped up and ordered their stupid snacks.

"As you were," Gideon said to the couple.

They gave him a nod, and he nodded back. It wasn't a fist, but it was close.

Φ

Gideon continued searching for the Daly home number in the theater as his mom and friends looked on.

"Dammit." Either Mac's parents were well trained in keeping a very low online profile, or they were so old school that they just didn't show up anywhere. He leaned over to Delia. "Any response from him?"

"None."

"His parents might have his phone," Seth said.

"It's scary to think that nowadays, if someone takes your phone, you are completely cut off. This is why I wanted you to get a landline in your apartment," his mom said. He was glad to see her worrying about Mac.

"Can you call Verizon and see if they've shut off his service?" Delia asked.

"His number would've been disconnected. All the messages went through." Gideon sunk his phone into the cup holder. He began picturing a world without Mac. It was a whole new layer of sadness.

"I'm sure he's fine," Delia said.

"But how would we know?" Gideon didn't know anyone back in West Virginia, only his parents.

"Have you tried Information?" His mom asked.

"What's that?"

She stared at the three of them dumbfounded. "Don't make me feel old. You can dial four-one-one and ask to be connected to Daly in Kingwood."

"That's a thing?" Seth munched on a SweeTART.

"Yes! It's not as high-tech as Google, but it should work."

The lights dimmed. Gideon cursed under his breath.

"I'm going in the hall."

Outside their auditorium, there was calm, a brief moment between show times when the ushers hustled to sweep up the stray popcorn and empty the trash. Gideon dialed 411 and asked for Daly in Kingwood. He held his breath until the operator put him through.

The line was ringing. Success!

He paced back and forth. He wiped his sweaty palms on his jeans.

"Hello?" A quiet voice answered. It had to be his mom. Right away, something seemed off. You could just tell when somebody was having a good day or bad day.

"Is this the Daly residence?"

"Yes."

"Is this the home of a Mac Daly or Cormac Daly, and his parents?"

"It is." It sounded painful for her to say that. "Who is this?"

"Please don't hang up. It's Gideon, Mac's boyfriend. I know I'm not your favorite person, but please don't hang up. I haven't heard from him, and I want to see if he's okay."

Gideon didn't hear anything. Seconds went by like decades.

"Please," he said again.

His mother didn't say anything back. She started sobbing.

Gideon covered his mouth and sunk to the floor.

CHAPTER
THIRTY-ONE

Mac

When Mac woke up, he felt pain. His back ached and legs throbbed and head pounded. His body was an orchestra of torture, and the overture wouldn't stop.

He looked around at the unfamiliar room. The blank walls and the smell of disinfectant slammed his senses.

Mac wailed out in agony.

A nurse ran into the room moments later. She tapped some things on the machine and greeted Mac with a wide smile.

"It's okay, it's okay. Just give me one second."

The pain was blinding, literally. Mac's vision turned white. He wanted to chop off his whole body and leave just his head. He looked down at the tubes and wires covering him. Red and purple bruising blotched his skin.

Just as the pain reached a fever pitch, it began to subside.

"That should be better," the nurse said, unfazed by his squirming and yelling. She had probably seen worse.

"What happened?"

Before the nurse could answer, someone grabbed his hand. He looked up at his mom, and his dad right behind her.

"Oh, my baby." She tried to lean down to hug him, but the wires and bed made that an obstacle. He still took in her warmth. His dad kissed him on the top of the head. Mac had to be on drugs because that did not just happen.

"You were in a terrible accident," she said.

The night came back to Mac in flashes of recognition. The headlights. Being chased. Something slamming into his back. Bits and pieces of a puzzle that wasn't complete, but was put together enough to make out what it looked like.

"It was Justin Weeks," Mac said. Saying that name was a deeper kind of pain.

"We know," his dad said. "He's been arrested."

"He has?" Mac tried to sit up, but it caused a sharp hit of agony. "How long have I been out?"

"Three days," his dad said matter-of-factly.

"I'm going to need a little more."

"I'll take it from here." A policeman stepped forward. He seemed to be in his thirties, with a sturdy build and a thick mustache that Mac couldn't stop staring at. "I'm Officer Calhoun."

"Hi." Mac winced from a general pain that he would deal with later. "What happened?"

"It seems that the Weeks boy hit you with a baseball bat when driving, and you stumbled off the road over the railing. You tumbled a ways down into the woods."

Mac caught flashes of trees and bare branches hitting him. He thought he dreamt that.

"How did anyone find me?"

"Well, a woman was driving on the road a few minutes after you were attacked. She found you and called nine-one-one. You were hit right by a private driveway, and the owners had installed security cameras, so we were able to get the whole thing on tape. Justin's currently out on bail, but we're watching him closely." Officer Calhoun had a tiny smile that only Mac seemed to catch. "I have to say, you are extremely lucky, Mac. That road doesn't get much traffic. If that woman hadn't stopped, who knows when we would've found you. And if Justin had attacked you just a quarter of a mile in either direction, we wouldn't have caught any of it on the camera."

His mom trembled behind the cop as that reality sunk in. His father held her tight. He looked at his son with warmth Mac hadn't realized he missed.

"How did she know to stop?" Mac asked.

"This four-leaf clover keychain was reflecting terribly off her headlights in the middle of the road. She had to stop to see what it was. When she got out, she heard you wailing." Officer Calhoun picked up the keychain from the bedside table. "This yours?"

Mac nodded. Words escaped him.

Officer Calhoun examined the four-leaf clover. "I guess these things really are good luck."

Thank you, Aunt Rita.

"That Justin Weeks needs to go to jail," his mom said to the cop, full of Norma Rae-type passion that was new for her.

"We're going to try to make that happen. We have a good case."

Mac wasn't buying it. "Bad things don't happen to the Weeks family, especially if all he did was beat up some gay guy. He'll probably get a fucking parade for that."

His parents didn't try to point out his cursing. They seemed to hate that Mac was right as much as he did.

Officer Calhoun gave Mac a heavy look. "Mac, I know what happened to you years ago. I know the stories going around about you weren't true. I couldn't sleep for weeks. I'd lived my life in the closet, but after your attack, I couldn't stay quiet. No matter how scared I was, I knew by staying quiet, people like them won.

"I came out to my squad six months later. They took it well. Not everyone, but most. I've been working with our unit to include LGBT sensitivity training. I've gotten guys who used to hurl Bible quotes at me to at least recognize that gay people shouldn't have to live in fear around here of being attacked. I won't let what happened to you happen to some other kid."

Mac was speechless. This guy couldn't be real. This couldn't be Kingwood. Mac had spent four years thinking the worst of this town, but maybe there were some decent people here.

"Thank you," he said quietly to Officer Calhoun. The cop nodded at him in understanding that transcended words.

"Anyway, I'll let you rest up and spend time with your family."

"Thank you, officer." Mac's dad shook his hand, and the officer walked out, leaving three Dalys.

His mom scanned his body. Mac didn't want to look.

"You're really here," he squeaked out.

"Of course we're here! It doesn't matter who you love. You don't deserve to get attacked!" She burst into a sob against his dad's shoulder.

"We love you." His dad kissed his head again. Mac yanked him down into an awkward embrace. It felt so good to hug his father again.

A few minutes later, a tall, black doctor with a shaved head waltzed into the room. Right away, Mac could tell he was a straight shooter who was too busy and tired to feed Mac lies.

"Mac, I'm Dr. Wright."

"Sounds like I'm in good hands already."

The doctor managed a polite smile. "Mac, you sustained a number of injuries. Fortunately, we've stitched up your cuts and gashes, and did surgery to repair the compound fractures in your legs."

Panic took over Mac, overrode all of the drugs flowing through his system. "I broke my legs? Will I be able to walk? People break legs all the time and still walk, right? That's why they say 'break a leg' in theater, because it's not that serious."

"Your legs should heal, and you're lucky there was no infection. However, you did suffer a spinal fracture when you fell. That will not heal on its own. I'm recommending you have a vertebroplasty procedure. We inject this special bone cement, and it will form an internal cast around the weakened vertebrae."

"You're going to operate on his spine?" Mac's mom asked.

"Yes, though it's not as involved as you're thinking. It's a minimally invasive procedure. Without the surgery, there's a strong chance you will have chronic lifelong pain and might need to use a walker to get around."

Mac pictured himself in a walker at twenty-years-old. "A few days ago, I was cleaning my apartment. I was thinking about finals. That's what I should be thinking about. What piece of furniture I can buy for my apartment, not if I'll be able to walk again without pain the rest of my life."

His mother squeezed his hand. He was scared shitless, but he wasn't alone.

"That's why we are recommending the vertebroplasty. Now that you're up and alert, we would want to get you into surgery as soon as possible," Dr. Wright said. "The orthopedic surgeon can come in tomorrow morning for it."

Mac nodded. His body felt like a junk heap, his tower of junk in Gideon's sun porch. He looked at his parents, and they gave tight nods of solidarity. "I'll do it. Tomorrow morning."

Dr. Wright put the clipboard with the consent forms on the bedside table and left.

Mac's dad sat in one of the uncomfortable hospital chairs, and his mom rubbed her back. He wondered if they slept in the room with them.

"How are we going to afford all of this?" Mac asked.

The dark cloud of money cast its shadow over the room.

"Now's not the time to think about that," his mom said. "We'll figure it out. What's most important is getting you healed."

Mac looked down at his bruised and battered body. The enormity overtook him, and he started crying.

"Now, son." There was his dad's firm voice, just as he remembered. "You're bent, but you're not broken. You're going to be okay."

This moment was almost perfect, except for the bodily injury. It was just missing one important person. "Can one of you hand me my phone?"

His parents traded looks. At some point, they stopped needing to talk each other. They were on some other wavelength.

"Your phone was destroyed. It was crushed by that idiot's truck."

"He ran me over. You can call him a fucking piece of shit."

His dad smirked at that.

"I want to talk to Gideon."

"I spoke to him yesterday," his mom said. "I gave him the whole scoop. I don't have his number with me. Do you remember it offhand?"

Mac shook his head no. He didn't know anyone's phone number. It was a scary thought. Damn cell phones.

"We'll call him tonight and let him know you're awake," his dad said. Mac couldn't imagine his dad and Gideon having a conversation. The thought made him smile a little.

"What day is it?"

"December 26th," his mom said.

"I missed Christmas?"

"Santa didn't forget about you." His mom pulled wrapped gifts off the window sill. "He left these for you under our tree."

"Santa is so thoughtful," Mac said with an arched eyebrow. He had trouble keeping his eyes open. Sleep was pulling him down. "I'll open these later. But I didn't get you guys anything."

His dad patted his arm and looked at him the way every son wanted to be looked at. "We got a great gift."

Φ

Mac was woken up first thing in the morning for surgery, before daybreak. Pieces of wrapping paper lay on his blanket from last night. His parents brought him presents. They ate McDonald's, while Mac fasted to prepare for surgery. It was a holiday to remember.

The nurse prepped Mac for the operation.

"I'm scared."

"Mac, think about all you've survived," his dad said. "You're more of a fighter than anyone I know."

He shook his head in dissent. "I ran. I ran away from you, from Kingwood. I didn't fight anything."

"You didn't let what happened stop you from living your life. You got yourself into a great school, you're doing things with your life. And you came back. You didn't give up on us. If you hadn't come back to Kingwood, we might never have spoken again." His dad's lip trembled again as he fought back emotions. "And I have to live with that. You are more of a fighter than me."

"Where'd you think I learned it? From watching you run the store day in and day out. I say this as someone on lots of drugs, but maybe it's time to close up the shop for good. Florida is lovely in the winter."

His dad kissed him on the forehead. His mom came in the room carrying a humongous floral arrangement. It couldn't fit on the table. She showed him the card.

Get well soon! Thinking of you up North! Love, Delia and Seth.

Mac rubbed his fingers over the card, wishing they were here. "Anything from Gideon?"

"No. But he's pulling for you." Something in her voice made him think there was more to that, but he couldn't tell. Drugs and all.

Mac held his parents' hands as the nurses rolled him into the hallway.

"Wait!" A distant voice called out. "Wait!" It got closer.

"Sir, you have to stay back. We are getting ready to wheel the patient into surgery."

"Please. Just one minute. You can time me."

Mac couldn't see what was going on. He was on his back. The ceiling provided no clues. But then there was Gideon's face and his crazy hair over him.

"Hey, you," Gideon said.

"Sir…"

"One minute. Please."

"Please," Mac said to the nurse. She stepped aside to let them have a private moment.

"Baby." Gideon ran his finger along Mac's cheek.

"You called me baby in front of other people."

"I love you, Mac. Maybe it's the extreme situation, or maybe I just fall faster than the average guy. I love you. And I don't care who knows it. Hey," he said to the nurse. "I'm gay, and Mac is my boyfriend."

"That's wonderful. Now can we please continue rolling your boyfriend into surgery?"

"Certainly," Gideon said. "I'll admit my timing isn't perfect."

"Yes it is," Mac whispered.

Gideon leaned down. Mac inhaled his familiar scent. "How'd you get down here?"

"I drove my mom's car overnight."

Mac ran a finger through Gideon's hair. He wanted to savor this moment.

"This surgery is going to go great. You're going to heal. And then we can spend the rest of our lives together."

The rest of our lives? Even Gideon noticed the slip. "That was jumping the gun. Dramatic moments call for dramatic declarations."

"Like I love you," Mac said.

"Did that count as you saying you loved me?"

"You have me on a technicality."

"I know." Gideon winked. Mac couldn't get enough.

"Are we ready?" The nurse asked. Mac caught her smiling.

"Yes! Hit it! Tally ho! I would say break a leg, but you have no more legs to break."

"You're a New York asshole," Mac said.

"I'm *your* New York asshole."

The nurse wheeled the gurney down the hall. Gideon jogged alongside it like a secret service agent in a motorcade.

Mac grabbed his finger tight.

"It's going to be fine, Mac. It really is. You have good doctors here."

"Gideon..."

"I'm here."

"Stop the gurney!" Mac yelled. The gurney screeched to a halt inches from the double doors to the OR.

"Last time. I promise," he told the nurse.

He nodded for Gideon to lean in close.

"I can't kiss you because of germs," Mac said.

"Understood."

"But as soon I get out of here, I'm kissing the fuck out of you."

"I'm holding you to that," Gideon said. His gaze nearly set Mac on fire.

"I'm in love with my best friend," Mac whispered.

"Me, too. Isn't it great?"

CHAPTER THIRTY-TWO

Mac

Mac's face crunched with agony as he put one foot in front of the other. His triceps flexed to steady himself. Gideon stood at the end of the bars, arms out, ready to catch his boyfriend.

"Come on. You got this."

Mac gritted his teeth together in pain. His arms wobbled in support.

"Three more steps. You can give me three more steps, baby."

"No. I. Can't."

"There is no 'I' in teamwork," Gideon said.

Sweat drained down Mac's temples and sideburns. Red on a rampage could best describe the color of his face. Mac lifted his leg to take another step and yowled in pain.

Gideon looked behind him for the physical therapist, but he stopped himself. They didn't need no stinking physical therapist. *I believe in you*, he told Mac with his eyes.

Mac's foot touched the floor. He gasped for breath like he just played a quarter of basketball.

"That was beautiful. First class step. Okay, two more. You can do two more."

Mac mumbled out something indecipherable. Gideon assumed it was "fuck," his curse of choice.

He lifted his left leg. Mac sucked in a deep breath of air. His leg hung above the floor.

"One and a half more steps to go."

"I. Can. Count. You. Cocksucker."

"That's right. I am a cocksucker. And I will suck your—" Gideon remembered there were other patients and therapists in this facility. Mac's therapist shot him a quiet look. "Let's keep going, baby."

Mac's left foot made contact with the ground. He was closer. Gideon smelled the musky sweat drenching his shirt, and he felt guilty for being turned on.

The right leg defied torturous pain and gravity and came off the ground. Mac and Gideon locked eyes, and the passion and love scorched between them.

"And the right leg is down! That's three steps!"

Mac collapsed into Gideon's embrace. He wiped Mac's sweaty hair and brow with a towel. Despite his agony, Mac's eyes shined with victory.

"Good job," Gideon said, his arms tight around his boyfriend.

"I couldn't have done it without you." Mac kissed him deeply, breathily. Gideon grabbed his sopping hair and flicked his tongue around his mouth. Not too much. They were still in public, and Mac was still catching his breath.

Gideon pulled out Mac's wheelchair and got it ready for him. The therapist came over and patted Mac on the back. "Great progress today! First week of physical therapy, and you are already walking."

"I wouldn't call that walking," Mac said.

"We do." The therapist chortled. "This is a process. Remember, you only came out of surgery two weeks ago. Since it was successful, there shouldn't be any setbacks to your recovery schedule."

"Twelve weeks?" Mac asked again. "I can't believe I'm going to be walking like my normal self in three months. I can barely take three steps."

"You won't be 100 percent, but pretty close. Just keep practicing and doing your exercises."

"You're fortunate you have to recuperate now," Gideon said. He pointed to the window where a gray sky and chunks of brown snow littered the sidewalk. "You don't have to go outside. You'll be better for spring."

"You can do it," the therapist said. "It may seem impossible now, but it will happen."

"That's basically the story of us," Gideon said.

Φ

One week later, Mac was able to take seven steps. Gideon tried to push him to take an even ten. Mac grunted out where Gideon could shove his even ten steps.

Back at the Daly residence, Gideon heated up soup in Mac's family kitchen. His mom came over to see if he needed any help.

"I got it, Mrs. D."

She stared into the saucepan like a curious child.

"You just have a seat with Mac and Mr. D. Don't ruin the surprise." Gideon swirled the matzo ball soup and watched it heat up.

Mac couldn't go back to school for winter quarter. His focused remained on his physical therapy and letting his body heal. He moved back in with his parents, who were not-so-secretly happy to have their son back, despite the circumstances. Mac's mom reminded Gideon of his own. She loved taking care of her son. Though Mrs. Daly could learn a thing or two about Jewish mother guilt from Judy Saperstein.

"Are you guys pumped? You excited?" Gideon called from the kitchen. He poked his head out of the swinging door. Mac and his parents sat around the dining table.

The soup boiled on the stove. Gideon breathed in the salty, dill-tinged aroma. He couldn't wait to send his mom pics of everyone enjoying her soup. Gideon had no idea soup could be shipped in the mail, but Mac's recovery was in definite need of matzo ball soup. It was part of the healing process.

Gideon scooted into the dining room. "How many balls do you want?"

Mac's father cleared his throat, and his mom's eyes bulged. Mac blushed with stifled laughter.

"Matzo balls," he clarified.

"Let's stick with two," Mac said.

"Old school. Good decision. One is not enough, and three's a crowd." Back in the kitchen he went.

He looked out the window at the snow coming down over the mountains. It seemed peaceful here, a far cry from the hustle and bustle of campus, or even Westchester. Gideon was going to miss Mac terribly when he went back to school on Monday. He had arranged his schedule to have no class on Fridays, and he planned to spend as many three-day weekends in West Virginia with Mac as possible. He wanted to take this semester off, but Mac wouldn't allow it. He wasn't going to let Gideon fall behind. He wasn't alone in Virginia anymore. Gideon was leaving him in good hands.

"You ready, Daly clan?" Gideon ladled soup into bowls and placed them on a tray Mac's mother had put out for him. He swung through the kitchen door butt-first and set the tray on the dining table. He passed around bowls. They poked at the matzo balls with their spoons, as if it were an alien life form. Around here, maybe everything Jewish was. Mac did find a temple on Google Maps the other day. It was only twenty-five minutes away.

"Are you ready?" Gideon asked the family. "Because once you taste matzo ball soup for the first time, there is no going back. Your life will literally never be the same."

"You're setting impossibly high expectations. I hope you know that," Mac said.

"I'm preparing you for a life-changing event."

"We're talking about soup here," Mac's father said. Gideon shook his head. The poor man. He had no idea how his world was about to be rocked.

Mac carved off a slice of matzo ball with his spoon, added soup, and ingested his first taste of savory goodness. "Shit," he said as if he just came.

Matzo ball soup was even better than sex.
Well, almost better.

They were in two separate universes and couldn't justly be compared, but they were both of superior quality.

Even frozen and shipped across state lines, the matzo ball soup was as good as Gideon remembered. His mom had told him that Christina wanted to learn how to make it.

"This is wonderful," Mac's mother said. Mac's father was already down to just one ball.

Gideon didn't have words. Each word he spoke would be another second his taste buds couldn't indulge.

"How did she learn how to make this? Is there a recipe online?" His mother asked.

"Nope. Passed down."

"I wonder how she gets the matzo balls so big and almost fluffy."

"Why peek behind the curtain?"

"These matzo balls are very good." His dad pronounced it *mahzzuh*. He sliced himself half of his wife's ball.

Mac squeezed Gideon's knee under the table. The bruising on Mac's face was fading away, but it didn't matter. He was as handsome as ever. Those brown eyes still radiated warmth. Gideon told him that his scars would make him look dangerous and extra sexy. He rubbed Mac's hand, over the table, in plain sight. Neither parent flinched.

"Is there enough for seconds?" his dad asked.

Φ

Later that night, Gideon helped Mac with his physical therapy at home stretches. It involved pulling his legs and arms with a thick rubber band to increase flexibility.

Gideon didn't want him to fall behind in his therapy. He was going to be worried and overbearing, just like his mother.

"So I was thinking," Mac said. He stretched his arm out and then in. "I wonder if you're right."

"About what?" Gideon sipped on a Sprite.

"Was I out of my mind for thinking we could be friends?"

"I think we've proven that wasn't true."

Mac squinted his eyes. "I'm not so sure. I mean, we're dating now. Romance and attraction got in the way."

"But maybe we weren't a proper example. I'm gay, after all. So there was never a straight guy in the equation, technically. What about Seth? We're both friends with him."

"But nobody wants to have sex with Seth except for Delia." Mac put the rubber band around his ankles and stretched his left leg, then right, to the side.

"I was a freshman. You should never take anything a freshman says seriously. Nobody knows what they're saying until they turn twenty."

"Oh, Gideon. You are a fountain of bullshit wisdom."

"I think I'll take that as a compliment."

Mac sat down on the bed. Gideon acted as spotter. He had a water bottle handy for his winded boyfriend. Mac gave him a look like he was off in a daze. He shook his head.

"What is it?" Gideon asked.

"I just got such a strange flashback when we were sitting on my bed that night we first met. It was just like this. You by the pillow, me over here."

Gideon could see it, too. Time had both passed and stayed still. "That was a good night. Well, up until…"

They both turned red.

Gideon took out his phone. "So I was looking up matzo balls on Pinterest right before you kissed me, right?"

"Correct."

He turned his phone around. A picture of a matzo ball was on the screen. It wasn't that different from the original all those years ago, except this matzo ball was smaller and plopping in soup rather than being raised out by a spoon. Gideon remembered those details.

"And then what happened next?" Gideon asked.

"I kissed you."

Gideon motioned for Mac to repeat history. Mac leaned forward and pressed his lips to Gideon's in a soft kiss that sparked with magic.

This time, Gideon didn't pull away. And he wasn't going to ever again.

SIX MONTHS LATER

CHAPTER THIRTY-THREE

Gideon

Gideon knocked on the bedroom door holding up a spoon. "I found this in the sink."

Textbooks and notebooks created a moat around Mac on the bed. "It's just one spoon."

"This is summer, Mac. We don't want to get ants. One spoon is all it takes for the cast of *A Bug's Life* to make an appearance."

"Can you put it in the dishwasher for me? I'm still recovering." Mac gave him his best *I'm sick* face and rubbed his leg in pain for added effect. Gideon rolled his eyes.

"Your legs didn't seem to hurt you last night when they were over your head." Gideon arched an eyebrow, and Mac blushed.

"You may have a point." Mac got off the bed and snatched the spoon out of Gideon's hand. "Is it possible that you've become even more of a cleaning Nazi since I came back to school?"

"Are you seriously using a Nazi reference for me?" Gideon slapped Mac's ass as he walked into the kitchen.

Bright rays of sunlight burst through every window of the apartment. Their window air conditioning unit was trying its best, but they were in the midst of a cruel summer. Mac wound up having to miss winter and spring quarter at Browerton since his recovery took a little longer than expected. He had made great progress with his physical therapy, thanks to Gideon's constant motivation. When he wasn't there on weekends, he was having daily Skype calls to get Mac through his exercises, even if it required some removal of clothes for added motivation. Dr. Wright said that since Mac was doing so well, if he took off spring quarter to keep concentrating on recovery, he would be able to return to Browerton in nearly perfect condition. He would be able to live in an apartment with stairs and attend his classes without help. They both decided it was the right thing to do. "We made it through one quarter. We can make it through another," Mac had said during one of their Skype calls.

"We can make it through anything."

There was Gideon, always with a reply that stole Mac's breath.

The patience paid off, as Mac moved back into Gideon's apartment with no problem and took summer courses to catch up for fall quarter. Except for some scarring on his face and legs, it was almost like nothing happened. Physically, of course. Mac would never forget, though.

"So I forgot to put the spoon in the dishwasher. It's not the crime of the century." Mac washed it in the sink with soap. He held up the shiny, clean utensil to Gideon. "See? All clean."

"Just remember the ants." Gideon grabbed it from Mac, brushing his fingers in the process, which sent a tingly feeling down to his core, and then further south.

"I thought you would go easy on me. I'm recovering. I have a heavy load of courses."

"I'm taking some summer classes, too, don't forget."

Mac wouldn't forget his sacrifice. Gideon had to drop two classes in the winter because he was tending to Mac as best he could.

"And I'm not asking for much. This was just one spoon." Gideon's eyes zeroed in on Mac's, like he could turn him to dust. Lust hung in the air thicker than the humidity.

Their lips were all over each other, right there in the hot, stifling kitchen. Gideon's shirt was blotted with his sweat, and the scent made Mac's cock stand at attention.

"I want to show you how well I've healed." Mac got on his knees and undid Gideon's pants.

"Your physical therapy…" Gideon gasped as his dick disappeared inside Mac's mouth. "I forgot what I was going to say. Oh, baby!" He dug his hands into Mac's hair. Mac went to town. Gideon's moans were fuel to his engine.

"You can't just do this every time you want to get out of cleaning…oh, shit!"

Gideon came, and Mac took it all. Mac wiped the corners of his mouth and stood back up. "See, I know how to clean up a mess. Now, I really have to get back to studying."

Φ

Later that night, Seth and Delia came over for dinner. They both had internships in nearby Harrisburg and were staying in Duncannon for the summer. Gideon and Mac ordered gluten-free pizza, while they brought over nut-free ice cream and gluten-free and regular beer.

"How's your family's store doing?" Delia asked. She enjoyed getting to ask these questions. Mac had spent years not talking about his family. She had told him it was a whole new side of him, one she was happy to hear about.

"This is going to be the last year, and then my dad's going to shut it down." Both Mac and his mom spent the past few months convincing his dad to come around to this decision. But eventually, his dad recognized that he couldn't do this forever and that he wanted to enjoy some type of retirement.

"This is so upsetting." Delia dug into her ice cream. "All of these family-owned stores all over the country are being wiped out by these mega corporations that are wiping out local economies and decimating employee wages."

"It's not all bad. My parents are thinking about getting jobs at Disney World in one of their gift shops. They still get to have a store, but they don't have to worry about it going under."

"Thank goodness for Disney, I guess," Delia said.

"And beer," Gideon said. "Let's not forget about beer." He and Delia clinked bottles.

"And ice cream," Seth said. He shoveled it in his mouth. "This is really good."

"I won't miss Kingwood, West Virginia. Florida is much nicer," Mac said.

"When do you go back to testify?" Delia asked.

Justin's trial was coming up. The prosecutor said they had a very strong case, and jury selection had weeded out any congregants from the church. Justin would probably play up the preacher's son angle. Gideon told him not to worry.

"Justin will get some kind of conviction, but no matter what, he'll be stuck in his pathetic life and small town forever. Mac still gets to have a real future." Gideon squeezed his shoulder.

"Our great legal system at work," Mac said. He wasn't scared about seeing Justin in court. Nothing worried him much anymore. He had Gideon, his friends, and his family. He was unstoppable. Strength in numbers.

"So Gideon, I have to ask." Delia took a swig of her beer. "Do you ever miss being with women?"

"Delia…" Seth groaned.

"I'm curious! You dated and hooked up with women for years."

Gideon scratched his chin as he deliberated. "Do you miss eating bread and peanut butter? You haven't had any since moving in with Seth last month."

"Yeah, sometimes I do."

Mac put down his ice cream and listened closely to his answer.

"Have you ever done something because you thought you liked it, but you realized you only did it because it seemed like the right thing to do?" Gideon asked. "Like getting drunk on your twenty-first birthday. I wonder how many people actually want to get trashed, and how many do it just because they think that's what they're supposed to do on their twenty-first birthday."

"Huh," Delia said. "Heterosexual intercourse. The ultimate peer pressure."

Next to her, Seth clutched his stomach and leaned over. "Hey Seth, you okay?" Mac asked.

"I don't feel so well." He lay down on the chaise.

Delia hopped up. "No, no, no. I double-checked the pizza, the beer, and the ice cream. No gluten, no nuts. You are fine."

"I don't think so," he said through controlled breaths.

"I love you, man, but you are not throwing up on my couch." Gideon went to get him a glass of water.

"What is it?" Delia held her boyfriend's hand. Their love was quirky and unexplainable, but something to behold. Mac wondered if that were true with all relationships.

"I think…" Seth knew how to amp up the drama. "I think I might be lactose intolerant."

Gideon burst out laughing. Delia fell back onto the couch.

"Nooo!!! Sweetie, you can't do this to me! I can't live a life of only eating dark chocolate and celery."

"I'm sorry." Seth drank some water. "I love you."

"Yeah, yeah. Pretty soon, the only thing you'll be able to eat is me."

Φ

Three weeks later, Gideon and Mac drove up to Westchester so he could hang out with his new nephew. Mac watched Gideon rock the baby back and forth. He was a natural. And naturally, Gideon's mom asked them if they were planning to have kids. She had no segues when it came to these types of questions about their relationship. She just spat them out.

He and Gideon were miles and miles away from kids, even marriage, although the thought had crossed Mac's mind. He smiled to himself whenever he thought of little Mac back in West Virginia, deep in the closet and hating life. One day, he would find love and actually have a shot of marriage.

"He's adorable," Mac said to Noah. "He has your eyes."

"He's going to be a ladykiller. Or a dudekiller. Is there a gay version of ladykiller?"

"Manwhore." Gideon said.

Noah tickled the baby's neck. Nothing was cuter than a baby smiling. "Doing good, uncle brother."

Gideon continued rocking the baby, like he never wanted to let go. His mom watched the scene from the corner as she gave Christina diaper changing tips.

"Is he sleeping?" Mac asked.

"For the most part. We've been lucky, because we've heard that some babies just cry all night. This guy has been a cool dude. We have a secret weapon, though." Noah motioned for Mac and Gideon to come over to the crib.

"The Big Bird mobile."

Mac's face was a cloud of red. Big Birds spun around in the mobile above the crib.

"Big Bird is awesome. I don't know where we'd be without him. What's so funny?" Noah asked his brother.

Gideon was crying from holding in his laughter. He had to give Mac his nephew so he could cover his face and wipe away his tears.

"What's so funny?" His mom asked.

"Nothing. It's a great mobile." Gideon laughed and cried into his hands. His whole head was a tomato. Mac joined in the giggles, too, until his stomach hurt. The baby smiled at them.

Everyone in the room gawked at them as if they were high. Mac and Gideon shared a look. They were oddballs, but oddballs together.

"You loved Big Bird as a little boy, Gideon," his mom said.

"And he loves him just as much as an adult."

THE END

Want to be the first to get details on the next Browerton University book? Become an Outsider. Outsiders always get the first scoop on my new titles, new covers, sneak peeks, members-only contests, and other cool goodies via my newsletter. Get in with the Out crowd today at www.ajtruman.com/outsiders.

Consider leaving an honest review at your favorite bookseller's website and on Goodreads. Reviews are crucial in helping other readers find new books.

Say "Hi" at www.ajtruman.com or on Facebook. And check out my Pinterest boards for each book, including inspirations for upcoming releases. I'm ajtrumanwriter on both FB and Pinterest.

And then there's always plain old email. I love hearing from readers! Send me a note anytime at ajtruman.writer@gmail.com. I always respond.

Thanks for reading!

A.J. Truman remembers his college days like it was yesterday, even though it was definitely not yesterday. He writes books with humor, heart, and hot guys. What else does a story need? He loves spending time with his cats and his partner and writing on his sun porch. You can find him on Facebook or email him at ajtruman.writer@gmail.com

Coming January 2017

Out for the Night

Book 4 in the Browerton University series

"For the night, I am yours…"

Meet Coop: Formal date. Wingman. Friend. Mystery man. He called himself the G-rated Gigolo of Browerton. He could be anyone you wanted him to be…for a price.

One night, his services are called upon for a unique assignment: distract a computer science nerd whose strong grades are killing the class curve. All Coop has to do is flirt with the guy, get him away from his books, save the curve, and collect the biggest payday of his G-rated Gigolo career.

Should be easy enough, right?

Matty has no interest in making friends or any cherished college memories that don't involve the Dean's list. Growing up, he withstood years of relentless bullying and loneliness to graduate from high school as valedictorian. His tough shell helps him excel at

Browerton, bringing him one step closer to his dream internship in robotic engineering—even if he has to do it solo.

When Coop stumbles into his life, he slowly breaks down the brick walls that Matty keeps concreted in stone. Sparks fly and quickly blossom into something deeper, but how long can their relationship last before the truth comes out?

Out for the Night is the 4th book in the Browerton University series, but can be read as a standalone. It contains humor, heart, and hot guys. The book is intended for readers 18+.

Made in the USA
Middletown, DE
03 June 2019